FU
FIXER UPPERS

FU : Fixer Uppers

by

Devon McCormack

Cover Design : Jay Aheer

www.simplydefinedart.com

Cover Photography : Allan Spiers Photography

Cover Model : David Romano

Editing & Formatting : Daryl Banner

www.darylbanner.com

Works by Devon McCormack

Romance

Between These Sheets
Filthy Little Secret
Tight End
Working It: Metropolis, Book II (with Riley Hart)
Faking It: Metropolis, Book I (with Riley Hart)
Weight of the World (with Riley Hart)

~

Non-Romance Titles

Bastards Series (Sadistic Contemporary)
Bastards (Two Dark Erotic Thrillers)

~

Young Adult Titles

The Pining
Hideous
When Ryan Came Back
The Night Screams

TABLE of CONTENTS

FU FIXER UPPERS

1

MIKEY

I kiss down the side of Tara's neck.

She rolls her head back, moaning as she grips onto my biceps while I bury my cock inside her.

I'm giving her what she's wanted since I saw her glancing at me from across the bar.

Adrenaline races through my body. Sweat slides down my face, and as a drop reaches my chin, it drips off and falls between her breasts.

I offer another thrust, and she screams out. She's screamed a few times while we've been fucking, and each time, I just want to hear her do it a little louder because I like knowing how turned on she is, how wet I'm making her.

"You like that dick inside you?" I ask.

"Give it to me, Mikey!"

"God, you're making me pre-come so fucking much right now."

She arches her back and tosses her head from side to side, her red locks waving as her wide green eyes roll back.

I pull out, wrap my arms under her legs, and flip her onto her stomach. Grabbing her hips, I pull her to me as she pushes off the mattress and gets on her knees.

"That cock is fucking massive," she says, gazing back like she wants to look at it one more time before I stick it inside her.

I could tell she'd be a good lay just by her game. The way

she posed while I chatted her up by the bar. The way she shifted her hips as she made her way to the restroom before returning, her expression filled with lust and hunger. Her lips seemed to beg for me to slide my cock between them—something that didn't take long once we got back to my brother's place where I'm staying for the next week.

He's out of town—doing field research in Belize for his Anthropology Master's program, and I needed to visit my sister here in Georgia, so it was a perfect opportunity to escape the stress of my job and give myself a little vacation.

Now that I'm here, pushing back into this gorgeous screamer from behind, I'm so fucking glad I had time to take this trip.

I lean down so my torso is flush against her back.

Reaching my hand around, I play with her clit, massaging it while I continue thrusting.

She moans before she starts screaming out again.

"You really like that, don't you?" I ask.

"Fuck, I'm coming." She stiffens before her body twists in a series of jerks. She calls out even louder as I continue giving her what she needs—what we both need. Her climax is just turning me on even more.

The pressure in my balls builds until I grunt out my own excitement.

I curse and groan, my hands moving across her torso as I spew into the condom within her.

"Fuck, fuck, fuck," I groan as I cling to her body.

We recover from the intense fuck before I head to the bathroom real quick, dispose of the condom, and return to the bed. She rolls off the side and collects her clothes off the floor.

"Where're you heading off to?" I ask.

"I've gotta work early tomorrow." She slides on her panties. "I didn't figure I'd be out this late."

"What time is it?"

She glares at me. "Two in the morning."

"Oh, fuck. Well, it was more than worth it."

She beams. "Oh, I agree. But I've still got a ton to do."

"You know, you could stay."

She smirks. "You're sweet, but no thanks."

With her blouse and skirt in her arms, she grabs her purse off the nightstand and pulls out her cell. She plays with it for a moment before handing it to me. She's pulled up her Facebook app. "Friend yourself." I do and then hand the phone back to her. "I'll have to hit you up again." She scans my body, which I'm pretty damn proud of right now considering how much time and energy I've put into it at the gym.

We make small talk as she throws on her clothes. Then I lead her out of the bedroom to the front door. She turns back to me, her hair slightly messy from our fuck session, despite her attempts to tame it in the floor-length mirror of my brother Jordan's room where we hooked up.

She glances at my dick. "You just want me to be reminded of that fat dong of yours, don't you?"

"Were you planning on forgetting it?" I ask with a wink, and she smiles.

I open the door for her, and her mouth falls open. She shakes her head. "You are a conceited motherfucker, but a charming one."

At twenty-seven, I'm hardly new to any of this. I know what I've got—and more importantly, how to work it.

Tara offers a soft kiss before pulling away and cocking a brow. "See you 'round."

"See you," I say, kissing her once more and letting it linger before she pushes against my chest.

"Wow. I'd better leave now before I get roped into something else."

"I could be down for rope."

Her expression transforms to something devious, as though she's giving actual thought to my suggestion. She bites her lip, grins, and then heads out the door. I peer out to keep an eye on that fine ass that captivated me at the bar as it moves down the hall of my bro's apartment building.

"Damn."

"Yeah, that was one hell of a fuck," comes a voice from behind me.

I spin around to a guy who leans against the wall across from the front door.

Shorter than me, he's lean but muscular, his arms folded. He's got a sharp jawline, which he seems to be tensing while he glares at me. His thin, light brown hair is combed across his scalp, his bangs curling over his forehead.

This must be Jordan's roommate.

I didn't realize my bro had such a sexy roomie, and I'm not ashamed to admit he's hot. I've always had impulses to test it out with guys. Never felt disgusted by the idea, but always happened to lean toward girls when I started realizing how amazing a penis could be, and they seemed like the most eager to help me discover just how incredible having a dick was.

This guy—can't remember his name—is so hot, he's making my dick twitch.

And I think I'm even more aroused by how he's obviously pissed, likely because of how loud I was with Tara.

"Hey, uh…" I say as I struggle to remember his name. "Shawn, right?"

"Scott." His lips barely moves as he tells me. My attention zeroes in on the groove above his upper lip right under his nose. It's the perfect accent on that cute face of his.

"Sorry. I didn't know you were here earlier, and I didn't hear you when we came in."

Even though I didn't get his name right, I know who the guy is. He's my bro's buddy from college. They moved in together during their sophomore year at Georgia State University, and they get along so well that they've stayed roomies for five years now.

I reach my hand out for a shake, but Scott keeps his arms folded, glaring at me.

"Sorry for the scene," I say, intending that to come out as a joke and to lighten the tension between us. Although, I wouldn't mind if we took this tension into his bedroom.

"A scene? Pretty sure I got to hear all three acts. At least I know the leasing office didn't give you any shit about getting the key Jordan left."

"Nope. Um… you got a problem with a guy getting a little action?" I was chill when we first started talking about this, but he's kind of being an asshole about it.

"Whatever. I told Jordan I didn't mind if you stayed while

you see your family, but I do like to get some sleep when I'm home, and I just had to deal with a family dinner, which is not the most fun experience to begin with, so if you could find a way to be a little... no, a *lot* quieter in the future, that would be great. Also, it's disturbing as fuck that you'd do that to someone in your brother's bed. No?"

"I changed the sheets."

"That doesn't make it better."

"I'm Mikey, by the way."

"It's nice to meet you, Mikey. Could you just keep it down?"

I could punch that foul expression right off his fucking face, but at the same time, I'd rather fuck him and watch him reel in the pleasure the way Tara did less than fifteen minutes ago.

What the fuck am I thinking? I've never done it with a guy. Fantasized, hell yeah. Plenty of times, but never followed through with it.

There's something about the way his full pink lips rest on his face. They're so fucking kissable.

And something about him being mad as fuck and hot as fuck at the same time keeps making my dick harder.

He takes a breath, like he's calming himself. "You're only here until next week, right?" he asks, as though it's clear all he wants to do is get rid of me.

"Yeah."

"Fine. Just so you know, I'm not a people person in general."

"Apparently."

His brows raise. "So… I was going to say Jordan gets that. He gives me the space I need. That's why we've been able to make this work. I was uneasy about you staying here, but if you keep out of my way, I'd appreciate it."

"Done and done, man."

"Thanks." He glances down, his gaze settling on my crotch for a moment.

Shit. I'm like a stone.

His gaze meets mine, and he looks confused. "She must've been really good." The dumbass doesn't realize he's the reason for why I'm rock solid right now.

"Pretty fucking good." It's not a lie.

"Okay. Night."

He heads through the living room and into the back hallway to his bedroom, which is directly across from Jordan's.

This is going to be interesting.

2
SCOTT

I'm falling.

Falling. Falling.

BAM!

I hit the floor.

When my alarm clock went off, it startled the shit out of me, and I went flying off the side of my bed.

This isn't a good way to start my day.

I hardly got any sleep last night thanks to Mr. Fucks-Like-a-Champ.

I rise to my feet and head to the window to open the curtains. A soft blue glowing light filters through the blinds.

My gym clothes from yesterday are still on the floor.

To most people, my room would look pristine. Neurotically clean. But having the small stack makes me feel like everything's fucked to hell.

I was so depressed when I got home from seeing my family that I didn't even bother with it. Why should I? It represented what a mess my life is—or what sort of a mess they make me feel like my life is.

I grab my gym clothes and take them to the basket in my closet before laying out a button-up and dress pants that I plan on wearing today.

Even though I can do my job from home, I prefer to at least feel like a professional.

And act like one, which is why I wake up at seven in the morning every day, because I don't want to slack off. I have the good fortune of doing something I love—graphic design. I'm going to take advantage of it and treat it like the job it is, even if Dad doesn't think it counts as one.

My eyes keep closing as my body begs for me to go back to bed.

Damn you, Mr. Fucks-Like-a-Champ, Mr. Giant-Dick, Mr. Hot-as-Fuck-and-I-Wish-You-Would-Fuck-Me-Like-That-Too.

Who the fuck does Mikey think he is? He knew Jordan had a roommate and must've known I'd be home at some point.

So why the hell did he and that girl have to be shouting like that?

I can act like this is about the noise all I want, but I know why I'm pissed.

I'm jealous as fuck. I haven't gotten laid in a while. Seven months now. And hearing Mikey calling out like that made me so envious. I wanted to be in there, taking it from him.

When I went out to talk to him about the noise, I got a view of that hot body, and it was hard to tell which looked better—the back or the front. I'd seen pics of him on Jordan's Facebook page. I even told Jordan that if he was gay, I'd fuck him.

But in person, he's even better. The image of his dark hair flashes through my thoughts—and those steel blue eyes. That light scruff that speckles across his face. And he's built like the fucking Terminator—beefy arms and thick muscles in all the right places. I noticed a tat just under one of his pecs that ran across his side and beneath his arm, but I was so distracted by the rest of his body—particularly his dick—that I didn't have a chance to read it.

Pissed as I was with him, I have to admit that the guy's hot as hell, and that's part of why I was so short with him. The moment my gaze got lost in those blue irises, I wanted to bail, but it actually made me even more on edge, more guarded and defensive. Like I wasn't attracted as much as I wanted to fight him.

And then when I saw he was hard... What the fuck was that about?

To have that in my mouth.

God, I've never been so frustrated with someone and wanted to blow them at the same time.

I feel like a fucking crazy person.

I don't like getting this way about my friend's brother, but I can't help it. It's like when I get in the mood to watch porn where guys are all tied up and being taken by men with stockings over their faces. One part of me says, *Fuck yes*, while another part of me cries out, *What the fuck is wrong with you, perv?*

I slide into a pair of boxers and throw on a tee before heading to the kitchen for some breakfast.

Mikey's on the other side of the kitchen bar turned partially away from me. He holds a ceramic bowl before his chin as he scoops Froot Loops into his mouth with a spoon, munching down like he hasn't eaten in days.

The grooves in his back are so defined, they're another reminder of how much he has to work that body out at the gym.

Act cool, Scott.

I walk through the entryway and around the bar until I see two tight cheeks.

He's naked.

Bare-ass naked.

And those are two of the firmest glutes I've ever seen in my life.

Saliva rushes into my mouth.

I'm fucking drooling over him. How pathetic.

I know from what Jordan's told me that he's an engineer, but I don't know when he has time for a job when his impressive physique suggests he spends most of his time at the gym.

I have to act like there's nothing weird. Although, surely Jordan's already told him I'm gay, so he's going to totally think I find him attractive. Well, as attractive as I really find him.

Bail. Bail.

As I spin around, the hardwood floor creaks beneath my feet.

"Scott?"

I whirl back around. My face must look like a cherry.

He eyes me curiously, the bowl right beneath his chin. He's such a straight guy—standing there, not having a clue why I'd be weirded out by him being naked in the fucking kitchen.

"Seriously?" I ask.

Anger has always been my defense mechanism. Just like with last night.

Now that I feel like I'm trapped, I'm going to lash out at him.

But I can't help but scan his impressive bod.

He's like a cover model for an Abercrombie ad.

He's got lines in his six-pack that would stand out even if he was sitting down, and his pecs are round and defined.

How much does he fucking bench to get that chest?

Even flaccid, it's huge. That cock belongs on a fucking horse! And damn that would feel good inside me, but considering my dry spell, any cock would feel good in me right now.

His eyes are wide like he's trying to figure something out.

His dark locks are tousled a little over his head, but it looks almost crafted. Like some hair designer intentionally made it appear ruffled for a photo shoot.

I can't believe anyone could just wake up with that hair.

He presses those thick pink lips together, seemingly revealing his uneasiness about my attitude—the only thing that reveals he's uneasy about anything right now.

"You're standing in the fucking kitchen naked," I say, my tone severe.

"That an issue?"

"Who the fuck does that? Were you raised in a nudist colony? You can't even throw some boxers on?"

He turns away from me.

"Better?" he asks.

And my dick lengthens even more.

Feels like it's a hundred degrees in here. Sweat beads across my forehead.

"You know, you could show a little respect, considering you don't even live here."

"Jordan didn't tell me there were all these fucking rules.

No loud sex. No walking around naked."

"Common decency, Mikey."

"Whatever."

Whatever? Oh, he sounds like my fucking ex. Now my face is hot, and not from embarrassment.

3

MIKEY

Shit, my dick is stiff as a board.

It's why I turned away from him. Because I could feel it getting hard.

If he thinks me standing here naked is weird, he's going to be real pissed when he finds out him seeing me like this is giving me a boner.

I don't know how to get out of this.

I didn't figure he'd even be awake yet. I just planned to come in here and grab a quick snack, then be back in my room in no time, not giving him any trouble today.

Cute as the guy is, his attitude is pissing me off, but something about how much curlier his hair is this morning gets me going.

Gotta stop thinking like that if I'm going to get rid of this raging boner.

I never get like this over guys. Girls, all the time. Guys, occasionally, but not like this. Never this hard.

"You know, you can cut me a break, Scott. I'm just trying to get a bite to eat."

I glance over my shoulder. He shakes his head, his face twitching.

"Okay."

"By the way, I noticed the pantry door is coming off the hinges. You guys planning to get it fixed?"

"We've talked about it, but we haven't gotten around to it."

"Oh, cool. I'll grab some shit at Home Depot on my way back from the gym. I don't know if Jordan's mentioned it, but I'm kind of *handy*. A little handsy, too."

I wink, expecting some sort of comeback or him to relax even a little, but he stares at me blankly.

"I used to work in construction." I figure since my sense of humor isn't working, maybe I can be real with him. "Are you okay with my doing that? I won't be stepping on your toes or anything?"

"Oh, yeah, yeah. Sorry. I was—You don't have to do that."

"It's the least I can do for you guys for letting me stay here."

"Thank you," he says like he's a goddamned robot.

How can a person live their life this tense and annoyed and weird all the time?

I just want to turn around and tell him to suck my dick.

I need to stop thinking like that, though, if I want this erection to go down, but the only thing I want to go down right now is Scott. On me.

"I'm gonna get back to work," he says.

I don't really understand why he's telling me. He can just go, but he turns and heads back into the main hallway.

I don't know how Jordan puts up with this guy. He's so fucking serious. So annoyed by everything. I'm not even trying to bother him, but it seems like that's the only thing I'm capable of doing right now. I remind myself that this guy will probably cool down when my bro gets back from Belize this weekend.

I scoop what remains of my Froot Loops into my mouth and put the bowl and spoon in the dishwasher because God forbid if I make a mess, too.

I hit the gym and then stop by Home Depot before returning to Jordan's apartment and fixing the pantry door.

Stuff like that bugs the crap out of me, and I figure, since they're letting me stay here, it's the least I can do. Maybe it'll even make Scott a little less grumpy when he realizes I can be helpful and that I'm not the fucking dickhead he seems to believe I am.

When I'm finished, I shower and head back into Jordan's room. Lying down on the sheets naked, I stroke my cock, thinking about how fucking hot the sex with the redhead was last night, enjoying images of her pussy and the way her face tensed up when she got all excited and screamed out. I imagine her writhing beneath me, clawing at my back.

My muscles tense as my excitement grows, the pressure in my balls becoming intense.

Then I imagine Scott's face—how he looked last night, his face tensed up, his shoulders squared off. My thoughts shift to a scenario where I rush him, throw him up against the wall, and force a kiss.

I want to savor the fantasy, but before I know it, I'm coming. It's intense. So fucking intense.

My load shoots up my body, dripping across my torso, the warm cum making it to my chin.

I reel in a powerful high that covers my body head to toe.

Despite how good it felt, I have this nagging feeling that my attraction to Scott is going to get me into a lot of trouble.

4

SCOTT

I sit at my laptop working on a design. It's a hot image of a bodybuilder that I'm transforming into a poster for Paradise Lost, a themed night at my client's bar. I've added some stock photos of foliage with vines hanging down from trees around him. I take my time getting the colors right in each image and cutting them together, attempting to unite the elements as seamlessly as possible.

My family doesn't approve of me being a graphic designer. Dad wishes I'd use my accounting degree to nab a cushy office job like my brothers or sister rather than wasting it and following my passion. It just makes me dread every family get-together—when I show up and remind them all what a failure the youngest kid is compared to my older siblings with their incredibly lucrative careers in real estate and finance.

But fuck them. I'm twenty-two years old, and I get to decide what I do with my life.

As I check out the model's body in the photo, I can't help but compare it to Mikey's.

When I saw him in the kitchen, I managed to read the tat under his pec: *Strength is Within.*

Hard to pay attention to it, though, when my eyes kept trying to look at the rest of that fucking gorgeous man-beef, particularly that big-ass dick.

God, I wish that hadn't been what I'd first seen this

morning. What I really hate is that I wish he'd tossed that bowl of cereal into the sink and come at me like an animal, ravaging me. It's not the most realistic fantasy in the world. That's not how real life works—at least, outside the world of porn—but it doesn't keep me from fantasizing about it over and over and over again, the scene running through my head and keeping me constantly hard, which is really fucking inconvenient when I'm trying to get this project done by tonight.

I manage to make some progress, and as I head into the kitchen for lunch, I see Mikey stretched out across the couch in the adjoining living room watching something on TV. He bites into the corner of a blueberry pop tart. A bowl with a bit of milk speckled with rainbow colors sits on the coffee table before him, assuring me he's had more of my Froot Loops.

I head into the kitchen and start fixing myself a ham and cheese tortilla wrap.

I glance over the bar between the kitchen and the living room and see he's watching Adventure Time.

I fucking love Adventure Time.

Mikey has his arm stretched out across the arm of the couch, and I'm a little frustrated with him for wearing a shirt.

I don't get to complain about that, though, since I'm probably the reason he feels like he needs one.

Even as he lies there appearing as chill as ever, I'm annoyed because he doesn't seem to have a care in the world. I'm always on edge—always stressed about money, work, and family. And here he is, relaxed as can be.

It's his vacation, I remind myself. Still, judging by his cool demeanor and suave attitude, I don't imagine he gets stressed about much. He seems like one of those guys who is comfortable in his own skin wherever he goes.

That's so not me. Never has been. I like who I am, but I definitely am not the kind of guy who can walk into any space and make it my own. I've never been that at ease anywhere in my whole goddamned life. Hell, I fucking feel out of place in my own home now that he's dominating it, claiming it as his own like the fucking alpha he is.

I should head straight to my room, ignore him entirely, and get on with my life.

He's not going to be here forever.

But I owe it to Jordan—and to Mikey—to make up for being such an ass the past few times we've talked. Because as much as I don't want to admit it, part of what has me so worked up about him is that I'm attracted to him, and I don't like that he reveals this weakness within me.

I finish making my wrap and pour myself a glass of unsweetened tea before heading into the living room. I'm not good at making conversation with people in general. It's one of the reasons I wasn't thrilled when Jordan mentioned the possibility of Mikey staying here, but it's only for a week.

"You mind if I sit in here with you?" I ask.

"It's your place." He doesn't sound thrilled about it, but it was a stupid question.

I sit in the cushioned chair that matches the sofa and face the TV.

"I like Adventure Time, too," I blurt out because I'm trying to make conversation.

"That's cool."

My face fills with heat.

I'm making a fool out of myself.

Why did I even set out to do this? I would leave, but I've already put myself in this awkward-ass position, so I might as well see it through. I just have to finish my lunch, and then I'll have a great reason to go back to my room and try to get him out of my head while really wanting to jerk off thinking about him again.

There's silence before he turns and asks, "Everything okay?"

"Yeah, why?"

I make eye contact with him for the first time since I've come out of my room, and I blush.

Goddammit.

He must know. He must see right through me.

He oozes masculinity and sex, and I'm not even sure if it has anything to do with him or if I'm just so fucking horny right now, but it bothers the fuck out of me how affected I am.

"I don't know. You seem a little tense. Like you're stressed about something."

"I'm kind of stressed about everything, all the time."

He smirks, and I have to shift my gaze away from him, because why the fuck does that have to be so adorable?

"Just some stuff I'm working on right now," I clarify.

"Yeah. Jordan told me you're a graphic designer. That's cool. Must be nice being able to have a job working from home."

"Yeah. It has it's pluses and minuses. Pluses being working from home. Minuses being that I have to motivate myself to do everything so I don't procrastinate."

"You don't strike me as the procrastinating type."

"No. I guess not. I mean, I feel like I am all the time, but I'm pretty disciplined with it. I have to be. I didn't get here by slacking off. I guess you didn't either, Mr. Big Wig Engineer."

"Yeah. Not so much. You know, you seem kind of nice when you're not being anal about shit."

As soon as the word "anal" escapes his lips, my dick hardens in my shorts.

Fuck.

"About that, I'm sorry. I'm not used to being around someone other than Jordan. And I'm kind of a clean freak, so I knew it was going to bother me a little already."

My gaze drifts to his bowl, and as soon as he notices, he hops up. "Oh, shit. I'm sorry."

He grabs the bowl and the wrapper for the Pop Tart he'd set beside him.

"Oh, no. I didn't mean it like that," I say, but I'm kind of charmed as he takes his stuff into the kitchen. He tosses the wrapper in the trash and rinses his bowl in the sink before placing it in the dishwasher.

Such a simple act sets me at ease.

That was incredibly considerate. And adorable.

As he heads back into the living room, I tell him, "You really didn't have to do that."

"It's the least I can do, considering I'm bumming at your place. I'm not trying to bother you, but I feel like that's all I've done ever since I got here."

"Well, thank you, but my neuroses are my own problem."

"Look, I do want to say that I'm sorry about that shit with Tara. I really should have been more considerate—"

"No. It's not a huge deal. Honestly, I was coming back from my family that night, and they were kind of a pain in my ass, so I was already on edge. Speaking of families, have you already met up with Kate?"

I already know the answer. If he had, he wouldn't be acting like this right now. What I really want to know is when he's going to meet with her.

Kate's Mikey and Jordan's sister.

I've talked to her a few times since I first met Jordan in college. She's a nice girl, and I didn't get started off on the wrong foot with her like I did with Mikey.

Nice as she is, her life hasn't been the easiest recently. That's why Mikey's here.

Her asshole husband ended up having an affair with one of his students. She had to move out of his place and back into Jordan's parents'.

It's why she urged Mikey to come and see her. She didn't want to tell him over the phone.

I feel kind of bad for Mikey, sitting here thinking he's going to catch up with his sis only to find out she and her four-month-old are entering into a rough patch. I kept telling Jordan he should tell his brother, but he didn't think that was a good idea, saying Kate wanted to tell him herself in person, which is her right. It just sucks for Mikey that everyone else in his family has known about it this whole time and kept him out of the loop.

"I don't see her until tomorrow," Mikey says, "so I was

gonna hit the gym later, I guess. Gotta keep this body for the summer. Competing with those LA gym rats."

"I doubt you can do much damage to that body over the course of a week."

We exchange a glance, and his eyes narrow.

I look away again.

Here I was, impressed with myself for making a lighthearted comment, and now he's thinking about how I just went all gay on him.

He must know. Jordan must have told him, but I don't have to go drooling all over him like this. God, when he tells Jordan about this, he's going to give me so much shit.

Mikey turns and notices a joke on Adventure Time. He comments on it, and we get into a discussion about the show, talking about our favorite episodes and moments.

"Yeah, I don't watch a lot of cartoons," Mikey says, "but this one is the shit."

"Oh, I watch a lot of cartoons. And anime, I have to admit."

"Really?"

"Yeah. That's one of the many dorky things I do."

"I think that's kind of cool, actually."

That wasn't what I was expecting him to say.

I finish my wrap and put my plate in the dishwasher.

"Guess I better get back to work," I tell Mikey, enjoying how relaxed I feel about him being here now and the ease within me that I don't feel threatened having a complete stranger in my apartment.

"Cool. Catch you later."

I start into the hall, but stop myself and turn back to him.

"Sorry," I say.

"What?"

"I can be kind of a dick. I know that. I just... I..."

...kind of thought you were hot and got weird.

I'm such an idiot. Even by the expression on his face, wide-eyed and with his mouth hanging slightly open, I can tell that he's as surprised as I am that I'm saying this.

"Anyway, sorry."

"It's all good. You weren't bad. And I've been the dick, so we're cool."

I head back into my room and get to work on another project I have a deadline for: the cover for a gay romantic comedy indie flick featuring two hot actors. The high-res images in the studio were done of them separately, so I've had to work hard to find shots that will gel together just right. The ones I found make it look like they're looking at each other, but I've had to do some color-correcting on top of shifting their heads ever-so-slightly to make it more convincing.

This is the kind of work I can get lost in for days. But my father's always there in the back of my mind, silently judging me for wasting my time on what he considers a hobby.

5

MIKEY

I sit in a booth at the Cheesecake Factory.

Finally, I get to visit with my little sis.

I haven't seen her new baby since right after he was born. It was also one of the few times I was willing to tolerate being around Mom or Dad since I left for college.

Kate enters the restaurant. Her dark hair, even darker than mine or Jordan's, hangs just past her shoulders, a lot shorter than when I last saw her. She glances around uneasily. She's the kind of person who's always felt out of place wherever she goes, which kind of reminds me of the way Scott is.

He's a nice guy, once he lets loose and doesn't take things so goddamned seriously.

It was nice to see that side of him today—that he can be something other than a d-bag—and after today, I feel like he's a pretty cool guy, someone I wouldn't mind hitting up a bar with. Although, there was a moment when the way he looked at me kind of made me feel like he was checking me out, and I hoped he was. What the fuck was that about?

I wave my hands until Kate sees me, and she heads over. She smiles, radiating this glow like an angel as she approaches. In a blue blouse and gray skirt, she looks so grown-up and put together—a far cry from the girl who always had pigtails and sported leggings like they were going out of style. Despite her groomed appearance, I can tell by some stray strands of hair and a patch of her face where she missed putting on foundation that she was in a little bit of a rush to get here.

I get up and slide out of the booth to give her a hug.

"Sorry I'm a little late," she says. "Roger had an accident when I was taking him to the sitter."

"Why didn't you bring him? I wanted to see the little guy." I detect apprehension in her gaze. "Oh my God, Kate, what happened?"

She hugs me again and bursts into tears.

I check around and notice a few restaurant patrons glancing our way, so I guide her into one side of the booth with me and keep her close, not saying anything. I just hold her because I know that's what she needs right now.

When she's settled down some, I remind her, "Don't worry. I'm here for you. Everything's going to be okay."

I'm relieved she mentioned Roger earlier because it assures me that he's alright. But is something wrong with Lyle? Or did he do something wrong? Because if he hurt her... Oh, even the thought of him doing something to her pisses me off.

When she stops crying, I slide the glass of water closer to her.

"Come on, Kay-bae. What's wrong? I figured there was something with the way you asked me to come out here. But I didn't know it was this bad, otherwise I would have come home sooner. I thought you and Lyle needed money or something."

"No, no," she says, sniffling. "Not that exactly... well, at all, really." She starts to say something, stops herself, and then starts again: "We're getting a d—"

She starts crying again.

I know what she's reaching for.

Divorce.

I grip her arm. "You don't have to say it, Kate. It's okay."

When she looks back at me, her face is bright red like she's embarrassed to talk to me about this, which I can understand.

"You don't have anything to be ashamed of," I tell her.

"I know. There's more, and it's hard to tell you why. There was a situation."

I'm not sure if it's because I know my sister well enough to get what she means, or if it's because her expression is that revealing and any stranger would know just by the way she says it.

Lyle had an affair.

I don't want to believe I'm right.

In an instant, I'm twelve again, and we're alone: me, Mom, Kate, and Jordan. Mom is in the kitchen crying against the counter because she can't keep it together, and I'm trying to pull Kate and Jordan's attention away from her, distracting them so that they wouldn't have to take the burden on themselves.

I pull myself from the memory, back to the present.

"What happened?" I ask.

"It was one of his students."

Lyle's a professor at USC teaching in the Film/TV department, so he never had a shortage of opportunities. But I'm livid that he finally took advantage of one.

"I found out a couple of weeks ago," she adds. "You

know, he's always played poker with some guys in his department, and I thought he was texting back and forth with one of his buddies. I never really thought about it. I guess that shows what an idiot I am, but one night, I saw that he'd left his phone in the kitchen, and I grabbed it to take it to the bedroom. It buzzed, and when I set it down on the nightstand, I saw this message that said, 'Miss you, too'. Obviously I didn't think that one of his gambling buddies was missing him that much, so I picked it up and went back. Back four months."

Meaning he was out having a field day while she was raising their child.

My face flashes with heat.

I want to hurry out of this restaurant, hunt him down, and beat the shit out of him. I have this need to defend my sister's honor. If we were back in the 1800s, I'd fucking grab my gun and have a duel with him because fuck this bullshit.

"I didn't know what to do," she says. "At first, I took his phone into the laundry room and replayed the past year, thinking, 'Was it because I was pregnant? Was I distant? What did I do?'"

"You didn't do anything." My tone is so serious, I sound threatening.

"He found me in the laundry room, and that was pretty much the end. She was in his intro class. A freshman. Some blonde thing who liked to send pictures of her boobs." Her face trembles before tears start sliding down her face. She wipes at them quickly. "Sorry."

"Kate, you don't have a goddamned thing to be sorry about."

I pull her close to me again, and she tucks her head against my shoulder.

As the waiter approaches, I shake my head at him. He nods, his expression sympathetic as he moves along quickly.

Kate takes a deep breath. "God, I thought if we met in public, this would be easier."

"Is everything okay outside of that? Do you get the house?"

"That's the tricky part. I can't afford to live in our house, even with him paying child support and alimony. Not on my salary at the school, so I'm moving in with Mom and Dad."

"What?"

She looks at me nervously because she knows how I feel about this. This is something she really knew she had to keep from me.

"No."

"I have to. Just for a while. I've already been staying with them since I found out. I haven't gotten my things yet."

"How can you even think that, considering—"

"I'm not thrilled about it, Mikey. I didn't think I'd be on my own in my mid-twenties, but I don't have a choice."

The despair in her eyes, the hurt, the pain. I know I need to be sympathetic, but all I can think is that she needs to keep away from their toxic environment. She needs to keep Roger away from it. He shouldn't have to be around their bickering and moaning—the sadness of their bitter, dead love. I remember the love being there when I was really young, but whatever was there died a long time ago, and now they keep up the charade.

We've already had to witness it throughout our childhood. She shouldn't have to endure it again. And the thought of her precious baby having to be around that for any serious length of time rips into my heart.

"It's just going to be until I can get some money from the divorce," she says. "And living off an elementary school teacher's salary in Georgia is hard enough as it is, so I don't have many options, especially if I want to keep from having a long commute."

"If money's the issue, I can pitch in. I'm not rich by any means, but I have enough in savings that I can loan you a decent amount of money at the very least."

"I can't accept that."

"It's nothing."

"Mikey, even if I borrowed money to get a place, I'd still have to have somewhere to stay right now. Lyle said I can stay at the house if I want, and he'll stay somewhere else, but I can't. Not after everything that happened. All it reminds me of are all my shattered dreams."

"Can't you stay with friends?"

"I'm not going to ask any of my friends to put up with a child who wakes up every night at two in the morning screaming. And do you really think that this is something I even want half the people I know to find out about?"

"But how can you do that to a kid? Have him around Mom and Dad?"

"I'm not excited about it, but I don't really have any options. And they have so many rooms, it's not going to be an issue for them."

My face fills with heat as even the idea that she has to spend more time around them enrages me.

"None of us have ever forgiven him, but he's not a monster. He's not going to beat the shit out of anyone."

"I know that. But still…"

"This isn't your decision to make, Mikey. I'm a big girl, and I made this decision on my own. If something happens that's going to threaten my child, I will take him somewhere else."

There's anger in her voice. I can tell she feels like she has something to prove.

She deserves a break, though, and not me barking down her throat about her decision, especially since she's had to make one quickly because of everything that's happened.

It doesn't make me feel any better about it.

I bite my tongue through the rest of our chat, accepting that she has a right to do what's best for her and her child.

She tells me she plans to move her things out of their home next Saturday. Evidently, she's been playing catch-up this weekend, trying to finish projects and grading she neglected right after her discovery of Lyle's betrayal. I might need to reschedule some things to make it work, but I plan on being there. I'm sticking around if only because she needs to know that there are people who are here for her.

But fuck if this hasn't made me pissed at my shitty parents all over again.

6

SCOTT

I'm still working on my Paradise Lost poster when my phone buzzes on the desk beside me.

Dad.

I should keep working. Something in me tells me it's the right thing to do, but I'm not going to ignore him.

"Hey. What's up?" I answer.

"How's it going, bud? What are you up to?"

I don't want to tell him. I already know how he'll respond, but this is my life, whether he likes it or not, and just like he had to get used to me being gay, he has to get used to this.

"A client I'm finishing a project for."

"One of those little drawing things."

He's trying to get to you. Don't let him.

"Yeah. One of those."

"I was calling because I talked to your sister, and she says there's a position opening up at her office for a new accountant. I figured with your degree…"

This is hardly the first job opportunity he's pitched to me, and I know it won't be the last.

"Dad, I'm not interested. This is what I do now. This is my job."

"I get that's what you want, and maybe the money is okay right now… for a while, but this isn't the sort of things you can create a life around. Self-employment isn't easy. Think of taxes alone. You're paying all that out of your pocket. And then you've got insurance on top of that, and rent, and a car…"

"I know all the expenses. I've been doing this for three years now."

"I want to make sure you're thinking about your future. It might look good for the time being, but what are you going to do when the market is full of guys on the internet with Photoshop competing for cheaper rates? You're not going to have anything set aside for retirement. You're not going to have any marketable skills outside of drawing…"

"I don't draw, Dad."

I draw a little, but not like comics and shit. He's trying to make it sound like I'm sitting around playing with crayons all day.

"I get it, I get it."

"No, you don't. We have this conversation week after week, and I don't want to have it tonight, okay?"

"Scott, I'm trying to help. Can't you understand that?"

"I know you think you're helping, but you're not. You're just frustrating me, and I'm already on a deadline, so I've got to get back to this."

"Are you going to come to dinner this weekend?"

"Yes. I'll be there."

So you can assault me with more of this bullshit?

I hang up, and fuck if I don't want to call it a night already. It's shitty that such a trivial conversation can set me off.

Even outside of that call, Dad's always in the back of my mind when I'm working, judging me, telling me that this isn't what I should be doing with my life.

It sucks, but I have to admit, I've probably had it pretty easy compared to Mikey, who I'm actually nervous for. I can't imagine what it must be like meeting with his sister to find out about what happened. Talk about a bitter pill to swallow.

I work some more until I hear the apartment door open.

Silence.

I hear rustling through the cabinets.

I should go out and talk to him. Even if he doesn't want to chat about her, I feel like he needs someone to be there for him. I can always pretend to be heading into the kitchen for something anyway. It's the least I can do, considering how I barked down his throat when he first got here.

I head out and see him digging through one of the cabinets. "Looking for something?"

"You guys got any liquor in this damn place?"

"I got it." I head to the pantry, which he fixed the other day just like he said he would. I dig into the back for a bottle of Svedka. "You're not going to head out on the town to pick up another easily excitable girl?"

His expression doesn't change.

"Sorry. That was a joke. Obviously not a good one."

"No. It was fine. Not fine, really. I got some bad news."

"Yeah, I know."

"*You* knew?" he asks, looking up at me, his dark brows pulling together.

I feel like shit, as if somehow I've let him down.

"Sorry. I mean, it wasn't really something I could say. I don't know you, and it was Kate's news to share."

"No, no. I get that. It's crazy coming home and feeling like

34

I was almost tricked into being told what might be the worst news that my family's had in... well, a very long time."

The way he says it, I can tell there's more to the story, but I'm not going to pry.

He walks around to the other side of the bar and sits on one of the stools, resting his elbow on the counter and burying his face in his palm.

"Soda okay?" I ask him.

"Yeah. That'd be great."

I'm quick with making a cocktail for both of us.

He scratches at the bar. "So I guess everyone but me knew the truth."

I don't say anything because I can tell he's still trying to make sense of it all in his head.

When I'm finished with his drink, I set it before him.

He takes a sip quickly. I think he's about to set it back down, but then he leans back, tilts the glass, and takes a gulp. Then another.

I add some soda to the vodka I've already poured for me before taking a modest sip, seeming to almost compensate for how much he just had.

He glares at his glass, apparently projecting his frustration on it.

"A little vodka isn't going to cut it," he says. "Whatdayasay we head to the bar?"

"I'm ready when you are."

He sizes me up. "You want to change into something a little more casual?"

I remember that I'm still dressed up for the day.

My cheeks warm.

"Oh, yeah. Let me do that and then we'll head on out."

I change into a polo and jeans. Mikey wears a leather jacket, which seems kind of warm for tonight, but considering how he looks in it, I won't question his judgement.

We walk to a bar a couple of blocks away. I figure it's the safest since I don't imagine either of us will be sober by the end of the night, not after I had to deal with my dad and Mikey got Kate's news dumped on him like that.

We don't talk on the way there, and I can tell by the expression on his face that he's stewing on something. When we arrive at the local pub, we sit at the bar and order drinks. As Mikey gulps down his tequila and water, and in an effort to keep up, I hastily drink my vodka Sprite.

"Much better," I say as the strong taste of liquor tingles on my tongue.

"Shit. I'm sorry. I've been so caught up with this bullshit with Kate that I didn't even ask you. What's going on? You looked as bummed as I feel."

"Well, not that bummed. It was just shit with my dad. He called before you got home, and let's just say he has a way with words."

"What'd he get onto you about?"

"My job. Well, what he doesn't even see as a job, I guess. He thinks my graphic design is a hobby that happens to earn me some cash. Sometimes, it's like he thinks I'm mowing lawns. Although, he might respect that more because then he'd at least understand that there's always going to be a need for someone to cut the grass. I know that's nothing compared to what you had to deal with today."

"No. I get having to deal with shit from your parents. That's part of what's pissing me off about this whole deal with Kate. It's not just about what her asshole husband did. It's what it brings up for our entire family."

"What does it bring up?"

He's quiet, like he's not sure he should say anything. "My dad cheated on my mom when we were younger," he blurts out. "Didn't just cheat. He left her for another woman. And we were on our own for six months before he came crawling back, and Mom, even after what he did to her... what he did to us... took him back. I can't say I remember my parents ever being really in love, but after that, it was even worse. The coldness. The clear disdain for each other. It's like they'd both given up on everything and were clinging to each other because that was all they had. And so we grew up around the nagging and the bickering, and I know a lot of people have it worse than that. Dad wasn't violent. Didn't ever raise a hand. His crime was in the total disregard and passive aggressive rage he had toward my mother. And hers was doing the same and having us live in a house of contempt until we were old enough to get out."

"That sounds miserable."

"Kate doesn't need to be around that, especially right now. And that's not the place for a kid to be, either."

He takes another gulp from his drink before setting it back on the bar.

"But it won't be for long, right?"

"That's what I keep telling myself. I'm going to do everything in my power to make sure that's really the case.

Kate's not the kind to ask for money, but I was thinking, if she can find a place, I'm willing to pitch in whatever I need to get her in there. Rental or whatever. I don't care. Not in my parents' house is all."

"Well, now I feel like my issues with my dad are kind of trivial compared to all that."

"No, sorry. That wasn't my intention."

"I know it wasn't, but I mean, my dad gets on my nerves and is always trying to get into my business, and it's frustrating. He and my siblings have always given me a hard time. I'm kind of the runt of the family."

"What do you mean?"

"Youngest. And they were always the star students. AP everything in school. Amazing at standardized tests. Sister and one of my brothers went into finance and my oldest brother went into real estate. They're all making six-figure salaries these days. And meanwhile, I'm making a low five."

"But you're doing something you love. Isn't that what matters?"

"You tell me, Mr. Engineer. Must help when what you love happens to be incredibly lucrative."

He smirks.

I'm not sure if it's because the drinking we did back at the apartment is hitting me or if it's because he's that hot, but I'm getting hard again.

Dammit, Mikey, how do you do this to me?

"I've had a lot of lucky breaks that got me where I am," he says.

"I don't imagine luck has much to do with it. From what

Jordan's told me, you're kind of a genius. Although, the leather jacket and ripped jeans kind of downplay that, don't they? Not to mention mooching off your brother's place when you could just as easily get a hotel."

"Eh. Just didn't want to book a hotel room. I would have rather bummed at my bro's place, you know? Meet his super-cool and friendly roommate."

He winks. I can tell he's making light of our less-than-friendly introduction, which I appreciate since I still feel like an asshole for how I reacted to him initially.

"But no, I was being serious about being lucky. I was a geeky science kid. I got into robotics in my Tech Ed class in middle school. Learned how to make one. And honestly, all the work distracted me from what was going on at home. And because Mom and Dad were impressed, they sort of left me alone, which was nice. I got some attention at a couple of robotics competitions in high school, and that led to an acceptance at Georgia Tech with a professor who wanted to mentor me. Worked my way through college doing gigs with a construction company while I got my bachelor's. And my professor and I were so active in robotic engineering that I got a lot of attention. So there wasn't really much of a job hunt after school. Got set up with a pretty sweet, stable job with a company I love."

"What exactly is your job there?"

"My company basically designs equipment for major corporations, so let's say... Coca Cola needed a new machine to produce coke bottles. I'd be looking at the designs, making sure they're reasonable and within budget. Of course, obviously we're not talking about Coca Cola here, because if we were, I'd be making a shit ton more money."

"Sounds like you're kind of a genius, though, to do that. So you've got it all? The brains? The body? The life?"

"The body?"

I blush, but I feel confident that the bar is dimly lit enough that he can't tell.

"Whatever. You obviously spend a lot of time at the gym is all I'm saying. Obviously you don't have any issue getting laid."

"Do you?"

"Shut up. I have plenty of issues getting laid. You don't even want to go there."

"Try me."

I shake my head and have another drink. "Not happening. I mean, you see how charming I am."

"Well, you can be when you don't have a stick up your ass."

I want his stick up my ass right about now. *Stop thinking like that!*

"But in all seriousness," he says, "don't stress about what your dad thinks about what you do. I mean, what does your mom think?"

It's like he jammed a knife into my chest and twisted it. What was such a light discussion has become a trigger.

"She… she passed away when we were little."

"Holy shit. I'm so sorry."

"It's fine. I was six when it happened, so I can hardly remember her." Not true, but it's something that's easy to tell people to shut down that conversation. Keep it light. Not so painful. "But it... it was really hard on my dad. He was on his own with four kids, and he did a good job raising us. He really did. And he loves us as much as a dad can love his kids, but that's part of why it gets so stressful when he gets on to me about shit like what I do for a living. I kind of feel like I owe him. I spent college following in the path he wanted me to go down. Majored in accounting. It wasn't satisfying, and I wasn't good at it. When I was struggling to get a job as an accountant after I graduated, I took on more freelance graphic design work, and it paid the bills, so gradually, I decided that, hell, if I could make money doing it, I should keep at it."

"And you were passionate about it. Sounds like you couldn't have cared less about accounting."

"Yeah. But he liked the idea of the security of a job like that. Dad's always worked for a company. Hell, his job's health insurance is what kept him from having to file for bankruptcy growing up. It's all he knows. But I question myself enough as it is, so he certainly doesn't make it any easier."

He raises his glass.

"To being two guys who are lucky enough to be doing something they love."

I clink my glass with his and we drink.

As he sets his drink back on the table, he says, "I think I need some shots. Hey, Barb!"

I'd forgotten the bartender had told us her name when we first got here. Mikey sure is a smooth operator. He's probably gonna work up her number before we leave. He orders some shots, which we down nearly as fast as Barb makes them—so

41

quickly that after about twenty minutes, I'm feeling tipsy. I can tell because I keep running my hands through my hair, a habit I get into—one that others are always eager to point out to me.

I should probably stop, but I'm enjoying this time I'm getting to share with Mikey, and I don't want to do anything to disrupt it.

7

MIKEY

Damn. Those shots weren't the best idea in the world.

We stumble up the stairs leading to the main gate of the apartment building.

"This was a really fun night," Scott says, his speech slurred before his foot catches on one of the steps, and he tumbles forward. "Fuck!" He falls to his knees.

"Oh, dude. You gotta watch it out here."

"Don't worry. The cement caught my fall." He giggles, assuring me that he either didn't get injured or won't feel it until tomorrow.

I approach him, squat down, and hook my arms under his, helping him to his feet. He throws an arm around my shoulder and doesn't seem to even think twice about it. I wonder how many times he and my bro have stumbled down this same path together.

"We didn't even drink that much," he says.

"Dude, that's not even close to true."

As I guide him to the gate, I retrieve the keycard Jordan left for me, but as I'm about to scan it, Scott loses his balance and catches me off-guard so that I drop it.

"Shit, sorry." He laughs.

"You don't sound sorry." Although, he's been apologizing since we left the bar. He's obviously an apologetic drunk.

I kneel down and grab the keycard off the concrete

pavement.

"Don't I? Sorry."

He's still leaning against me for support, and as I turn to him, a smile sweeps across his face. He looks like he's thought of something really clever to say.

The curls in his hair are messy from running his hands through them repeatedly after we got deep into our drinking. His hazel eyes glisten in the security light that hangs beside the gate. I detect something in his gaze, something I'm used to seeing in guys or girls who are interested in me, like he wouldn't mind if we fucked around right now.

Surely, Jordan would have mentioned that his roommate was gay. But maybe he's in the closet. I figured he would have mentioned something when I was talking about him getting laid, but he gave an ambiguous reply.

I've never done anything with a guy before, though. I've been around some guys I thought were hot and wouldn't have minded doing things with, but nothing ever happened.

Should I go for it? Kiss him and see how he reacts? But if I'm misreading his being drunk for being interested and go for it, I could be in a shit-ton of trouble. And I've already pissed Scott off enough as it is with my antics. There's no need to make him pissed about something like that if I'm wrong.

But maybe…

I'm about to lean in and just go for it when he shifts his gaze to the gate. "You gonna open this up or what?"

"Shit, of course."

I'm glad he interrupted me. I'm not thinking this through. Even if he is interested, I could be putting Jordan in a really awkward position. What if we fucked and things got weird?

I could have made a massive mistake.

Regardless of whether or not Scott would be interested, maybe it's better that we just be friends. I've never been good at being able to be friends with girls and hook up. I have to hit it and quit it. If we did anything, I imagine I'd push him away like that too.

Not that anything else could happen. And I'll be out of here in a week and probably never see him again, but why play with fire?

I lead Scott back to the apartment, and when I open the door for him, he releases me and starts inside. He stumbles into the living room and falls onto the couch. "Oh, shit."

I close the door, head to the recliner adjacent to the couch, and collapse onto it.

"You know how long it's been since I've been this drunk?" Scott asks.

"How long?"

He glances around the room, as though he's searching for the answer on the wall. "Eight months ago... after I broke up with my ex."

"Fuck, really?"

"What about you?"

He's so carefree right now, so far away from that version of himself who seemed all uptight and rigid when we first met and he gave me such shit about fucking Tara. I like this side of him. It arouses me even more.

My dick's getting hard. I figured I would have whiskey dick after all we had to drink, but it's as functional as ever, and it's not helping that he looks so fucking cute lying on that couch, his muscles tight in the sleeves of his polo.

I'm not ashamed that I'm attracted to him, especially when he's like this—uninhibited, free.

He chuckles. "It feels good. I need to do this more often."

"You're hot," I blurt out.

His eyelids flutter a bit before he turns to me. "What did you say?" Judging by the expression on his face, he doesn't believe what I said.

"You're really hot."

He stares at me. He doesn't even blink. It reminds me of that morning when he was looking at me in the kitchen.

"Whoa, you must be really drunk if it's taking you that long to process that."

He opens his mouth to say something, but stops himself, just lying there with his mouth hanging open.

"Is that an invitation?" I ask, my gaze fixed on his lips. I'm joking, but kind of serious at the same time.

He doesn't seem to get what I mean. Damn. I was fucking wrong.

I'll play it off. He seems fairly oblivious right now, so it won't be a big deal. Hell, he might even forget by tomorrow. "I'm shittin' you, man."

His cheek twitches, and he smirks. "Oh. Shitting me? Got it."

He eyes me suspiciously. Like he doesn't believe me.

Now I know I've made it awkward.

"God, I should get to bed, I guess." I start to get up and head for Jordan's bedroom.

"Were you making fun of me?"

I turn back around. "What?"

His forehead is scrunched up as he slides his legs off the couch and stands. "That was a dick thing to say."

"I didn't mean to start anything."

Fuck. Now he thinks I was being an asshole? I can never win with this guy.

"I'm sorry, Scott. I didn't meant to—"

"I don't need a fucking apology. I actually thought we were having a good time tonight, and then you start up that bullshit. Why are you making fun of me?"

Oh, shit. He feels like I was calling him gay. If I did that to some of my friends back home, I could see them acting the same way. Defensive. Freaking out.

"Can we drop it?" I ask.

He approaches me quickly, and I back up against the wall, not because I can't take him, but because I don't think it's a good idea for us to get into a drunken brawl in the middle of his place. Then I really will have to stay at a hotel for the night.

But the angrier he looks, the more I want to kiss him to diffuse all this tension.

"You think it's funny that I'm gay? You think my life's been easy because of it?" His words are severe, but now I'm really fucking confused.

"Wait. No, I was saying—"

He holds his finger in front of him like he wants me to shut my mouth. "Oh, you were just shitting me? You know, Jordan at least has the decency not to fucking insult who I am."

Now I'm starting to get pissed.

"How the fuck did I insult you? I called you hot. I said I was joking because you acted like you weren't interested, okay?"

His brows push together as he looks even more bewildered than before. "Why would you call me hot? What could you possibly have to gain by saying something like that?"

"Have you never had a guy find you attractive?"

His expression relaxes, as though he's starting to listen to what I'm saying, as though it's taking some time for his drunk brain to realize what's going on. "You're not straight?"

Is he really this dense? I lean into him and whisper, "If I'm attracted to you, I must not be entirely straight."

His gaze wanders like he's still trying to figure it out, so I decide to make this a lot easier on him.

I move quickly. Easy to do with my liquid courage.

And holy shit, his lips feel so good.

Just as kissable as I thought he'd be.

My cock grows harder by the second.

I cup my hand behind his head and pull him close.

He's tense, rigid, and it just turns me on even more as I think about drilling into him, helping him relax.

8

SCOTT

This can't be happening.

Jordan's brother is bi?

I guess I can't question it as his tongue slides between my lips.

He spins us so that we swap places and pushes me back against the wall, firming our kiss.

As he presses his tight body up against me, I can hardly believe that I can feel his stiff, lengthy dick against me.

My cheeks fill with heat, not from embarrassment like usual, but from the passion of our kiss.

I hope he's enjoying it even half as much because my awareness of all the bullshit in my life evaporates, and I'm just in the moment, tasting him, feeling him, needing him.

It's been a while since I've been with a guy.

I haven't stepped out of my comfort zone. Haven't put myself in the position to get hurt again.

Not like my ex hurt me.

But right now, being here with someone as hot as Mikey, I don't figure getting hurt will be an issue.

We're just two guys who need to get off. I want that giant cock inside me. I want him thrusting, forcing it deep. I want him making me cry out the way he made that redhead cry out.

I feel so irresponsible right now, but it's also freeing. The scent of tequila on his breath as he moans into my mouth makes me even harder.

He grabs my hips and pulls on me like he's trying to press my body as close to his as he can.

"How many… guys… have you been with?" I ask between kisses.

"None." He offers me another kiss so much stronger than the ones before it. The intensity has me kicking my head back, and he kisses down my neck. I roll my head back and forth on the wall while he tugs at the hem of my shirt, pulling it up.

I submit to him. I don't care what he wants from me. Between the sensations his kiss and touch stir, he's free to do whatever he wants to my body. It's fucking his.

I throw my arms up as he removes my shirt. He throws it onto the floor before kissing down my body, my abs trembling with excitement as he nips and offers the occasional light tease with his teeth.

He kneads at my flesh with his hands.

For someone who hasn't been with a man, it's clear he's had plenty of experience to be good at what he does.

When his lips return to mine, it feels so surreal that I'm wondering if this is even real. This tipsy feeling makes me seriously consider the possibility, but if it's a dream, I don't want to wake up.

Just let me get to the best part. Let me enjoy it as much as I can, revel in it before my eyes open and I'm forced to face the bitter reality that none of this even happened.

I'm lost in a pool of sensations as he guides me back into Jordan's room.

I break away to say, "I think we should do this in my

room."

He laughs awkwardly. "Oh, of course. That could have been really weird." This makes him look even more adorable because I think that's the first time he's looked flustered about something. There are so many sides to him—so many that I'm eager to explore.

But I'm so impatient. Why are we still in our clothes? And why can't he already be inside me, jamming the head of his dick against my prostate?

We head into my room, our kisses reckless, sloppy, and so fucking delicious. He pulls me to the bed, taking charge the way I want him to.

I want him to dominate me like he dominates a woman, to make me his screaming bottom. Considering how long it's been since I've bottomed, it's gotta be tight for him.

He'll probably be impressed with how it feels, especially if it's really his first time.

I don't know why, but that makes it so much fucking hotter.

We end up on the bed, him on top of me, his weight heavy against my body. I slide my hands up and down the back of his leather jacket, and he pulls back so that he's straddling my right leg.

He removes his jacket and throws it behind him. Then he grabs the hem of his shirt and pulls it off slowly, displaying those muscles before he throws the shirt.

The light in my room casts sharp shadows beneath his eight-pack abs.

He collapses on me, his skin against mine, and it's like I'd forgotten what it felt like to have a man's body on top of me.

I'm painfully hard, my erection pinching in my briefs.

We scramble out of our remaining clothes until we're both standing, and as soon as I remove my socks—the final inconvenience—I turn to Mikey and see that thick cock hanging between his legs.

He tosses his boxer briefs on the floor.

"Oh, really? I took you for more of a briefs guy," I say.

A sly smirk spreads across his face. "Well, it won't be the first thing you've been wrong about when it comes to me." His gaze shifts to my crotch. "Nice cock, by the way."

"Not so bad yourself." Which is bullshit, because he's way more hung than I am.

He comes for me and kisses me, skillfully turning me and pushing me back onto the bed.

I laugh at the playfulness of our little game as he crawls on top of me and assaults me with another series of kisses. I throw my head back against the foot of the bed while probing his back with my hands, feeling the dips and grooves between his thick muscles.

"How often do you get to the gym? Damn."

He snickers. "Oh, you're obviously appreciating all those lat exercises I've been doing."

He lifts his ass into the air and repositions before planting his pelvis, and fully erect dick, firmly against my leg.

He doesn't let up his gaze as he says, "God, you're making me so fucking hard, Scott."

I like hearing him say my name and the way his hot breath chases the words across my face, warming my flesh.

As I glance down at his dick, wedged between our pelvises, a horrifying realization hits me. "Shit. I don't have any condoms."

He grins before pushing up off of me and crawling off the bed. He grabs his jeans and retrieves a condom out of his back pocket.

"Someone think he was getting lucky tonight?"

He sneers. "Gotta be ready for luck. And there's plenty more where this came from."

I haven't thought about protection since I broke up with Sam.

He glances at the condom and then at me.

I wonder what he's thinking.

"You know," he says. "I've never really done it with a guy, so I'm not exactly sure about... mechanics."

"Wait. You're a virgin?" I ask in an overdramatic tone, trying to give him a hard time and yet make light of it.

"You're so weird, Scott. But I like it."

"I've had a few drinks, so cut me a break. But seriously, considering what I heard you do with that girl the other day, I don't think you're going to have any issues."

He grins again.

"Oh, fuck you," I say. "You really are so fucking conceited, you know that? You might be one of the most arrogant assholes I've ever met."

He crawls back onto the mattress, moving over me. "Obviously something you're into."

His lips slam down against mine again, reminding me how much my body wants him.

He pulls back, sets the condom beside him, and as I look at his girth, I'm reminded of something just as important.

"You don't have any lube?" I ask.

He cringes. "I ran out with Tara. I needed to go grab some at the store, but…"

"Fuck."

"We don't have to do *that* then, I guess."

I look at the condom he got out. "At least it's lubricated. But still, it's not going to be like with a girl. You're gonna need to go real fucking slow… and do a little more legwork."

"I doubt it's my leg I'll be using."

I laugh so hard that I cup my hand over my mouth to stifle it. I'm so fucking giddy right now. "Please be careful. Unlike with the hottie girls you mess around with, this hole doesn't lubricate itself. When I say slow… I mean, like, careful and slow or no one's going to be able to get in there for a while."

"Okay, okay. Only one way to figure this out, I guess."

He kisses down my body to my cock, then studies it like he's not ready to have it in his mouth—or like he's wondering what that will feel like.

He wraps his arms around my legs and raises them so that my hole is on full display for him. He takes a quick lick, like he's testing it out, before continuing with a smooth sweep around the rim. He explores, then probes, taking his time as he buries his face against my ass. As he eats me out, he stimulates all the right places, and my nerves erupt with sensation.

"If this is how you work a pussy," I say, "then you've been with some lucky women."

My encouragement makes him work even harder.

I roll my head back, enjoying the feelings that shoot through me, feelings that I didn't ever get with Sam, feelings that I've never felt before.

9

MIKEY

Well, this is intimidating as fuck.

I want to please Scott. I want to give it to him the way he needs it. But how the fuck does this work with a guy? What will he like? I know what I like, but I don't want things in my ass. Not like this. At least, I've never tried it before, so I don't fucking know.

I keep licking at the tender flesh inside him, which is tight as fuck. I'm curious to see how much of my dick I'll actually be able to get in there.

It's definitely not going to slide right in.

Although, I know from what porn I've watched that I can find a way to make it happen, despite how impossible it seems right now.

I'm don't have experience with this. Hell, I've never even had anal with a girl.

A hole's a hole, I figure, but I'm wondering if, because I haven't fucked any guys, Scott's even gonna enjoy it.

What if it's totally different and I can't satisfy him?

That's one of the reasons I avoided his cock. I've never given a guy a BJ before. Eaten out tons of pussy, though, so I figured I could give him something he'll like, and he seems to be enjoying it with the way he's rolling his head back and forth on the bed as he moans.

I lick my finger and slide it inside him. It takes some work to get it in there.

"Damn, you weren't kidding about being tight."

He chuckles as I pull out, lick my forefinger and middle finger, and stick them both in.

"Oh, fuck yeah," he says, arching his back to display the lines in his torso. It's not a six-pack, but it's defined with creases between his muscles. He must hit the gym, but doesn't seem obsessed with it like me. He just does enough so that his biceps and pecs have nice curves to them.

While pushing deeper inside, I shift my attention to his dick, my mouth watering. I've never hungered for a cock like this before.

I lick across the shaft, tasting it.

Not bad.

I enjoy how it shifts and grows at the tease of my tongue. I lift his cock with my free hand and stick it in my mouth because if I'm going to do this, I need to go for it. I move my head up and down, creating a rhythm and picking up speed. I'm cautious about teeth since I fucking know how a less experienced girl can get when she's going at it. While I suck on his cock, I move my fingers in and out of his hole.

"Jesus fucking Christ," he says.

A bitter taste fills my mouth, and I quickly slide it out of my mouth.

"Holy shit, you're pre-coming."

He gazes down at me with wide eyes. "That a problem?"

"Sorry. No. It just shocked me. A lot."

I see it leaking from the head of his cock and down his shaft. I lick it, curious to taste it again.

"You like it?"

"It's not bad."

I press my fingers further within him.

"God, you're good at that." His words encourage me to slide my ring finger in between my other two, pushing them together as much as I can.

"Just wanna make sure you're ready to take me."

"You can stop teasing me and put me out of my misery."

I thought my dick was as hard as it could get, but I was wrong, because the moment he says that, it grows even stiffer.

I snatch the condom beside me and suit up.

Just like a pussy, I tell myself.

I offer a few more spits and add it to the modest lubricant that's already on the condom.

Scott lifts his legs and grips onto his thighs. He's the expert here, showing me the ropes, and I'm glad he's so willing and inviting, not making me feel pressured or uncomfortable.

Am I seriously doing this? Am I really about to fuck a dude?

I can just imagine what some of my guy friends would say if they could see me now.

It's a momentary thought because pretty soon, I'm pressing the head of my dick inside him.

His lips make an O as I push.

It's a slow process, and I have to add some more spit onto the condom before I manage to make progress.

He takes deep, steady breaths.

"You okay?" I ask.

"Keep going. I want it. It's just so fucking big, so I'm

trying to relax."

But as I push, my dick doesn't go farther in. I pull back out and wipe my hand across the condom.

"Dry as fuck," I say. "Dammit. We're seriously going to need lube."

"Wait, wait."

He rolls off the bed. He's unsteady in his movements. Crouching, he scurries across the room and slips out the door. When he returns, he's holding a bottle of lotion that I'm guess he grabbed from the bathroom across the hall.

He tosses it to me. "This'll do the trick. It's water-based."

"What does that mean?"

"It means it won't weaken the latex like oil-based lotions."

I smile. "You clever ass."

He approaches the other side of the bed and places his forearms against the wall, pushing his ass back to display it for me, his hard cock poking out.

He gives me a seductive gaze. "What are you waiting for?"

I grab the lotion and stand up, approaching him from behind. I lather the condom with lotion and keep some on my fingers. As I approach him from behind, I slide my fingers back inside him, filling him with some of the lotion so that it can help ease me in.

"Don't worry," he says. "That'll be more than enough. Just do it. I need you inside me."

I obey, working my way in until I'm pushing my cock into him with so much more ease than before. He presses his hands firmly against the wall as I take his ass. Even though I'm making much more progress, it's still so tight, like the tightest pussy ever.

He tilts his head back, and as I get in balls-deep, I wrap an arm around him and pull him in close, tucking my face against his cheek.

I move my hand up and down his abs, enjoying every slight shift they make as I thrust.

I slide my nose across his face until I reach his ear.

I whisper, "You have one fucking hot body."

He turns his head and kisses me. It's a firm, passionate kiss that's easy to get lost in—almost as easy as it is to get lost in this hole, now that I'm in all the way.

Scott's so incredible at this. I wonder why he's not already snatched up.

I set my hand on his throat, offering a light grip. Some girls like it when I hold them like that, letting them know that I'm dominating them. I can tell by the way he arches his back even more, his shoulder blades pressing tight against my chest, that he fucking loves it.

"Harder," he begs.

I thrust quickly, sharply.

He raises his hands over his head, reaches back, grabs the back of my head, and stands there, absorbing every thrust.

I like how he surrenders his body entirely to me. I never would have expected him to give his everything to me so willingly. All that anger and frustration was just waiting to dissolve so that we could share such an intimate experience, but it still isn't enough for me.

I pull on his hips and guide him back to the bed, bending him over so that he lies flat across the mattress, his ass hanging off the side of the bed.

I'm still inside him, but in our movement, my cock slid out a little.

I squat slightly to adjust to the height of the bed and fuck him good.

With one hand, he grabs onto the sheets. He balls the other into a fist while cursing.

"God, you feel great, Scott."

I stroke my hand across his back. I can feel that I'm getting close—so fucking close.

I pull out, wrap my arms under his legs, and flip him onto his back, quickly getting back inside. His eyes roll to the back of his head as he twists and turns and jerks his cock off.

"I'm gonna fucking come," I say.

"Me, too."

He looks directly into my eyes.

I don't want to get lost in this moment. I don't want him to see me come, but the pressure is too much, and soon, I'm cringing and grunting as I fill the condom with my spooge. I shout out even louder than I did the night with the redhead.

He curses again before he shoots his own load across his torso.

We settle with me staying inside him, leaning down and kissing him. His lips feel so good still. I don't want to stop kissing him, but I can feel that the room is starting to spin.

Now that the hot, passionate sex is over, I'm realizing how wasted I really am.

"Oh, shit." I collapse on top of him.

He pants. "Oh… my fucking… God. That was insane."

I tuck my head next to his and close my eyes, trying to block out the spinning of the room. "Sorry," I say, recognizing that he probably wants me to get off and out of him.

"You can stay right there until you're ready to go again, if you want."

He shifts his head so he's looking me in the eyes, a sly smile spreading across his face.

I like this guy.

10

SCOTT

My head and my ass are in pain.

My ass in the good way. My head, not so much.

Mikey really did a number on me with that massive cock of his.

I was so wasted that, if it weren't for the sore feeling I have now, I'd think it was a dream.

It wasn't, though, and I'm forced to face the fact that I made a big mistake.

Really? Jordan's brother? His brother who fucks girls?

Jordan gets back from his trip today. What the fuck would he say if he found out about what we did? He'd be pissed that I turned his brother gay. I know I didn't, but that's totally what he would think.

I didn't even like him two nights ago.

Maybe I'll be lucky and he'll want to forget about it as much as I do.

Although, it was too fucking hot for me to really want to forget about it. It was steamy, passionate, in-fucking-credible. But I'm sure that half the reason it felt so good was because of how wrong it was.

I don't do this. I don't hook up, and I'm not the kind of asshole to throw my friendship with Jordan away for some stupid fuck with his brother.

Isn't that, like, Friendship 101? Don't fuck your friend's

siblings.

I dread getting up.

Can't I just lie in bed all day?

I head into my bathroom to grab some Tylenol. But as I search through my drawer, I realize I'm out.

This day isn't going to go well. I can already tell.

Although, I guess the shitty turnout with the job was a dead-giveaway that it was going to be a crap weekend.

I throw on some clothes and head out of my room, hoping Mikey is passed out in Jordan's room so that I won't have to deal with him.

He sits in the living room wearing a pair of black trunk boxer briefs, eating Froot Loops from a bowl, and looking totally relaxed as he watches some more Adventure Time on Netflix.

He glances up at me and smirks, like he's proud of the work he put in last night. I would say he should be proud if it wasn't totally inappropriate and I wasn't feeling so guilty about my moment of weakness—a moment that never would have happened if we hadn't had so much to drink.

"Morning," he says. "I stopped by the store and grabbed some ibuprofen."

He glances at the kitchen bar. Bottles of ibuprofen and Pedialyte lie partially out of a plastic bag.

"Thanks," I say quickly.

"That Pedialyte is for you too," he says. "Gotta hydrate."

Now he's my fucking hero, too?

I down five pills of the ibuprofen, chasing it with the Pedialyte.

I can tell by the knot in my stomach that my body's nervous about me attempting to do the same sort of damage that I did to it last night.

"I know," he says. "My skull still feels like it's about to split in two. Sorry I didn't grab anything to eat. I forgot my card, so I had to use what cash I had on me. If you want, we can go grab something."

Grab something?

I turn back to him, and he appears surprised by my confusion.

"Everything okay?" he asks, sounding totally cool.

"I just fucked my roommate's brother, and you're asking me if I'm okay?"

"Well, technically I'd say I fucked you. And... damn."

"Are you not freaked out, even a little bit?"

"About?"

"Um... having sex with a guy for the first time? Having sex with your brother's friend? Neither of these things feel weird or wrong to you?"

He sets the bowl of Froot Loops on the coffee table and pushes to his feet. "Everything felt pretty right, actually."

He approaches slowly, an eased expression on his face, those perfect abs shifting with his movements. As he nears, he wraps an arm around me and pulls me to him, offering a kiss, one I don't fight.

I enjoy the fruity taste of his mouth.

But then I pull away. "What is going on?"

"What?"

"What are we doing?"

"I assumed going for seconds."

"Mikey, really? You don't see anything wrong about what we did last night?"

"Is this a joke?"

"No. It's not. Look, you were awesome and perfect and everything, but Jordan would kill me if he ever found out what happened."

"I wasn't going to race to the airport and shout it at him, if that's what you're thinking, but more because I don't think he'd want to know about who I fuck, not because I think it's something we need to keep from him."

He doesn't seem to get what I'm saying. "It was wrong and inappropriate, and we should have thought twice about that before jumping into bed together."

He scrunches his face up. "Scott, I really had a good time last night. And I was totally aware of what I was doing, and happy as fuck that I did it because it helped me finally put something into place that I've always known but never really gotten to validate before."

"Oh my God. You would be the one guy on the planet who doesn't have any hang-ups about having his first experience with a guy. Really? Come on. You're not a little worried about being bi?"

"This isn't my first time knowing that, even more than it was your first time realizing you were gay before you ended up in bed with a guy."

Very valid point.

"Come on, Scott. It wasn't that big of a deal. It was fun."

I'm kind of mad at how casual he can be, not just about

what we did, but about sex in general. It's like how his laid-back attitude gets on my nerves because I can never be like that. I always feel high-strung, especially right now.

"You know you liked it," he says with a smirk. He reaches up and grips my chin between his finger and thumb. "The way those eyes rolled to the back of your head, and you opened this mouth to call out my name."

My face flashes with heat.

"You're blushing," he notes before moving in for another kiss.

I pull away. "Mikey, what are you doing?"

"I think you know the answer to that."

"But we can't."

He tightens his jaw, his eyes narrowing. "Why not?"

"Because I don't want to fuck around behind your brother's back."

"We're not doing anything behind his back."

"Oh, are you going to be all kissy-face when he comes back here?"

"Not right in front of him, but I mean, if he finds out, it's not going to be the end of the world. It'd give me a chance to tell him that I'm bi."

How can he be so easygoing even about that?

It fucking nearly killed me to spit the words out to my father.

"Look, I just don't want to do anything like that, and I mean, you're only here for a few more days."

"So? Just means more time to have fun."

I roll my eyes.

"You're going to think this is dumb, but I don't do this, Mikey."

"Have sex with guys?" he asks, eyeing me skeptically. "That didn't seem to be an issue for you when you were sticking your ass out and begging me to get inside."

His words remind me of how much I wanted to be his— totally his, having him owning my ass.

"That's not what I meant. I just don't hook up. Normally. When I'm sober. And I… couldn't stop drinking those damned shots. And then—"

"Then you asked me to fuck you. And then we got off two more times."

I reflect back on each fuck session and how good they felt.

I'd feel better if I had at least blacked out. Then it wouldn't feel like I had actually participated in making him get off with me again and again… oh, and I can't forget that last "again".

"I don't hook up like that normally, and I'm not interested in doing anything else. It complicates things, and if it gets weird, Jordan is in the middle of it, so can we pretend it never happened?"

He stares at me blankly. I'm trying to figure out what he's thinking, but I don't fucking know.

"Totally," he says, his voice deep, almost a growl—one that gives me a little chubby.

I'm not as relieved as I thought I'd be by getting that off my chest. I feel like an idiot for turning down more sex with Mikey, but it's the right thing to do.

Despite how cool Mikey's acting, I have this awful feeling that somehow Jordan will know when he gets back later today.

That he'll have this feeling that something happened between us. All I have to do is remind myself that there's absolutely no reason for him to suspect his seemingly straight brother would have done anything with me.

"I think I'm gonna hit the gym before I head to the airport," he says, avoiding eye contact as he heads to his room.

I can tell he's bummed, probably because he really did want to go again, and I did too, but it's not like he's going to have a hard time finding some other hot lay.

I'm just another notch in his headboard. Someone who won't even cross his mind once he's on to the next one.

11

MIKEY

"You guys have a good time while I was gone?" Jordan asks as he sits in the passenger seat of my rental car.

"Yeah," I say through gritted teeth.

I'm not mad at him. I just can't get over what a total asshole Scott was this morning.

Really? After we had such hot-ass sex, he wants to say fuck it and pretend it never even happened? Didn't he enjoy it as much as I did? He sure as fuck seemed to love the way it felt.

"Haven't gotten to do all that much," I say. "Just trying to figure out this situation with Kate."

"Sorry about that," he says. "She made me keep it a secret. She didn't want you to find out over the phone."

He wears a polo and cargo shorts with a Braves baseball cap turned backwards. His skin's tanned to a nice bronze color. We're not the sort of family that burns easily in the sun. I imagine he was red for a day before his skin changed to that nice, even color. He looks totally relaxed as he slumps back into the seat.

"No, I totally enjoy being lied to," I add.

"We didn't technically lie. Technically, we just neglected to tell you."

Then I guess I care even less about not telling you about how I fucked your friend.

Not that it's even any of his business to begin with, because if I thought it was going to affect him, I'd be out with it.

"Oh, yeah," I tell him. "That makes me feel a hell of a lot better. Thanks."

"That's not an easy thing to say over the phone. You don't think I was feeling the same thing when that happened? You think I was excited about facing Mom and Dad after all this shit came back up? And we knew you'd be the worst of everyone."

"The worst of everyone? Because I actually remember what it was like when Dad left us. You guys were five and six. I was the one who would walk into Mom's room and catch her crying. I was the one who saw the dead look in her eyes when she wandered around lifelessly, incapable of making a decision because she was trying to figure out how she could kill her soul enough to stay with that bastard. And then she finally did kill it."

"You're being a little overdramatic about this whole thing."

"You just don't know what Mom was like before all that happened. How much she smiled and laughed. How eager she was to play and have fun with us. That's not the woman she is anymore. She hasn't been that woman in a long time. I don't even think you can remember what she was like before."

"I think we've all grown up and realized life's a little more complicated than that. Everyone stops smiling after a while."

"Not everyone stops smiling because of some twenty-something assistant that their husband refuses to fire and runs off with."

Jordan presses his lips together. Whether he's willing to admit it or not, I'm in the right. He and Kate like to play pretend and act like we're just an average American family, but we're not. If we are, America's fucked.

"Whatever," I say. "I want to be there for Kate. I called into work today and told them I'm staying. I'm going to help her move her shit out of Lyle's place and into Mom and Dad's."

"You haven't said anything weird to her about that, have you?"

"What do you mean?"

"She doesn't need you digging up all that shit about Mom and Dad. We knew that's what you'd make this about, but—"

"I'm not the one bringing it back up. Her husband having an affair is what's bringing it up. And you're blaming me for it?"

"No. It's come up on its own, but everyone kind of knew, without any of us talking about it, that you'd want to drag all that shit from the past back up."

I hate it when they all act like it's in the past, because it's not.

I see it every time I'm in their house.

I get that it's easier to act like it isn't real, but that doesn't make it any less difficult for me to grin and bear it as I'm subjected to that environment all over again.

"Just don't flip out when we move her in to Mom and Dad's, okay?"

I quiet my rage.

I've been known to have a temper when I go back home,

but between Dad's attitude and Mom's uneasy silence, they have a way of stirring all those old memories.

Mad as I am, I know the situation with Scott isn't helping matters.

On top of the stress of dealing with Kate, what I had initially thought was improving my mood turned into this bullshit with him acting like we did something wrong. And it fucking sucks balls that something that felt so good—and gave me such a feeling of empowerment and ease after such crap news—had to be taken from me.

I had a good time—a *great* time—and he did, too. I'm not ashamed of what I felt. The passion. The excitement. I'm amazed it's the first time I've ever felt so aroused by a guy, but for him to want to act like we should pretend it never happened, that's something I've been told all my life regarding this shit with my family. He may have spent the night rubbing me the right ways, but today, he rubbed me the wrong way, and I'm mad as fuck.

"You know what?" I say. "I'd rather not talk about this right now."

"Good, then can I tell you about how awesome Belize is?"

This is how he always got through the hard times: changing the subject and pretending nothing was wrong.

I don't like living like that.

It doesn't feel fair that it's how I've always been expected to act, but I roll with it like I always have. He tells me about his trip, and I do my best to set aside our differences about the family drama even though it keeps playing in my head and making me tense, just as it did when we were growing up.

Once again, I'm playing quiet while the rage against Mom and Dad rises within me, building pressure until it will finally explode, usually on Dad.

When we get back to Jordan and Scott's apartment, I'm on edge, wondering if Scott's gonna be there or not. That's what sucks about him working from home. He's always around, and I bet Jordan will want to catch up with him, meaning I'll have to be around him and holding all my anger in—the very thing I hate doing.

There's no sign of Scott when we enter the apartment.

He's probably hiding in his room.

"Hey, Scottie!" Jordan shouts. "Scottie, you home??"

Fuckin' A.

He heads down the hall and knocks on Scott's door, and when it opens, I tense my fists.

Not like I'm going to do anything. It's just a knee jerk reaction. I might be pissed as fuck at Scott, but I'd never lay a hand on him. Well, only the good kind.

Scott steps out, his gaze shifting everywhere but me before finally meeting mine. He forces a smile. If he thinks that's a convincing act, he needs to go back and check that shit in the mirror. If I was Jordan, I'd be asking, "What the hell were you doing fucking around with my brother last night?"

"How was the flight?" Scott asks.

"Not too bad. It's five hours, so it's whatever. Mikey told me about what happened last night, by the way."

Scott's jaw drops.

Not that, you fucking idiot.

"Whoa, whoa, relax," Jordan says. "It's not a big deal."

Scott stares at him, his face white as a ghost.

I'm about to say something to ease his concern, but I'm enjoying this too much. I kind of like him squirming a bit, especially after what a dick he was about what we did.

"Wow, I didn't think it would be getting to you this much, dude," Jordan says. "I mean, it wouldn't be the first time you got hammered…"

I see the shift in Scott's expression as he realizes what Jordan's talking about. "Just pissed that you didn't wait 'til I got home."

"Oh, yeah," Scott says before letting out an uneasy laugh. "I know, right?"

"I was just telling Mikey on the way here that it'd better not keep you from getting wasted tonight. Or at least buying me a few drinks."

Scott laughs, but I can tell it's more from relief of being wrong about what Jordan was talking about, not because my bro said anything particularly funny.

"Well, I don't know," Scott says. "I think it might be better if I stay in. I have to finish up some of these projects, and—"

"Nope, nope, nope. I call bullshit. You're coming out with us. I need a drink and to tell you about this girl I met. Hot as hell, and she's from North Carolina. Invited me to stay with her in Asheville. Oh my God. We didn't do much but make out one night, but damn it was sexy as hell."

"I guess you have to come out then," I tell Scott, and his expression tenses up. He looks like he wants to punch me in the face, but also like he's trying to conceal that part of himself that's so fucking pissed right now that I would encourage

Jordan to bring us out together. He would rather just crawl back into his room and hide until I leave, but I'm not planning on making this easy on him. He's making this weird for me, so I'm gonna make it weird for him.

12

SCOTT

I sip on my vodka Sprite, drinking as little as possible since I'm not eager to get trashed like I did last night.

Jordan sits between me and Mikey at the bar. A tuft of his dark brown hair, as dark as Mikey's, twists out of the hole in the cap he has on backwards.

As he talks about his adventures in Belize, all laughs and smiles, he doesn't seem to notice the tension lingering between me and his brother.

Through my periphery, I keep noticing Mikey gazing at me, but I avoid looking at him because I feel like I need to put on a good act to keep Jordan from suspecting anything. He's known me for so many years that he can read me better than most people, and while I feel guilty as fuck for what I did and how I want to keep it from him, I know he wouldn't want to know this. He's fine with me seeing guys, but he's never wanted to hear any of the details about my sex life. And I know for sure he wouldn't want to imagine me going down on his brother or taking that dino-cock of his.

I wish I could move on, but thinking about Mikey and the possibility of another moment alone where we can share an experience like that again—filled with that same passion and intensity—excites me. Of course, fat chance that can happen after what a total ass I was to him this morning.

I know that wasn't the best way to handle it, but I was

freaking out.

And if I hadn't put my foot down, Mikey sure as fuck wouldn't have. Hell, he wanted to go again right after I got up.

There was some relief in knowing he still wanted me. It let me know that the hot sex wasn't just in my imagination, that he experienced something powerful, too. I guess I should have figured out he was enjoying himself by the third time we fucked, but I was so consumed by our passionate kisses and the feel of his flesh against mine that I wasn't doing much thinking, and if I could have stayed up, I would have totally gone again. Unfortunately, it was so late and I was so drunk that I just passed out. And that was the last time I'd ever fuck him.

"It's amazing," Jordan says, "the way you can lie out in the middle of the jungle, look up into the sky, and see all the stars. So many beautiful stars. In the city like this, we can't really appreciate that. You don't even think about how weird it is that you never see them, and I'm not talking a few here and there. I'm talking so many, and then it's like you can see the depth to them. You can see that it's not just this backdrop of white dots, but this constantly moving lightshow that is better than the most epic fireworks display."

Mikey snickers. "Obviously you and Asheville girl did more than make out."

Jordan laughs before taking another drink. "I wish. I mean, she was pushing for more one night when we were really drunk, but then a few of the other guys we met there came around and wanted to stay up chatting. God, I wanted to sneak off into our cabin and have a go at that, you know?"

He's like his brother, with his cool attitude and ability to charm anyone in the room. Although, since he's dedicated his life to getting his doctorate so he can be a professor of anthropology, he doesn't seem to have much time to date. One of the reasons we both get along so well is that we're both workaholics.

"Sorry, Scott," Jordan continues. "Don't mean to bore you with all this talk about girls. There was one guy down there in my team who was gay, and he had a six pack and this massive chest. You would have fucking died." He turns to Mikey. "Scott loves a beefy guy. Oh my God, when I showed him your picture on Facebook for the first time—"

"He gets it, Jordan," I interrupt, my face burning from the intense blushing.

"No, no," Mikey says. "Go on. I want to hear more about Scott's interest in beefy guys. Is that what his other boyfriends looked like?"

"Oh, no. Sam was pretty lean."

Now we're talking about my ex?

"Sorry. We won't talk about that," Jordan adds. "Sam was kind of a bastard."

"Jordan, please." I'm begging him psychically not to say anything else. I figure my body language must tell him he needs to let it go, but he persists.

"No," he says. "You need to move on and forget about that bastard." He turns to Mikey. "He met Sam in college, and they were together for what? Like three years, I guess. Sam got this job as a medical sales associate, and then suddenly he was too good for my man Scott here. Scott evidently wasn't going to make enough money for them to have any sort of real life together, so Sam broke up with him."

"That's really shitty," Mikey says, and as I make eye contact, I can tell he means it.

This is the first time I've felt something from him other than anger about what we talked about this morning.

I wish I hadn't told him about my dad, because now he gets that Sam's judgement just further solidified all those things that I have to hear already—how they make me feel like what I'm doing isn't worth it.

I feel vulnerable—something I don't feel a lot since I haven't truly opened up to anyone since Sam.

It reminds me of how nice it felt talking to Mikey about my design work, that he doesn't think I'm just some guy dicking around all day in Photoshop. Of course, it's easy for him to be encouraging when he's not really in my life. It's one thing just to be someone he's having a conversation with. It's another to be in a relationship with him. I doubt I'd be the kind of guy Mikey would ever consider dating.

As soon as I have the thought, I wish I could take it back.

Dating? I shouldn't even be associating the idea with Mikey. Although, I guess it's only natural, considering he's the only guy I've done anything with since Sam.

Jordan shakes his head. "You were too good for him."

"Thanks. I appreciate it." I'm hoping that placating him will make him change the subject.

"You are too good for that," Mikey adds, and he sounds sincere.

God, what the fuck is he? A dick? A nice guy? One minute

I want him fucking my brains out, and the next I want to get into a wrestling match with him… or is that the same thing? Part of why I think he gets under my skin is because I'm so attracted to him. But it's more than how hot he is; it's moments when he reveals there's more to him than this body—this incredible body.

"You'll find someone worthy of you, Scott," Jordan says.

"Yeah, you never know what life's gonna throw at you," Mikey adds, and our gazes meet again.

And now I feel all sorts of weird.

Even worse, I feel guilty for how I treated him this morning.

Here he is being supportive and encouraging with me, and I should have been the same way, especially after his first time with a guy.

I was so busy worrying about my selfish concern over my friendship with Jordan that I wasn't taking his feelings into consideration. He acts so chill and cool about everything that I thought he wasn't considering the consequences.

But he's not an idiot. He might look like some dumb blockhead jock, but he's a fucking engineer. A hell of a lot smarter than me, that's for sure.

"You never mentioned Scott was gay, by the way," Mikey says.

"What? Didn't I?"

"Not that you needed to. I kind of figured it out."

"What gave him away?" Jordan asks. "Were you walking around bare-ass naked and he was drooling all over it? Or did he help you get rid of a raging boner?"

Jordan bursts into laughter, but we're both quiet for a moment—too long of a moment—before I ham up a laugh so that we come across as totally chill.

"You have no idea," Mikey says, which only makes Jordan laugh even harder. Then Jordan stops and thinks about what he said and says, "Wait. What?"

"I'm just teasing you, Jordie."

Jordan laughs some more. "The thought of you two together. Oh my God, that's gotta be your wet dream, Scottie. Mikey, you don't even know the way he drools over your Facebook pictures. When I pulled up the summer pics of you at the pool, I thought he was going to jizz all over himself on the spot."

"Oh, really?"

"Can we not talk about this?" I ask.

Jordan can't know how uncomfortable this is making me—and how weird it is, considering everything that's happened.

"Come on. He doesn't care, Scottie. It's not a big deal. And it's not like I'm blowing your chances of getting laid. I think it's funny as shit, but Mikey, if you do need anything, any service at all, Scottie's right down the hall, and you can have your way with him. He won't mind."

How can I crawl out of my skin and escape this conversation?

"Tell me, is he hotter in person?" Jordan leans out of my way so that I can see Mikey sitting there looking hot in that leather jacket. "Just honestly."

"I don't think he wants to play this game," Mikey says.

"Humor me and let my buddy objectify you for, like, two seconds. Scottie, what do you think of my sexy bro?"

"He's definitely hotter in person," I say, playing along.

Mikey smiles like he appreciates the compliment. Not that I think he needs it or doesn't know how attractive he is. Maybe he just enjoys that Jordan's putting me on the spot like this.

I look into Mikey's eyes a little too long as my thoughts race back to last night.

Jordan glances between us.

"Oh, looks like I just made a love connection. You getting tired of roping in the girls, Mikey?" He laughs as if the thought is so absurd, he's not even considering it.

"You never know," Mikey replies.

He's playing with fire and igniting something else in me as he doesn't let up his gaze, so I have to first.

Jordan is oblivious. He takes another drink.

We hang at the bar a little longer before heading back to the apartment, Jordan with either arm around our necks as we walk him up to the front gate.

Mikey and I are pretty sober right now. I don't think either of us wanted to go overboard after last night. Hell, I still have a phantom hangover.

We carry Jordan into the apartment and into his bedroom, laying him in the bed. "It was a really amazing trip," Jordan says. "I had a great time. I so wish I'd stayed. I don't want to TA this summer. Or work on my fucking thesis."

Mikey chuckles. "I'm sure, and we can complain about it some more tomorrow."

"Okay. Night guys. Love you. Not you, Scott. I mean, I do.

But like a friend. God, now I'm sounding gay."

I laugh and roll my eyes.

"Night, Jordan," I say before we head out, Mikey closing the door behind him.

I feel like we have so much to say and like I have so much to apologize for. But how the fuck am I supposed to do that with Jordan in the next room?

13

MIKEY

I was being hard on Scott.

We were both in over our heads when we messed around, and even though my pride has been wounded all day, tonight, when I saw how hurt he was when Jordan brought up his ex, I couldn't help but sympathize with him. Not just because of what a dick that guy was, but because it so perfectly represented what he'd told me about his dad's feelings about his career. In so many ways, he feels like he's on his own, and that's how I've always felt. Like I have to fend for myself and fight for the life I want to live.

As Scott and I stand outside Jordan's bedroom, I'm trying to think of something to say to make up for this whole ornery day when he blurts out, "I'm sorry."

"No, I'm sorry. This was a lot to think about, and…" I glance around uneasily. "This might not be the best place to do this."

"My room?"

"Let's go."

We head into his room, and I shut the door.

He looks like he's surprised at how comfortable I am in his space.

"Sorry my brother was kind of a dick tonight," I tell him.

"No. It's how he gets sometimes when he drinks. And it probably wouldn't have bothered me if… if last night had gone differently."

"Do you wish it had?"

He shakes his head. "I was freaking out, Mikey. I didn't mean anything by it. I'm sorry that I was an asshole. The only reason I made a big deal this morning is because I did it without even thinking about Jordan. He's my friend, and the thought of doing something that would hurt him or make him uncomfortable... that hurts me."

It touches me that he cares about my brother that much. I was so pissed about him trying to act like it was a mistake, I didn't consider that it was because he was such a good friend to my brother. Amazing, how I can go from being pissed to appreciative in such a short time. Jordan's lucky as fuck to have a friend like him.

"So... if we could, tonight... would you want to?"

He stares at me for a moment, clearly considering my invitation.

"I told you, I don't normally do this kind of thing. Just hook up."

"Well, I mean, I gotta go back home—"

"No. I wasn't saying this wasn't okay. Just more of a dumb observation. Maybe I should stop talking."

"It's cuter when you talk."

His face turns red again.

"You've blushed a lot tonight."

"Well, considering Jordan said that shit about Facebook right in front of you. I mean, that was kind of embarrassing."

"What was embarrassing about it?" I ask, feeling kind of cocky knowing how hot he thinks I am, but also figuring that he should be confident knowing I want to bang him still. It's not sending me running.

"Shut up. You know you're hot. You don't need me to tell you."

"But I thought it was cute when you said it."

He's still flustered. I like how cute he gets when he's uncomfortable like this. I like knowing how much he wants me.

And I like how all the tension that stretched between us from earlier has dissolved.

I move toward him, and he flinches, so I stop.

"What is it?"

"This is such a shit idea."

"Why? It's just for a few days. Why can't we have fun? I want to make you feel good. Let me make you feel good."

His gaze meets mine, and considering how timid he looks right now, I know I'm going to have to push this.

I move in and kiss him, and he doesn't resist me.

His tongue slides past mine, assuring me that he's not fighting tonight.

I'm glad.

We have this hot chemistry, so why not enjoy it? Why not let ourselves get lost in the passion for what little time we have?

The sound of our kisses seem so loud—like, surely Jordan has to hear them—as we scurry out of our clothes.

When we're naked, I push Scott back onto the bed and crawl over him.

He looks so beautiful lying beneath me, his curly bangs falling back to reveal his smooth, pale face. His eyes sparkle in the glow from the streetlight that shines through the window beside his bed, casting sharp shadows around his abs.

By now, I think we're both pretty much sober, especially since neither of us were throwing the drinks back like we did last night.

It actually feels better because of it. The numbness that came from being wasted isn't there, and there's this electric energy that ignites every time I kiss him, every time my flesh touches his.

Not that it wasn't there last night; it just wasn't this intense, racing through me like some sort of drug, awakening every sexual impulse in my body, and making me want to take Scott like an animal.

I grab his legs, lifting them before pressing my face against his hole. I slide my tongue around inside, exploring, appreciating how good his flesh tastes.

His soft moan is the only assurance I need to know I'm giving him what he wants. That moan hits my ear just right.

I pull away briefly to remind him, "Don't forget to keep quiet for my brother."

He cringes, like the thought that we're having to consider my bro weirds him out, but better him be like this than how he was this morning.

"I'm sorry for being an asshole," he whispers.

"All good now." I lick his hole again.

He rolls his head back on the bed while I continue my work. My dick grows even harder, but I remain patient. I want him to be good and ready to take me.

I release one of his legs and suck on my forefinger and

middle finger before pushing them inside him.

"I figured I might have loosened you up a bit," I say. "But I guess not."

"Fuck. Just stick it in me. Please."

He doesn't have to ask me twice. I suit up and add some lotion before inching into him. He's so tight that it takes some effort to get things started, but with a little determination and a couple of thrusts, I find it's easier than it was last night. Soon, I'm in deep with Scott whimpering, clearly trying to keep from shouting out in pleasure.

I wrap my left arm under his thigh and stroke his torso and chest with my right hand. "Fuckin' A," I say. "How do you keep it so tight?"

"Negligence," he says, smirking.

I chuckle. I can't help how much I enjoy his sense of humor.

I lean down and kiss him. He reciprocates. It's like he just wants to lap up my saliva.

Like with last night, he doesn't hold back.

He wraps his arms around me and strokes his hands up and down my back.

I pull away from the kiss. "Why don't you get on your knees and take my cock like that?"

He obeys, and I enter him from behind. He's kneeling before the headboard, his hand pressed against it. I wrap an arm around him and place my hand against his taut torso. He arches his back, revealing all those defined lines in his back, all those lines that are amplified by the shadows the light from outside casts across it.

"You feel so good," he mutters.

He leans back and raises his arm, wrapping it behind him and gripping onto the back of my head and pulling me close to him. He turns and greets my mouth with his. His kiss is like a fucking firework as our bodies press together. I cling to his firm torso, appreciating how beautiful his body is.

I offer powerful thrusts, forcing him to break our kisses and return his hand to the wall as he matches my movements his own push back.

Apparently, being a relationship-guy hasn't hurt him in the fucking department.

He glances over his shoulder to make eye contact, but still scrunching up his face.

As I speed up, he grinds his teeth together.

"God, how do people take that big cock?" he asks.

"You don't seem to be having too much trouble."

I stroke my right hand on his ass cheek.

I lean down and reposition my arms around his chest under his arms. I thrust some more, and he turns his head to face the window, throwing his head back.

His body tenses up.

"That's more like it," I say.

"Oh, Mikey," he mutters, and it's him saying my name that gets me even more worked up—that has this powerful surge of energy rushing to my pelvis.

As good as it feels, it isn't enough for me. I don't just want to take Scott; I want to dominate him.

I pull out.

"Turn to me," I instruct. "And put your arms around my

neck."

He does. I grip onto his thighs and hoist him into the air.

His lips curl as he smiles. He presses them together because I can tell he's about to burst into laughter.

I step off the bed, moving slowly and carefully as I carry him.

"What are you doing?" he asks as I make my way across his room.

He glances back, and as he sees his desk, he must realize what I'm plotting.

He looks back at me, his eyes filled with desire and excitement. "You're full of surprises, aren't you, Mikey?"

I lift his laptop and move it to the side of the desk and push some of his papers and pens to the side. Then I set his ass on the desktop. He releases me and lets his arms fall, pressing his palms down on either side of him.

He gazes at me, and I can tell he's a little nervous.

"What?" I ask. "Never fucked on this desk before?"

"No."

"Well, I guess you gave me a first, so I should give you one, too."

This fun, frisky experience makes me feel like it's a shame I'm spending such little time here.

I push back into him. He bites down on his lip in a way that makes me even harder than I already am. As I start to thrust, the metal handles on the desk rattle against the wooden drawers.

Shit.

I move slower, the sound becoming less intense, but I'm

worried it'll wake Jordan and have him running over here to see what all the fuss is about. It's clear by the way Scott glances around that he's thinking the same thing.

Regardless, I don't stop moving in and out.

I lean forward and wrap my arm around him, feeling his breath against my face, just how I like it. I can smell the vodka on his breath. I can feel his body heat.

A bead of sweat falls from my bangs and drips onto his abs, sliding down to his navel.

"You're having quite the workout," I whisper before he kisses me again.

I can't help myself. I know we should be quiet. I know we should be good, but I fuck him. Hard.

He reaches up and presses against my shoulders. I snatch his wrists and pin them back against the wall, fucking so that the desk handles rattle loudly against the drawers again.

I don't know why I can't stop.

I'm waiting for him to tell me that we have to be quiet, but he doesn't. He just absorbs everything that I'm giving him as he rolls his eyes back and turns his head in a way that assures me I'm hitting his prostate just right.

We kiss in a frenzy, hardly breathing, and he breaks away finally, gasping for air as I penetrate him deeply, powerfully.

Yes, I want this so much. This is so much better than any of the girls I've ever fucked. I wonder if it's just like this with Scott or if it's always better with guys. How could I have gone all these years without ever knowing how amazing it could be to fuck a dude?

"Fuck. I'm gonna—"

"Do it," he tells me, and I explode into the condom.

He grips onto his cock, and I'm worried I came too soon until his cum rushes out of the head of his dick, shooting across him.

I watch his expression as it twists and cringes, his mouth opening but obviously stifling the sound to keep from waking Jordan.

I lean down and enjoy the taste of his lips and tongue once again.

They're mine right now—mine to savor, mine to enjoy— as much as I'm Scott's to take pleasure in.

As we settle, I pull back and gaze at him, noticing the satisfied expression across his face, much better than the way he looks when he's tense and stressed out.

He pants. Another drop of sweat falls, this time from my bangs onto his face. He flinches, and I shake my head. "You are too fucking adorable." I offer a soft kiss.

He breathes heavily. "Guess that was a nice way to end the night."

I chuckle. "Uh-uh. Our night's just beginning."

And I see the lust in his eyes, the invitation to keep on exactly like I want to.

His body still trembling beneath me, I know I'm going to get to savor it all and enjoy it like I want to. And yeah, we might feel tired as shit when we finally wake up tomorrow, but I feel like it's no different than if we fucked all night and got trashed the night before.

This will be way more worth it than spending the night drinking.

Scott's still shaking, his body occasionally spasming like he's recovering from his climax.

"You good?" I ask.

"God, this is just so embarrassing." He starts to look down, but I grab his chin and pull up, and his gaze shifts back to me. "Nothing to be embarrassed about with me."

I kiss him again.

14

MIKEY

It's a shitty idea, but I have so much fun messing around with Scott.

He's so playful and easily excitable, especially in the bedroom.

We've spent the past week leading up to Kate's move fucking while Jordan's been at work or attending his summer classes.

Scott working from home is a blessing, and even though he's had time to work on his own shit, he's made time for a little fun, too. I've made sure he hasn't regretted that.

The intensity of what I feel with Scott isn't like anything I've ever felt with a girl before.

The power, the heat, the way he gets my dick hard makes me realize I'm gonna have to give this fucking-around-with-guys thing a shot when I get back to Los Angeles. Clearly, I've been limiting myself all these years.

I lie on the mattress of the fold-out couch, my nude body over the covers as I watch an episode of Family Guy on Netflix. The bright morning light shines through the sheer white curtains of the living room.

My body's still on LA time, and I haven't adjusted to the east coast, so I keep waking up around nine in the morning. Last time I checked my phone, it was a little after ten.

We have to head over to Kate's place at two to help her

move shit out of her bastard ex's place.

I hear a bedroom door open in the adjoining hall. I'm kind of hoping Scott's woken up and that I can at least see him a bit before Jordan wakes, because this is the first day since last Sunday where Jordan will be here with us.

Jordan stumbles into the living room, groggy-eyed and looking like he's about to fall over he's so tired. I'm surprised he even bothered to get up at all.

"You want an omelet?" Jordan asks as he heads into the kitchen.

"Sure, that'd be great. What time do you want to leave here for Kate's?"

"I was thinking noonish. Maybe one."

"Let's say twelve thirty. That'll give us time to pick up the moving truck."

"Works for me."

We'll have to check to make sure that works for Scott. I really hope it doesn't because I don't even like that he's coming with us. Our fucked-up family isn't any of his business. Although, considering he's seen Kate a hell of a lot more than I have in the past few years, I know he's doing this as a friend.

I'm going to have to suck this up and be appreciative.

While Jordan makes omelets, Scott wanders into the living room. His curly hair is all over the place, and I realize I need to get under the covers, if only to keep anyone from noticing my dick getting hard just thinking about how much he got me worked up last night. Even though he's obviously tired, he appears refreshed, and I take pride in knowing I'm at least partly responsible for why he got a good night's rest.

He glances at me briefly, his lips curling upward like just looking at me makes him a little giddy.

"Morning," Jordan says, and Scott's lips become a sharp line.

I want to laugh. God, he's fucking cute with how weird he is about keeping it from Jordan. Not that I want him to know, but I certainly don't feel like it'd be the end of the world.

"Morning," Scott grumbles.

Jordan steps out of the kitchen with a plate and a cheese-and-jalapeno omelet with ketchup on the side. Just how I like it.

"I'm making you one, too," he tells Scott on his way back into the kitchen. "No Froot Loops this morning."

"But I love Froot Loops."

"I do, too," I tease.

Scott sits on one of the two barstools in front of the kitchen bar.

"How'd you sleep last night?" Jordan asks Scott.

"Pretty damn good." He glances at me, and I smile.

"I just have this headache. God, it's like when I was hung over last weekend. I'm so not looking forward to this."

"Yeah, me neither," I say. "And Scott, you really don't have to come."

That's the first time I've said that this past week.

"What? No. I want to help you guys out however I can."

"Mikey, how the hell are we gonna do all that work by ourselves?" Jordan asks. "You know I'm only going to do half as much as you, so you might as well not fight free labor." He winks at Scott. "Just playin', man. I seriously appreciate it, though. And Kate does, too. She wants to get this over with so that she can move on with her life."

"I more than understand that."

"Yeah. And then we're having dinner at Mom and Dad's, which I know Mikey is excited about."

I groan, and Jordan rolls his eyes. Such predictable responses for both of us.

"You can come on back here and just skip it if you want," Jordan says.

"No. I want to be there. Someone has to protect the two of you from them."

Scott glances between us uneasily. He can't understand just how true my words are. I've always felt like I have to protect Jordan and Kate from how Mom and Dad are. I know I can't really. But even when I was younger, I felt like I couldn't abandon them, like they needed someone in their life who could remind them that life was going to get better than the world that we saw in Mom and Dad's house.

I took on a lot, and I think it's partly responsible for the resentment that I feel toward our parents.

***

Kate hugs Scott with one arm since she has Roger in a carrier strapped across her chest. "So good seeing you again," she says.

Despite the smile on her face, I can see the sadness in her eyes, the disappointment that she has to see him under these circumstances.

We stand at the rear of the moving truck I backed into the driveway.

Kate and Lyle's two-story home looks like something off of the cover of a magazine. Light-blue paint on the siding. Black shutters. Lush grass covers the lawn leading up to a small bed of rose bushes that grow beside the brick front porch. I remember how excited she was about their new home when she sent me pictures of it on Facebook, talking about how eager she was to close on the place. She would take pictures of magazine photos she liked and email them to me, and chat with me on Facebook about ideas she had for the renovations.

It's hard to think about how happy she was and then how her dreams have been crushed because of that asshole Lyle. I'm just glad he's not going to be here so I don't have to beat the shit out of him on her behalf.

"I appreciate you guys helping me with this," she says. "You really didn't have to, though. I told you I could hire movers."

I unhook the latch at the bottom of the back door on the truck and pull it open. "Whatever, Kate. We're family. This is what we do."

"I mean, it wouldn't have killed us to have hired movers," Jordan says with a cheeky grin.

I shove against his shoulder.

"Ooh. You wanna wrestle like the good old days, big bro? Come on. You remember when I fucking pinned you when we were younger."

"Jordan! Language!" Kate scolds.

I smile. "I let you win that time."

Jordan's eyes narrow. "You never would have let me win."

I turn to Scott. "Okay, maybe I didn't let him win."

Even though I totally did, I don't see a reason to brag about it. It's pretty clear by our stature who won that wrestling match.

"I have to wait for the sitter to arrive and then I'll get in there and help you guys," Kate says.

Jordan grabs the bill of his Braves cap and spins it around. "We got this, kiddo. Just let the men handle it."

She sizes him up. "You remember who won when we wrestled?" she asks, and he looks to the ground.

"You know what? We don't have to relive that. And come on, I clearly—"

"Say you let me win, and I'll hand Roger to Scott so we can go again."

He presses his lips together, and I have to laugh. Kate might be a lot of things, but she was never afraid of stepping up to a challenge or wrestling with one of us when we thought we were so much bigger and stronger than she was. And what she may have lacked in strength, she always made up for with ruthless determination.

It's one of the things I've always admired about her.

And as much as I know this tragedy is killing her, I know she's strong, she'll beat this, and somehow she'll find a way to spin this whole situation into gold.

Kate leads us into the house. She already has a stack of boxes piled up in her fully-furnished den. Jordan takes those while Scott and I carry larger pieces of furniture—things Kate purchased during her marriage or ones that belong to our family.

We'll be taking most of this stuff over to a storage unit

Kate's renting until she can find a place to stay permanently, which I hope is sooner than later. I've mentioned that if she needs any financial help, she just needs to let me know, that I'm more than happy to help in whatever way I can. I'm lucky to have such a good job. What's the point of having this kind of success if I can't use it to help my own sister out of a crappy situation?

As Scott and I carry a sofa up the basement stairs, I note how easy it is to do this with him. Like in the bedroom, we read each other's nonverbal cues amazingly well. Either of us are able to lead without too many issues, and when they come up, we solve them fairly quickly.

We reach the top of the stairs, and I enter the hallway before I say, "Shit. We're not going to have room to turn."

"Prop it up on its side and then we'll roll it and carry it up that way."

It looks like it'll be close, but someone got it down here somehow, so I figure we might as well try. We position it on its side, and he says, "Now step down on that first step and grab it at the bottom."

"Trust me," I say as I obey, "I'm not worried about topping."

He chuckles. "You conceited motherfucker."

He stands on the steps, sweat rushing down his forehead. There's a patch of sweat in the middle of the tight gray t-shirt he wears. It's too small for him—in just the right way, hugging close so that it's effortless for me to keep picturing what his body looks like.

"We make a pretty good team," I tell him. "Wonder if

there's a correlation with why we have such fucking hot sex."

"I'm going to pretend you didn't say that. Now I'm about to push it toward you, okay?"

We finish carrying it into the hallway, Scott's arms trembling, clearly wearing down from all the work we've put into this.

"You good?" I ask.

"As gold."

15

SCOTT

Damn, this is getting tough.

My neck feels tense from when I pushed the couch up to him on the stairs.

I should ask for a break, but I can take a breather once we finish.

As we make it into the kitchen, a sharp pinch in my neck catches me off-guard.

"Fuck!"

"You okay?"

"Fine." But as soon as I say that, the sensation intensifies before I start screaming out, "Fuck, fuck!"

We set the couch down as the pain radiates in my neck. I press my hand on it.

I've pulled it and effectively blown my whole reason for being here.

I shouldn't have pushed through, I know that. I should have told Mikey I needed to set the couch down for a minute, but I was determined to be useful and not wuss out, and I pushed myself too hard.

Mikey approaches. "Here, let me feel it." I don't want him to make it worse, so I keep my hand in place, guarding it until Mikey says, "Trust me."

And I do.

I know even just from our sex that he wouldn't do

anything to hurt me.

He rests his hand on my neck and rubs his thumb in circles where it's tender.

I grind my teeth.

"Sorry. Is that hurting?"

"Yeah."

"It's definitely tight. I don't think you need to be lifting for the rest of the day."

"No. I can do this."

"Sorry, Scott. I appreciate it, but we got a lot of the big pieces. It's fine."

Once again, I've disappointed myself.

"Hey, hey, what's wrong?" Mikey asks, his voice so soothing.

"Nothing. Just feel kind of useless."

"No. You helped so much, and you didn't even have to do this. This means a lot. Hell, most friends would have made up an excuse to get out of doing something like this for a friend."

"No, they wouldn't have."

"Yes, they would have, and you know that's true. It means a lot to me."

I'm still looking at him, enjoying the feel of his hand on my neck, but then his gaze shifts to it and it's clear that he didn't realize it was there.

I figure he's going to take it off, but he moves close and kisses me instead.

I enjoy the taste of his lips and tongue—greedy for them like I always am.

He sets his hand on my waist and I move closer to him.

Nearby footsteps catch my attention, and I pull away quickly.

Jordan rounds the corner of the hallway into the kitchen. He glances between us uneasily. It's almost like he knows something is up, but his gaze settles on where I'm holding my neck. "You okay, buddy?"

"I pulled a muscle."

"Fuck, that's got to hurt."

"Hey, Kate!" Jordan calls.

She enters wearing a tee and gym shorts, her hair pulled back into a ponytail and her arms around a box. After the sitter arrived, she threw on some old clothes and started moving shit with Jordan.

"What's wrong?" As soon as she sees where my hand is, she says, "Oh, no. I'll get the painkillers."

"You seem to need a lot of those," Mikey teases, and I know he's referencing the morning after I was hungover—the morning after we fucked for the first time.

"I know, right?"

Kate fetches the pills, and we head into the living room for a break.

Seems like we all need one of those.

We've been going nonstop for two hours, which is surely part of the reason why I hurt myself. Jordan removes his baseball cap and wipes the sweat off his forehead before lounging in the loveseat beside the walkway from the living room into the kitchen. Mikey and I sit beside each other on the sofa on the adjacent wall while Kate sits in a recliner positioned in the corner opposite the loveseat.

Kate glances around the room, seemingly taking note of the chandelier and the beautiful pieces of décor—accessories, statues, obelisks—that are spread throughout on side tables and a console in front of the wall-mounted TV screen.

This isn't the kind of home I grew up in.

Dad was never much for design.

"He really did have good taste, didn't he?" she asks.

I see the sadness in her eyes.

The hurt. The pain.

While she was working, I didn't notice it, I guess because she was so busy that she didn't have time to stop and think about everything that was going on—something I don't imagine is easy to do, especially when she's having to walk away from such a big part of her life, the only life she knew, really.

"Fuck him," Jordan says. "I'm surprised you didn't take a baseball bat to all this fancy shit the moment you found out what he was doing."

"Oh, I thought about it," she says. "Believe me. You see that horse statue."

On the media console in front of the TV sits a large sculpture of a horse rising up on its hind legs.

"I thought about how beautiful it would look smashed across the floor, but I was really responsible and restrained myself. I thought, 'I'm not stooping to his level.'"

"You should reconsider," Jordan teases.

A flash of something wicked shifts across her face as her lips curl at the edges. It's like she's thinking of how easy it would be for an accident to occur.

She shakes herself out of her fantasy.

"You know what I need? A fucking drink."

"I got it." Jordan hops off the love seat and hurries into the adjoining kitchen. He opens the fridge, in view through the entryway. He leans down, and I hear him opening what sounds like a drawer.

"You know I meant unsweetened tea, right?" Kate calls. "Not Mike's Hard Lemonade."

"Oh, really? I figured you're nursing, so you wanted to make sure to get some of that good stuff to Roger. Just trying to help my nephew out."

She laughs.

And it's nice seeing her mood disrupted by Jordan's sense of humor.

He makes us all glasses of unsweetened tea, and while he keeps busy with that, I notice the space between me and Mikey on the couch.

Feels like after all we've done, we should be sitting closer. But it's only been a few days, so I might be getting some weird relationship impulses since I'm not used to just hooking up— not like Mikey, who can have a sexy redhead every other night.

When Jordan finishes with our drinks, we sip on them, making small talk before Kate says, "Mikey, you should've been here for the housewarming party. It was a real hit. Everyone in the neighborhood came and then some." She says that in a particularly bitter and biting tone. "Went into this thinking I was going to be living here for ten, maybe fifteen years. That this was where we were going to spend the rest of our lives." She sighs before taking a large gulp from her tea.

When she finishes, she sets the glass on her knee and says, "God, I wish this was a fucking shot of tequila."

"You and Mikey are definitely related," I joke, and she chuckles.

"Too true." But as quickly as she delighted in the joke, her expression turns serious again. And I totally understand. Today's rough for her. She's saying goodbye to the life she thought she was going to share with Lyle. It reminds me of Sam. I thought we would share our lives together, that we were fine, but then he told me that he didn't feel the same way, that he'd lost that passion for me—that spark that he felt in the beginning.

Because I'm too serious and don't know how to cut loose and have fun.

A boring lay, something he mentioned more than once. Mikey doesn't seem to think I'm boring, though, but it just might be because he fills me with an eagerness and excitement that I never felt with Sam.

"Thanks again for coming, Scott," Kate says. "We'll have to have a far more exciting Sunday Funday once I get situated in a new place. I'm looking at a condo in Midtown next week. Maybe we can go after I see it."

"What are you talking about?" Jordan asks.

"I want to go to Blake's or Ten."

"What are those?" Mikey asks.

"Oh, shut up," Jordan says. "Don't act like you don't know where all the gay bars are in this town. Are you just so straight that they aren't even on your radar?"

"I seriously didn't know about them."

"Oh, we all should go together. I would love to see the boys crawling all over Mikey. God, they would eat him alive. Although, I have to admit that I feel pretty fucking attractive whenever I go."

"You've been to these bars?" Mikey asks.

"Fuck yeah. Scott and I went a few times after his breakup. It's a lot of fun. They have the best music, and they actually pour decent drinks. I got trashed off two vodka sodas."

"Oh, I need to dance soooo much," Kate says.

"Then definitely hit me up when you're in town," I say. "I'll meet you out."

"That'd be nice. I'll get the sitter." She slaps her hand against her face. "But God, no drinks is going to fucking kill me."

"I'm sure you need one, especially right now."

"You have no idea. I think this would have been easier if I'd been able to go out and get trashed after it all happened." She laughs, but then her expression turns serious. "You know I'm kidding about that, right? I know we don't know each other that well, so I don't want you thinking I always need a drink in my hand. It's just that nothing has made me want to turn to liquor more than this situation."

"Oh, no. I totally get that."

"But dancing will definitely cheer me up."

"Well, then we have to do it. Although, I should tell you that I'm not much of a dancer."

"Oh, you're gonna dance," Jordan says. "That's how you're gonna get you a new hottie." He turns to Mikey. "I keep telling him he needs to go out more to snatch up something good, but he's all work and no play. You're a hot piece of ass, Scott. You gotta get out there and own it."

"You should get out there, Scott," Mikey says, and I can tell by the amused expression on his face that he's just enjoying having our little secret.

I sip on my tea.

"Like Jordan said," Mikey adds, "you're a hot piece of ass."

I start to laugh when the tea hits the back of my throat, and I pull the glass down, coughing and spitting it across the floor. Thank God they're hardwood.

As I recover from his comment, my neck pinches even more from the movement. Kate bursts into loud, boisterous laughter, and Jordan isn't far behind.

"You're not the first person Mikey's made choke like that," she says, tears rushing from her eyes.

"Kate!" Jordan exclaims.

"It's not like we all didn't see that thing growing up. It was practically falling out every time he wore gym shorts. Do you know what brothers like you guys do to a girl? I went out into the world thinking that they all looked like that."

Jordan covers his ears with his hands, even though his glass prevents him from actually being able to cover one. "La, la, la, la, la," he sings.

Kate giggles some more, rolling her eyes at him. I think she's enjoying that she's getting to him. Whenever I hang out with them, it's obvious that she likes making him a little uneasy. I think she believes that's her job as his older sister— although, only by a year.

"Well, there are worse things you could be saying about me," Mikey points out, grinning.

We chat for a few more minutes, Kate telling stories about when they were younger and the hard times they used to give each other. Her eyes are filled with life, reminding me of the times I saw her before all this shit went down. It's probably helpful to have her brothers here. I think, at least in this moment, she feels safe and relaxed and like she can set some of that shit behind her.

I've always liked Kate. We never hung out much because she was married, but we had fun whenever we did hang out.

We lose track of the time until Jordan checks his phone and says, "Okay. It's four thirty already, guys. We need to get back to work if we're gonna be at Mom and Dad's by six."

"Okay," Kate says. "Scott, you think you can handle some boxes? I can help Mikey with the sofa and the rest of the furniture."

"Shouldn't I be the one helping with that?" Jordan asks.

"Wouldn't want you to hurt your pretty hands," Kate teases as she pushes to her feet and starts toward the kitchen. On her way, she stretches her hand out and smacks the glass horse she mentioned previously so that it falls. As it hits the floor, it shatters, the pieces scattering across the floor.

"Oops," she says, a wicked smirk spreading across her face. It's the sort of smirk I've seen on Mikey when he seems particularly pleased with himself.

"Holy shit," Mikey says.

"Good girl," Jordan adds before we all get back to work.

16

MIKEY

After we drop the furniture off at the storage unit, we head to Mom and Dad's with the remainder of Kate's things she'll need while staying there.

I white-knuckle the wheel.

Just thinking about dinner with my parents is stressful as fuck. I'm only at their house for brief periods like this—holidays and special occasions, this definitely counting as the latter.

I don't like staying here long, but I know it matters to Kate and Jordan, so I do it for them.

When we enter the front door, Mom and Dad approach. Mom hugs Jordan and Kate before they move on to Dad. Mom wears a white blouse and jeans. Last time I saw her, her hair—dyed so it's nearly black—came to her shoulders, but now it's in a pixie-do. And although she's smiling, I can see the uneasiness in her expression and feel her tension as she hugs me. She's wondering the same thing as I am: will I be able to control my temper and keep from going off on Dad?

She doesn't get it like he does because she doesn't test and pick and push. She knows what she did was wrong, and as bad as it was, I still consider his treatment so much worse.

Dad makes a friendly smile. His head that used to be full of the same dark hair as me and Jordan has turned white. He wears a cream-colored polo tucked into a pair of light gray slacks that he has his hands in. He has a crease between his eyebrows—one that becomes more pronounced the longer we're around each other, like being around me is stressing him out.

While Mom and Dad seem relatively calm and collected in this moment, even as they greet us as calmly as they can, I sense their disdain for one another. It's something I've never been able to shake since I had to spend so much of my life witnessing it—Mom filled with silent disapproval for what Dad did, like she's using it as leverage for the rest of their lives, and Dad constantly on the defensive, as though he's a moment away from shouting that he never did anything wrong.

Kate hands Roger to Dad, who makes faces at him. "Oh, haven't you grown up big in such a short time!"

As much as I wish I could allow myself to fall for this charade, I can't get the old arguments out of my head.

The fighting. The bickering. The anger.

Most of the times, they can put on a good performance, at least for a while, but then there are the times where they get into fights. And even worse, when it was just the two of them in their room having their screaming matches. It can be about anything, but I feel like it all goes back to that dark time in our family's history with the unresolved issues that linger between them.

Sometimes, I want to put my hands over my ears because I can still hear them like they're right down the hall from my condo spewing their hate for one another—both so wrapped up in the heat of their passionate hatred for one another that they can't hide it from the rest of the world.

And then, of course, there were the arguments I had with Dad. Those were epic, and I'm not ashamed of having been responsible for many of them because I'm still mad as hell, and I feel like I have every right to be.

Even though I can't escape this, at least I know that I don't have to put up with it for long. As soon as we get back to Jordan's place, he can help me release this tension through a good fuck.

We unload the remainder of the shit from the U-Haul into the house, packing most of it in the upstairs bonus room where Kate will be staying. It was my room initially since I was the oldest, and it went to Kate after I moved out. Jordan never stayed there since Kate lived at the house for freshmen year of college, something she makes a point to tease Jordan about while we're packing boxes in there. Once we're finished unloading the truck, we head downstairs into the dining room where Mom has a dinner of steak, mashed cauliflower, and Brussels sprouts waiting for us. She's gotten out the nice china—a set of white plates with silver curly designs around the edges. Glasses of water are set beside wine glasses at each plate. Jordan's already agreed to drive the moving truck back to the rental company where we have his car to get back to the house. He won't be drinking, which is good because I could use a little alcohol right now.

That would be a nice escape. But knowing me, the alcohol will make me more likely to start a fight with Mom and Dad, so maybe I should just leave it alone.

I sit by Scott on the opposite side of the table from my parents. I intentionally positioned myself here hoping it'd create less tension and that it'd be easier for me to bear being around everyone.

I can't tell if Scott's tense because of his neck or if he's worried about how I'm going to handle dinner, especially after everything I told him. I can't say I'm feeling too good about it, but I'm going to do my best to keep my cool for everyone's sake.

Kate and Jordan sit on either end of the table acting as physical barriers between me and our parents. Roger sits in a high chair glancing around the room, his eyes wide like he's in awe of being in a new place.

Mom keeps the conversation moving, which she's good at. She asks Jordan about his trip to Belize and Kate about how work's going. She avoids mentioning the reason Kate has to move. She's never been the sort who liked to talk about uneasy subjects, but particularly if they were ones that would drag out her own issues.

Still, things are going pretty well. Maybe I can get through this after all.

"How's LA?" Dad asks me.

I tense up.

I figured when I didn't approach him after we arrived, he would have taken the hint. I'm not here for him. He's just the bastard I have to see while I'm here. But he's obviously not going to let me skate by without stirring up shit. I can tell by the expression on his face that he's testing me. And it's a test I don't mind failing.

Keep it together. Keep it together for Kate and Roger.

17
SCOTT

It's shitty that Mikey had to come back into this toxic environment. But I'm impressed that he's willing to be here, knowing that it's what Kate needs right now.

Tension lingers in the room, especially now that Kirk has singled out Mikey.

Kate sits sideways in her chair, facing away from me as she holds a plastic spoon of mushy sweet potatoes in front of Roger's face. As she guides it to his mouth, Jordan glances between Kirk and Mikey. His question was harmless enough, but I can feel Mikey's tension—his frustration—about having to even be around his father, let alone having to discuss his life with him.

"It's fine," Mikey says, his words cutting through the air like knives.

"You enjoying your job out there?"

"Yes."

Kirk takes a breath, as though he's realized he's not getting anywhere with Mikey. "Mikey, I figured we might be able to have a conversation, considering how long it's been since we've talked."

"I think you know I'm not interested in having a conversation."

Kirk tenses his jaw. "Is it so wrong that I want to talk to my son about his life in my own home?"

I can tell he's irritated with Mikey—almost like he doesn't get why his son is still so mad at him after all these years.

"Dad," Kate warns, her tone severe.

"What? I just want to have a conversation with my kid who I haven't seen in God knows how long."

Dara chimes in with, "He's just asking him about his job."

"Always so eager to defend him, aren't you?" Mikey asks.

Kirk and Dara are acting oblivious, like they can't possibly understand why Mikey is lashing out like this, but they must understand that what they did to him when he was a kid is the whole reason why he's so estranged from them.

"Mikey, don't be like this, please," Dara says.

I set my hand on Mikey's leg. I don't even know why I do it. I guess I want him to know that he's not on his own right now. That at least, even if I can't say anything because it's none of my business, I'm on his side.

"I'm not doing anything," Mikey says, taking another breath.

"You all have fun with this," Kate says, pushing to her feet. "I'm going to take Roger upstairs until you can all work this out of your system."

"You don't have to do that because Mikey's acting this way," Kirk says.

"I just don't want to be in the middle of this. I'm taking Roger upstairs to let you boys figure this out."

She lifts him from his high chair and heads off.

"You couldn't let us have one quiet dinner together as a family?" Kirk asks. Mikey sets his fork down. "And you're not going to eat this nice meal your mother spent all this time preparing now?"

"I'm not hungry."

Kirk's face flushes red, his jaw tense.

In the few times I've been over, I've never seen him like this before.

"I don't know what I ever did so wrong to you, Mikey, other than put a roof over your head and food in your stomach."

Mikey clenches his fists at his side.

I don't understand why this is escalating so fast, but all I know is there has to be a hell of a lot more to this than what Mikey's told me.

Kirk shakes his head. "Sorry. Jordan, why don't we go back to discussing your trip? That seemed to be an easier subject for everyone."

Even the way he says that, it's obvious he's blaming Mikey for ruining the conversation, but Mikey didn't do anything wrong.

Jordan tells the story about the girl he met who he plans to see again in Asheville before Kirk says, "You know, Jordan, you need to be settling down with a girl pretty soon, don't you think? You don't have much time left to have kids. Especially you, Mikey Can't hold off forever."

"Who says I want kids?" Mikey asks. His tone assures me we're on our way to a really uncomfortable place right now, and I'm not sure how or if there's even a way to get out of it.

"Oh, of course you want kids," Dara says.

"Why? So they can grow up one day, and we can all do this together? Have this awkward-as-fuck dinner while pretending that everything's okay and we're all one big happy family?"

"Don't you curse at this table, Michael." Kirk's lips barely move as he speaks.

I bite my tongue. This is too much for Mikey, and I can tell by the way Jordan and Dara's eyes wander that they're both wishing they could sneak out of the room like Kate was smart enough to do.

"Oh, is my cursing what the issue is?" Mikey asks. "That's what it is? You're sitting here trying to get at me and—"

"No, I'm not. You're imagining things."

"You think this is easy for me?" Mikey asks as he sits upright in his chair. "I was asked to come here only to get ambushed about this stuff with Kate? You think that doesn't bring up anything from the past? You don't think that reminds me of what you did to this family?"

Kirk's jaw tenses and his nostrils flare. I've hung around him a few times, and I've never seen him get like this. I didn't even think he had this sort of fury in him. It kind of freaks me out, and now I understand what all the tension was about.

"You know what, Mikey," he says, bashing his fist against the table and making the plates and utensils rattle as well as causing the wine and water in the glasses to shake about. "I thought after all this time, you might have grown up a little and stopped trying to stir up trouble in our family, but it's obvious that you're still that same poisonous brat you've always been."

Dara looks right at me from Kirk's side, her shoulders high and tense. I can tell she's embarrassed by this explosion, but for Mikey and Kirk, it's like I'm not even there. Like they've been teleported back into the past where perhaps these fights were a regular thing for them. Like they're just following an old, familiar script, playing it out with the passion and conviction that they're used to.

Kirk shakes his head and stands. He tosses his napkin on the table.

Mikey sits, his body tense as ever as he gazes Kirk in the eyes like he's challenging him.

"It's been how many years, Mikey?" Kirk asks. "How long since I have seen my son? And then only because your sister had a baby? And this is what you bring back here? Hatred and contempt?"

"I didn't bring any of it here," Mikey replies. "It's been here all along, and you both know it. And you always knew it. You can put on this show for yourselves and the rest of the world, but you're not fooling anyone, especially not yourselves."

"I'm your father." The veins in Kirk's neck push forward as he says these words softly, almost like a threat more than a fact.

"And what a great one at that." Mikey's words drip with sarcasm.

Kirk walks around the table, moving quickly and with an intimidating stance. I've never seen him like this before. He looks furious.

His fist clenched, he approaches Mikey standing tall, like he's trying to intimidate him with his stature. Mikey hops up and steps forward, making it clear that he's not backing down.

"Why did you even bother coming if you just wanted a

fight?" Kirk barks.

"I'm here for Kate. That's the only reason, so why don't you back off?"

I'm paralyzed by the intensity of their fight. This isn't how things work at our house. I've never had a fight with my dad, and he's never raised his voice to me. He expresses his disapproval through sighs and lowered glances.

Jordan jumps out of his seat and approaches me, widening his eyes and nodding toward the door, letting me know this is probably a good time to leave.

I know I should go with him, but I don't want to leave Mikey right now. I feel like he needs someone to be here for him.

"No one else go anywhere," Mikey says. "I'm outta here."

"Mikey!" Jordan calls after him as he heads through the walkway between the dining room and the den toward the front entrance. He's out the door, slamming it behind him. "Looks like he's on the run."

Kirk waves his hand through the air. "Let him go!"

"I'll go check on him," I say.

"You sure, man?" Jordan asks. "I already feel bad enough that we dragged you into this. He just… He gets weird like this sometimes."

Jordan doesn't realize that I know why he gets weird, that he isn't freaking out over nothing, that his dad hurt this family so much, and that it was too much for Mikey.

Surely Jordan and Kate can understand that a little bit.

"I'm dragging myself into it," I tell him. "It's not a big deal. I think it might be better if someone not involved talks to him right now. I'll see how he is and text you, okay?"

"Thanks. I don't think he'll talk to me if I go."

"He just does this sometimes, Scott," Dara explains.

Kirk shakes his head. "Don't worry about him. He'll blow off his steam and be fine. Then he can go back to Los Angeles and pretend his family doesn't exist like he always does."

I acknowledge his comment with a nod, stifling every urge in me to defend his son from his dismissive attitude before I head out to find Mikey.

He's already made it down the road a bit, walking downhill alongside the curb of the similarly designed suburban homes as he makes his way to a cul-de-sac at the end of the road.

I jog to catch up with him. I don't know what I could say to make this better, but at the very least he could use a break from his family.

With his hands in the pockets of his leather jacket, he powerwalks, his gaze fixed ahead of him. The sun's still up, and judging by its position near the horizon, I figure we have about an hour until it sets.

When I catch up with Mikey, I slow my jog until I'm walking alongside him, moving rapidly to keep up. I don't say anything because I'm not trying to make things worse. And I really want him to know that if he needs someone here for him, he can turn to me. But if he wants me to keep my mouth shut and pretend nothing happened or get my ass back to the house, I'm fine with that, too.

He glares at me with a look that nearly makes me back off, but I remind myself he's hurting right now.

Why can't anyone else seem to understand that he needs sympathy right now?

"They think I'm fucking overreacting," Mikey says.

He's not wrong. Jordan didn't seem like he could help because, if anything, he was just annoyed. He had this expression on his face that said: *Why is Mikey starting shit again after all these years?*

"I understood what was happening," I tell him. "Trust me, I know a father's power to get under his kid's skin. Sometimes I think mine is trying to win an award for it."

I was trying to make him smile or smirk, or anything other than the rigid expression that's on his face, but it doesn't change.

He stops in front of a driveway two houses from the cul-de-sac. "Look, I know you're trying to be help me out, and I appreciate that, but I need some space right now."

He turns and continues down the road.

I should go. I should let him think this through on his own, but something possesses me and I pick up my pace again, catching up to him.

"You have a problem understanding what I mean by alone?"

18

MIKEY

Why is he bothering me right now? He knows I don't want to talk about this.

Not with him. Not with anyone.

I'm not just ashamed of my family. I'm embarrassed as fuck that I came back here. I only did it for Kate, but now I know that was a stupid move. Things haven't changed; they're exactly right where they were when I left for college. It wasn't that Dad was trying to get on my nerves. I was just so pissed because he was acting like we could just pick up where we left off, as if nothing had changed. And to see Mom take his fucking side, like she always does, was just too much for me. It sliced open a wound that's still never fully healed. I'm sure Jordan and Kate are frustrated as fuck by how we keep doing this over and over again, but I'm not okay yet. And I don't know if I ever will be.

I have this horrible knot in my gut—one that makes me want to vomit because it reminds me of how weak and stupid I was when I was a kid and he took advantage of me. And when Mom made me feel like I'd done something wrong.

Dad's never treated Kate or Jordan the way he's treated me because they've never challenged his authority. They've never betrayed him the way he believes I did, when really, he's the one who betrayed me. They both did, and now they suffer in their miserable lives in that home, pretending to love each other

124

while Mom stocks up on as many pills as her psychiatrist will liberally prescribe to her to help numb the pain of living a loveless life.

I don't want Kate or her son to have to be around that sick environment for a single day, confronted with the horrifying reality of what happens when two people who once loved each other feel nothing anymore but hate and resentment.

It's not good for either of them, not after all she's already been through with Lyle.

I side-eye Scott as we reach the end of the cul-de-sac, then guide him onto a dirt path that leads through a gap in the woods where the power lines are. It's the path I used to take when I wanted to get away from it all after a shouting match with Dad.

When I needed to get far away so that I could forget how they treated me… what they did to me.

Dirt crushes beneath my shoes.

"Roger doesn't need to be here," I say.

I wait for Scott to say something. Anything.

At this point, I'm not sure that he can say anything that's right.

But he doesn't talk. He just walks with me, being patient and supportive, which is all I really need as a mixture of emotions race through me—rage, guilt, sadness, defeat.

But vulnerability wins.

I lash out at Dad like that because I feel so hurt and wounded, and I need to do something to take my power back.

As we come to the path I usually take into the woods, I turn and start along it, Scott following me and not questioning where we're going, though I can tell by the way he keeps glancing around that he's curious.

I lead him to a small clearing. There's a fallen tree that stretches alongside the creek. Moss and weeds spread across the soft earth.

"This is where I used to come to think," I tell him. "When we would have a fight and I wanted a place to hide. To regroup. Don't know why I'm even telling you this."

"Can be nice to talk to someone, especially a total stranger who you've only boned a few times."

"Sometimes it feels easier to talk to strangers about crazy shit than people you've known all your life. How fucked up is that?"

He's quiet. He doesn't know what to say, I know that. Figure he doesn't want to set me off.

I take a breath. "It's not just about some cheating or even about the fights with him," I admit. "There's a lot more to it than that, but I—"

I stop myself because I know I shouldn't be telling him any of this. He doesn't care or want to know how fucked up my life is. But considering how I feel right now, and how I don't ever feel like I have anyone to share this with, I want to tell Scott.

I have to get it off my chest.

"It was much more than cheating," I blurt out.

"Um... I think you should be a little more specific because that could mean a lot. Did he touch you...?"

"Oh, God no. Nothing like that. No. He didn't do anything sexual or beat me. But what he did was pretty fucking shitty. And Mom isn't innocent either."

"What did they do?"

"When I was in middle school, Mom was taking Kate to a sleepover at one of her friend's houses. It was just Jordan and I playing army. Jordan took the walkie, and Mom had thrown out the other since we'd smashed it a few weeks earlier, so I was going to use Dad's cell phone, which he'd left in his laptop bag. I knew it was in there because that's where he usually left it. Back then, he'd still use the landline for work. I knew I wasn't supposed to be playing with it, but I was eleven and I figured Dad was so busy on his call that he would never know the difference.

"My and Jordan's game was basically hide-and-seek, but I'd pretend I was radioing to my fellow soldiers in battle while we were looking for him. During the game, Dad got a message. And I was curious. I was a kid, so of course I was. I wanted to see what it was, and when I clicked on the message, a picture of some girl popped up. She was very young, and she wasn't covering up the fact that she had some nice boobs. I knew what I was looking at was wrong, and I scrolled up the messages. There were a lot of pictures, not just of her, but of Dad, too. And messages from him saying how much he missed her... and then other things that are like the pictures... I can't block them out of my mind if I try. I couldn't really process what I was looking at. But Dad came out of his office, like he fucking sensed what I was up to, and I guess he knew by the look on my face.

"He sure as hell knew when he snatched the phone from me and saw what I'd been looking at. I was stunned. I couldn't think straight, and I was scared as fuck about what he was going to say. He got quiet, then found Jordan and got him to watch some TV. He said we needed to talk, and pulled me into his office where he told me that I had to keep this a secret from Mom. He said if I didn't, she would leave and take us and that she didn't have any money or anything to survive. That I'd be basically making us homeless. He said he was sorry and that it was an accident, and I mean, I believed him. He was my dad. But he kept making it about how I was going to destroy our family if I said anything. I was so fucking dumb."

"You were a kid," Scott says. "And he was your dad. You trusted him."

"That's not good enough for me. I should have been smarter. I should have thought about it more. But I was so fucking thrown by it when he said all that, and I knew he was wrong. Deep down, I knew. I felt it every night when I went to bed. It was keeping me up, and I was throwing up for the next few days. I worked up the courage and finally told Mom what I found, and I told her what Dad said about us being homeless."

"Oh my God. Is that when she made him leave?"

I cringe at his words.

"She didn't leave. She called me a liar. She said I'd misunderstood and all this other bullshit. It wasn't until a year later that he left with the girl he was cheating on her with. That's how it all really happened. And Mom, even after how she humiliated me and made me feel like a liar, admitted she knew I'd been right all along, but that she'd needed Kirk. She didn't apologize or anything. And then when he came back after that girl ditched him, she took him right back. She was never the same after it, though. They fought a lot, but they clung onto each other like the co-dependent scum they both are. So forgive me if I can't be all roses and sunshine when I see them. They want to pretend that everything's fine and like that shit never happened, but I just can't grin and bear it the way I always have."

"Strength is Within?" he asks, referring to my tattoo, I assume.

"I got that in college when I was finally free of them. Kind of a badge of honor for surviving so many years with them. Putting up with all the bullshit. Made me realize that I can be tough when I need to be."

"I'm sorry you had to deal with that on your own. Have you ever talked to Jordan and Kate about this?"

"It's not something I've ever been proud about sharing. Not something they should have to deal with. It's one of the reasons I don't want her to be here with them."

"And you don't think they should know?"

"What good does it do them?"

"I think it might at least help them understand all this pent up rage you have. Know that you're not being a dick. Although, I think it was clear from what happened in there that your dad was instigating it."

"I think it bothers him that he knows he can't control me like he did back then."

Although, in a way, he still controls me. I have to keep this a secret from Kate and Jordan because some part of me still believes that telling them would bring about the end of our family. I already lost Mom and Dad, so in some ways, I don't want them to live that same fate.

"I just wish Roger didn't have to be around him," I say. "Dad's—"

"He's a monster for what he did to you. You're right to be mad at him. You didn't do anything wrong. To ask his kid to cover for him… and to put all that pressure on you…"

"I was so fucking dumb."

"You didn't know what was going on. And he made you keep that awful secret. And then for your mom to act like that when you found the strength to finally tell her? No, I definitely get why you're so upset. Thank you for sharing that."

He's the first person who's been here when we've had one of those explosions—the first person outside of it who I felt I could open up to about this thing I've kept to myself for so long.

I'm glad he came out here to get me. I needed this. I've carried this with me for so long, and I haven't ever shared it with anyone. I think the only reason I even shared it with him was because he found me at my weakest, when I needed someone the most. And I never have anyone there for me.

It's me against the world. Always has been. But Scott's friendly and kind, and obviously understanding. And it's such a relief to hear someone be on my side in all of this.

In some ways, I'm still that eleven-year-old kid thinking that it's all on me, that I'm the one who's done something wrong.

"She's not going to be here forever," Scott says. "She'll find a new place soon."

I take a heavy breath. He's right, and I know a part of this is me projecting how hard it would be for me to be back in this house reliving all those shitty memories.

"It's the worst place for a kid to be. It's not even just the fights they get into... or the screaming matches. It's the little things. The nagging. The way he talks to her like she's nothing, and how she nags him with so much hate. You can hear how angry she is at him still when she asks him to fucking take out the garbage. You can hear how much she's never gotten over what he did to her. You think a kid should be around that?"

"Kate will be here for a few months, maybe, and you know they're going to try and act a little more chipper around their grandson. They're not going to be their usual selves during this honeymoon period."

He's right. I just need to keep reminding myself that it's not going to be as bad as I'm thinking.

"It's more than that, though. I worry about Kate. After what she's been through, is this really the house she needs to be in? With this bitter couple who remind her that this is what life is? Sadness and misery? Doesn't she need something positive in her life right now?"

"She just needs a place to stay."

"You think I'm thinking way too much about this?"

"I think you're making it hard on yourself... and Kate, too. It's temporary. No one wants to live with their parents. It's not the best situation, but at least it gets her out of an even worse one."

I'm amazed at how at ease Scott's words are making me feel. He's done a good job of bringing me down, soothing all that rage that built up so quickly when I was back at the house yelling at Dad.

"Thanks," I say.

"For what?"

"For following me out here. For not letting me be on my own right now."

"I honestly wasn't sure if you'd want me chasing you down like this. Thought you might have seen it as annoying as fuck."

"No, it's helping. Making me breathe a little more. Feel a little more at ease in this whole crap situation."

"I'm glad. And I'm sorry that you had to deal with all this tonight. This week. I know that wasn't easy when Kate dumped that shit about what was going on with her on you."

"What an understatement. In the past few days, it feels like everything's sort of fucked me over from every angle."

"Hey, I'm the one who's been fucked from every angle," he reminds me.

I smirk. "Trust me, that's been the only good thing to come out of any of this."

"And there's definitely been a lot of *cum* out of this." He pats my crotch.

I chuckle. God, it feels good to go from that intense hate toward my father to being lighthearted with Scott.

"There we go," Scott says. "This is the Mikey I prefer to see."

"I don't want to go back there."

"We don't have to do that. We'll figure something out. Maybe Jordan can come pick us up… or maybe we can Uber. It doesn't matter. I don't think anyone is going to be asking you to go back there and revisit any of that."

"Right?!" I laugh at the truth of it.

"It'll be okay."

I believe him. "Kinda sad that I'll be leaving for good on Wednesday."

"Well, at least it gives us time for some more fun."

He glances around. I wonder if he's thinking what I'm thinking.

He approaches me slowly, a shy expression on his face, but considering the way he moves, I don't imagine there's anything shy about him right now.

He pushes up against me, and I lean down and kiss him.

It sets me at ease—chases away all those thoughts that have been running through my mind, making me obsess about them, making me dwell on the fear that had returned to me. He frees me of the imprisonment of these thoughts and the hold that my father's sins had on me once again.

19

SCOTT

I didn't know if this would work, especially while he's so stressed out about Kate, but as he reciprocates my kiss, I know this was the right decision. Plus, his reminder about how little time we really have, about how we need to savor this while we can, just makes me want to do this even more.

His kiss destroys the uneasiness that I started feeling back at the house.

I want him to relax. I want him to feel like he does when we fuck—like he doesn't have anything to worry about and can be free from the pain that just worked up in his mind as he was forced to revisit his past.

He pushes me back against a nearby tree and moves his hands under my shirt, his fingers massaging my skin. It's hard to focus on his kisses and touching at the same time because they both generate such powerful sensations, like explosions within me, overtaking my senses and leaving my thoughts scattered.

His touch feels so warm on this cool evening.

As he kisses my neck, I say, "Let me help you forget."

He drops down onto his knees, unfastens my belt, and unzips my fly.

What is he doing? I thought I'd blow him, but if this is what he wants, I sure as fuck am not going to fight him.

He pulls my jeans and boxers down, and I glance around to

make sure this place is as private as it seems.

Nothing in sight but the woods around us.

My cock sticks straight out, begging for him to take it in his mouth. But he goes for my balls instead, licking, playing, teasing. He moves the fingers of his right hand up my leg before reaching that sweet spot just behind my balls.

The rush it stirs forces me to clench my ass cheeks together.

"God, you taste good." He licks before glancing up at me like he wants to see if what he's doing is stimulating me.

"That feels fucking amazing, Mikey."

I can't tell if it's the physical chemistry between us or if he's this fucking good at what he does, but there's a heat that covers my body, leaving me filled with anticipation and excitement. Whatever Mikey does for me fills me with an energy I can't explain, a powerful force that races through my entire body.

It leaves me begging for more. Wanting him to take me. All of me. In whatever way he wants.

He licks from my balls across to the bottom of my shaft before sliding my dick into his mouth and moving his head back and forth.

His mouth is so wet, like he's been salivating for this cock ever since we started kissing.

I lean back against the tree as he cups my balls tightly with one hand and then brings his other to stroke my shaft in sync with his sucking.

"How did you fucking learn to work a cock like that?" I ask.

It seems like he wouldn't be this good since he's only been with women. But I guess this is a talent he's picked up from listening to women's bodies, seeing what works and what doesn't.

He slides the hand on my balls back and pushes his middle finger up to my asshole, massaging in circles while continuing his intense blowjob.

"God, I wish you were inside me right now," I say.

He pulls my cock out of his mouth and gasps for air. I don't know why that turns me on even more. I like the thought of him being that invested in my dick.

"Let's do it then." He reaches into his back pocket and retrieves a condom.

"What the fuck?"

"I try to always be prepared, especially when I'm fucking someone who turns me on as much as you do."

The look he gives me—playful, filled with desire—arouses me even more. He reaches into his side pocket and fishes out a small packet of lube.

"Where the fuck did you get that?" I ask.

"That gas station we stopped at when we took the U-Haul back. I figured we might get a chance to use it tonight when we got back to the condo, but looks like Christmas came early."

"Oh, it'll come alright."

I'm thrilled he had the foresight to think of it. Probably because he's a fucking sex machine. This is his life with women. This is the kind of stud he is. The kind who could run into sex at any time and just needs to be ready for the occasion. But it certainly benefits me that he's prepared, so I can't complain. In fact, everything about his previous sex life is why he's such an incredible lay now, so I'm more than happy with the manwhore he's been.

"Are you serious right now?" I can't believe what we're going to do. Getting a BJ in the woods is one thing. But anal? I never did that in public, and was certainly never prepared enough to give it.

I don't wait for him to respond to my question, though. I whirl around and toss my shirt off before leaning up against the tree.

"Damn, you're ready for my cock, aren't you?" he asks.

I glance over my shoulder, seeing that look of desire in his eyes, that lust that makes me feel like I'm the hottest guy in the world.

"Don't make me fucking wait for it," I tell him.

He rises to his feet and comes up behind me, glancing down my body.

"Taking in the view?" I ask.

"Thoroughly enjoying it is more like it."

Even with just my pants on, I feel like I'm totally vulnerable. I like when he's in charge, making me feel submissive to him.

He licks his middle finger and forefinger and pushes them between my ass cheeks, sticking the tips in my hole and moving them in circles inside me.

"Jesus Christ, Mikey. How do you fucking do this to me?"

He moves in close, kissing behind my ear.

The nerves he stimulates erupt with tingling sensations.

I toss my head back, then shift it to the side and kiss him.

He continues pleasuring my hole with one hand, and I hear him undoing his belt with the other.

The thought of nearing that moment where he's pushing into me fills me with excitement.

He doesn't leave me in suspense for long. Soon, he's suited and lubed up and ready to go, sliding his cock into my willing ass.

The pressure is powerful. My body is tense from a chill in the air. Goosebumps prick across my flesh as he slides inside, the lubrication making his work so much easier than when we used lotion those first few times.

I wrap my arms around the tree and cling onto it for support as he presses within me, offering a gentle stroke down my back to my ass, which he squeezes gently.

Pushing deeper and deeper, he arouses and excites all those nerves within me that feel so good.

The pressure he fills me with makes my cock hard as a rock. I let one arm fall, and I stroke my dick to offer it some ease.

"You like me inside you like this, Scott?" I like the playfulness in his tone—so carefree compared to when we first came out here. He's obviously enjoying this experience as much as I wanted him to—taking me, possessing me. "Groan for me," he orders.

I've kept quiet because I didn't want to rouse any attention if there was anyone nearby, but now that he's requested a performance, I fully intend to give him one worthy of what he's giving me. I offer a light groan first, but as he digs into my ass, I offer another much louder one that, if anyone was nearby, they'd easily hear.

"Give it to me, Mikey. Harder."

He fucks me like the stud he is, pushing that fully erect girth deep within me, as deep as he can, and I moan because damn, it feels so good.

I notice him shifting about through my periphery, and I turn to see him removing his shirt.

Sweat rushes down his face.

He's already put in quite the workout, and I'm pleased to see his energy isn't waning.

He pets my ass as I accept him eagerly and greedily as every force that hits my prostate stirs and excites nerves that ripple up my body.

My arousal climbs and climbs.

"Give that dick to me." He leans down so that his torso is against my back. Reaching around, he snatches my cock from me, and I don't put up any resistance. He strokes with such skill. I keep thinking, *Where did he learn this?* But I realize he has his own dick, and this must be what he does to get himself off. And it works like a fucking charm as he twists his wrist, rubbing his thumb over the head, exciting it, thrilling me to a point where I don't know how much longer I'm going to be able to keep from coming.

I can feel my balls shifting, tightening.

I'm so close. "You've got to stop. Please. You're gonna make me come."

He positions his face beside my ear, whispering, "Isn't this what you want?"

That's not helping any, having his hot breath hit my ear,

that voice stirring a whole other level of arousal within me.

I can feel the pressure moving up my shaft…

"No, no." I grab his hand on my cock, stopping him. "Just stop for a second. You don't know how close I am."

He smiles beside my ear.

I remain still, and he stops fucking me for a moment. The pressure remains in that same spot before finally settling. I breathe hard, furiously. I'm trying to control myself, trying to calm myself down. I'm relieved that he didn't take me too far too quickly. I would have hated myself if I'd disappointed him.

Deep, steady breaths.

Then he starts pushing in again.

I roll my head back as I enjoy the sensation once more, now that I can enjoy it without having to worry about spooging everywhere.

He rubs his hand across my abdomen, and the sensations his fingertips stir is incredible. So fucking incredible.

"I don't think I can keep it in much longer," he says.

"Don't."

"Fuck."

Shifting, twisting, I know he's spewing within the condom. I rub my dick, spilling out before me, my come dripping onto the moss-covered ground.

He pushes up against me, shoving me against the tree, and I relax against it, catching my breath.

God, that felt so incredible. He's always incredible.

As we fall from our climax together, I think about how nice it is that I could be here to soothe Mikey after that shitty dinner with his family.

20

Three Weeks Later...

I sit at my desk, looking over some notes from our logistics department.

I compare them with the specs our company's client sent over and their needs for this piece of machinery we're designing for a glass bottle manufacturer. The new machines will work quicker and integrate several stages rapidly, along with faster sorting into packaging. If we can do it right, we're talking about creating a goldmine for the company we're selling it to, but as always, the real obstacle is finding a way to make the changes practical and on a budget. The budget is where the real issue lies. We got back the deets from the owner of the company, and there was a major oversight in the annealing stage of the machinery—something that will cost a lot more money to fix. I'll have to review this with my boss and smooth things over because he's not going to be happy.

While I go back through the specs and create my report on this particular design, my phone vibrates. I pull it out and see it's from Scott. *How's it going, stud?*

We've been texting back and forth for the past few weeks. Since our conversation in the woods near my parents' place, he's become more than my brother's roomie. He's a friend of sorts, at least.

The other day, I sent him a Lamb Chop/fisting meme, and

he replied with a Mean Girls meme that read, "Why are you so obsessed with me?" It cracked me up and kept me laughing throughout my day.

It's a shame we're thousands of miles apart.

What we shared was fun and playful and frisky.

I miss that cute face of his, and I wish we could have shared a few more nights together. Not that we didn't have a few good throws after the night at my parents', but I hadn't grown tired of fucking him.

Not even a little.

I've had plenty of sex in my life, but it's hard to get the hottest sex I've ever had out of my head.

And I've never been able to be this cool with someone afterward. Usually, we don't chat beyond the fuck. Although, I don't ever go on the sort of sex-fest that I went on with Scott after that shit weekend with my family.

His text reminds me that I need to call Kate. She called last night, but it was well past midnight by the time I finished my conference call with my guys in logistics about this project I'm trying to sort out. As I'm about to pull up her number, she calls and I answer.

"Hey, there, Katie."

She doesn't groan like she normally does at me calling her Katie instead of Kate, and it's got me concerned.

"Everything okay?"

"Oh, yes. No. Everything's fine. I had kind of a crazy morning. Like in what could be an amazing way."

"Okay, don't be vague, sis. Spit it out."

"A friend of mine, she used to be my neighbor, told me

about this house that just came on the market. It's a friend's house. Now don't get crazy. It's not incredible. A little bit of a fixer upper, she said. But it's in the right school district for Roger, and the neighborhood is really nice."

"How much of a fixer upper are we talking about?"

"I'll send you a link on Zillow."

I pull up my email and skim through the images.

"Here's the thing," she says as I peruse what appears to be a really nice place. Not perfect, but nice. "I can't afford the down payment right now, but based on what my attorney says, I'll have the money once I finalize the divorce, and between that and my salary, I can pay you back."

"How much are we talking about here?"

"I can get FHA funding for it, so it'd only be, like, seven-thousand. But I'd need help with the mortgage until I can get it on my own."

I like the sound of that. Although, anything sounds better than her staying with our parents right now—something that's still itched at me since I left Georgia.

I inspect some of the information on Zillow. "Two stories, .73-acre back yard... doesn't look like it's been on here long."

"Is that a good thing?"

"I mean, I'm not a real estate agent, but I remember when I was buying my place, my agent told me that sometimes if it's been on there for a long time, it's because there really is a problem, and that's the reason no one's put up an offer yet. But that price does seem really low for the area. Definitely a red flag, so I wouldn't get your hopes up too much."

"She says they want to sell it quickly. They have a few

showings already, but they managed to book me today. I'm going to run over there and look, so please just get ready if I call, because they want a quick offer."

"Well, don't go racing into it. You want to make sure it's actually a good deal before you wind up with a place that might need a little more than a few quick fixes, you know? But fortunately, if you need to make an offer, you still can get an inspection done in your due diligence period, so don't sweat it too much."

"I will, I will. But look at that yard. Isn't it beautiful? Roger would have a place to play. I could even put a little swing and a play area up for him. Can't you see it?"

"That would be really cool," I admit. And it's not just something I think would be nice for Roger. I can tell by her enthusiasm that it'd be just as good for her. She needs something to be excited about, something to give her some hope about their future together.

"There's even room for a kiddie pool when he gets older. I mean, Mikey, I'm talking about a place where I can start a new life. Where I can put the past behind me. I feel like this is somewhere I could spend my future."

It kills me to hear her enthusiasm return like this, because I'm scared as fuck that this place might not live up to her expectations. Maybe I'm just a pessimist. Or maybe I've had my own hopes dashed too many times by contractors overselling products and designs to be jumping head over heels about this yet, but for her sake, I hope she's right.

All I want right now is for her and Roger to have a life—a real life where they can be happy together—where they can put

Lyle and all that fucked-up shit he did behind them and move on.

"I know. It could be amazing, Kate, but I want you to be careful and be on the lookout for a con. Check it out and if you like it, put in an offer. I can wire you however much you need for the down payment. We can work a repayment plan around that. I have the money for it, so don't stress about thinking you're gonna need to pay me back right away."

"Are you sure? It's not too much?"

I can tell by the way she says it, it's like when we were kids and she would ask to use a toy. She doesn't want to hurt my feelings, but she also wants this so bad.

Even if I didn't have the money, I would be doing everything in my power to get it to her because I love her, and she deserves this.

And because, as pessimistic as I am about this being a great opportunity, I want to believe that maybe somehow she deserves this, and that it might be a situation of her being in the right place at the right time.

"This is not a big deal at all," I tell her. "And you know I'll do anything to get you out of Mom and Dad's place right now. Don't want you mooching off of them until you're in your forties."

I was expecting a laugh or at least a chuckle, but I think I activated something she's already been concerned about because she's totally silent.

"I'm sorry. That was a joke."

"I know. I just—I really want this to work out. And if it is too much—"

"I'm not Daddy Warbucks, but I can pinch this if it turns out to be as good of an opportunity as it sounds like. Although, promise me if you decide to make an offer, you'll get someone to come out and inspect to make sure it really is this good. I don't want you to get excited and it wind up being something that isn't as great as it looks on Zillow, you know?"

"Their real estate agent said it'll probably cost a couple thousand dollars to renovate. There's a leaky roof and some water damage, but I figure it's stuff we have to patch up here and there."

"Like I said, it *sounds* great. Just don't get your hopes up until you get out there and make sure that this place is as amazing as it seems, okay?"

"I'll check on it and get back to you."

She makes a squealing sound that's sweet to hear.

I smile.

It's nice knowing that she's filled with this much excitement—so different than when I talked to her at that lunch when she had to tell me the truth about what that bastard Lyle did to her. I like that she feels comfortable sharing that with me. And I like that I can be here for her right now when she needs me.

21

SCOTT

"Miranda was telling me earlier she has a lead from work if you're interested," Dad says.

I sit at the table with Dad, Miranda, and Conner. Miranda and Conner are my siblings who still live in Atlanta. Josh, my eldest brother, lives in Seattle now, so he can't just swing by for one of Dad's occasional dinner get-togethers—ones that remind me of when we were all in high school sharing our success stories. Well, they were sharing their amazing success stories, and I was more detailing a progress report of how my grades had steadily improved through my normal human efforts—since I didn't inherit the genius genes.

I love my family more than anything, and I know my Dad, despite how he can be sometimes, loves me. He's not a fucking ass like Mikey's parents were to him.

"No, but thank you," I tell him, reminding myself that he's trying to help out.

"With your bachelor's in accounting," Miranda says, "I could get you a good in with the company. You should definitely consider it. It's not too late to put your foot back into the business world."

There she goes again. As if, because I chose a different path, I'm sitting here pining away at my missed opportunity. The thing my family will never get is that I don't need to have their success to feel successful. Not that I'm making a ton of money, and hell, I'm barely paying the rent as it is, but I've made enough connections in this industry to believe I can make this work.

"And I offered to talk to some guys at the bank," Dad adds.

His hair, graying at the sides, has the same curl to it as mine. I'm the only one of the kids who inherited this gene. Everyone else's hair is about as straight as they are. I used to envy how much easier it was for them to manage their hair, but now it seems simple and boring. I like my curls, even when they are a little wild and unmanageable.

"I don't know how many times I have to tell you, but I don't need any help. I'm doing fine," I tell Dad.

I don't normally snap like that, but I feel like it's the only way I can get them to shut up and shift the conversation onto something other than me.

Dad eyes me uncomfortably. It reminds me of when I came out to him, that silent disapproval. That feeling like all the work he'd put into me, his investment, was for nothing.

Like Mom's death was for nothing.

"I say these things because I love you, Scott. I don't want you to wake up one day waiting tables. You can do really well in a serious career if you apply yourself like you did in school. You're always going to have to work a little harder than your brothers or sister, but you can get through it. You don't have to be a CPA like your sister... or the head of your department like your brother Josh."

"Or an accounts manager like Conner. I get it, Dad," I say.

He has a way of making me feel like a dummy. And I

know he's trying to be practical, but how does he expect me to feel when he's sitting there, comparing us like this, making me feel like I need to be a second-rate version of my siblings instead of a first-rate version of myself. I have enough insecurities without him adding this to the mix.

"I'm going to be fine, Dad. I'm working and I'm happy, so can you back off?"

He quiets before running his thumb and forefinger through his goatee, which is graying as much as his hair.

And that's the end of the discussion about me.

Thank God. I didn't know how much more I could bear. When I finish up with dinner, I head back to my and Jordan's place. He's stretched out on the couch, his laptop on his thighs as he types away. He has his glasses on, which he typically only wears when he's actually working on something and never when we go out. He's types quickly. As cool as he always acts, I don't imagine people who didn't know him well would realize just how dedicated he is to what he does and his continuing education. He has a similar attitude as Mikey. They act too cool for the world but then are still totally successful within it. I envy their attitude towards life.

"How's the fam?" he asks, not letting up on the keyboard.

"Fine."

He shifts his attention to me. "How about you?"

"That's a whole other thing. For some reason. They're all trying to get on to me about getting a real job right now more than usual. I don't know if Dad had a talk with them or what, but I kind of snapped."

"You snapped? Oh, I'd like to see that."

"Shut up. How's your day? Working on your thesis for a change?"

"When am I not working on it? I'm trying to knock out some ideas I got while I was in Belize. It gave me time to put together some chapters I hadn't really figured out how to go about. This gets the structure down, but I'm going to have to go back and add citations and some more research, but from what I've done, I know it'll all come together pretty well."

"Cool, cool." I head into the kitchen, carrying a plastic container Dad gave me with some leftovers. "There's some chicken and mashed potatoes in here if you want any," I tell Jordan.

"Ooh. Fried chicken."

"Does Dad make any other kind?"

"God, you know I'll be stealing all of that in the middle of the night. Nothing like his homemade fried chicken. You manage to sneak me any cornbread?"

I chuckle. "You should have come with me. Didn't have anything left to steal by the end."

"I should have. Hell, I fucking owe you after that clusterfuck dinner you came to with me the other week. Oh, speaking of which, Kate had some good news today."

"Really?"

"Evidently she found a house that she might be getting a good deal on. She'll need Mikey to front her some money, but it sounds really promising. She just went out there today, and she loves it. They're working something out with the real estate agent who's repping the clients who own the place."

Hope rises within me. "Would he come back to help her

move in?"

I did my best—summoned every bit of self-restraint within me to make that sound casual, but I could tell that my tone was strange, because secretly, I want him to come back, even if only for a few days.

It's not just the sex, either.

That was fucking unbelievably amazing. But also, behind that chill, cool attitude, there was something more, something I caught a glimpse of that night when he revealed the truth about the burden his father and mother forced upon him. But it only made me want to get to know him better.

Although, maybe it's for the best that I didn't get the chance because I was starting to develop a little bit of a crush, but considering our lives are so far apart, there was no point in exploring each other any further when there wasn't really a chance anything could ever come of it.

"He mentioned coming back for a few days," Jordan says, "just so we can get that stuff out of storage. I keep telling him we need to hire movers, but he was saying it's more about being there for Kate, and I agree. She really needs us right now. Why you asking about my bro? You digging seeing him prancing around here half-naked again?"

"Whatever," I say, trying to play it off. "I'm glad he'll be here for Kate."

But really, as glad as I am that he'll be here for her, there's a selfish part of me that just wants to have more sexy-time with Jordan's brother.

It's kind of nice, even if there isn't anything more to it than that.

"But we'll see if it really pans out," Jordan adds. "She has to close on it quickly, and there are a lot of people looking at this place. It's a good deal, so if she doesn't get it soon, it's liable to get snatched up. But if she does, you mind helping us out again? I know that's a lot to ask, but I don't think that we could have done it without you last time."

"Oh, absolutely. I really don't mind helping out. Anything I can do to help your sister, I'm in. I'm impressed with how she's getting back out there and trying to find a new place as quickly as she can. I can't imagine that it's easy with everything she's been through to just dive right back into trying to create a new life, but she's not afraid of anything, which is nice. She keeps saying that she wants to hang with me in town, but I've been so busy trying to get some of these projects out that I haven't really had time."

"Yeah. Kate's a fighter. Always has been. And she sure as fuck won't let this keep her down for long. I'll keep you posted about what happens with this lead."

"That'd be really great."

"For sure. Oh, and about my bro…"

I tense up.

Did I do something? Say something? Was it when I asked about him coming to visit?

I thought we did a good job of keeping everything under wraps. Jordan was so busy during the week that it gave us time to fuck again and again and again, to fully enjoy each other's bodies and share some intense passion that I know from my own experiences I'll never be able to forget—so much so that I feel bad for the next guy because he's got a lot to live up to—

but did something happen? Did Mikey say something that made him catch on?

"Yes?" I ask.

"He told me to tell you hi."

"He did?"

God, sometimes he's too fucking adorable.

"Yeah. Right? I guess you two really hit it off."

More than you could possibly know. Or would want to know.

I head into my room to start working on a few of the projects I need to wrap up by the end of this week. I have to commit probably another five hours tonight to make my schedule on these.

I can do it, though. I may not be as smart as my siblings, but what I've always lacked in genius, I've made up for in dedication.

But before I get to work, I text Mikey.

> **ME:**
> Why didn't you tell me about Kate's place?

It's not that he needed to, but I considered, since we've been texting back and forth since he got back to Los Angeles, that he might have brought it up with me.

> **MIKEY:**
> Just didn't want to get your hopes up in case it doesn't pan out. She's kind of head over heels for this, so I want to

be sure before we get everyone excited.

ME:
It'd give you a good excuse to swing by
for some more booty.

MIKEY:
Not that I need an excuse. ;)

God, why am I grinning like this?

He has a talent for making me feel like I'm not just any lay. Like I'm special. I'm sure he has the same talent with girls, just having those blue irises on you, making you feel like you're the only one he's thinking about—which is a bunch of bull, but that doesn't keep it from feeling good.

I get to work on one of my new projects: a series of Christmas cards for an erotic art company. They have all the models picked out, and they need someone to create the layout and the design for the cards. I've gone through about a thousand fonts trying to find the right ones that go along with the text they want to use. Nothing seems to fit. I want something classical, but that doesn't look outdated like something you'd see on a website back when people were first starting to create their own shitty websites. And I don't want a font that's too wild like someone who just figured out how to design is trying to overcompensate for something.

I need something elegant.

I make my way through my database of fonts, taking my time, trying out a few with the images until I narrow it down to three that I really like, and create a mock to send over to the client.

Here I am spending all this time on something that my family thinks is pretty much useless. They don't realize the work that goes into it, and they don't really care.

22

One Month Later…

I sit in the moving truck next to Kate. It's been a long-ass time since I've been this excited about something, and I appreciate that Kate made sure to schedule a moving time when Dad wouldn't be home so I wouldn't have to see him when I picked her up from the house.

I can deal with Mom, and someone had to watch Roger.

"You're totally going to fall in love with it the way I did," she says.

She's glowing, her eyes lit up with excitement. And I have to admit I'm just as excited since I haven't seen the place since she closed on it two days ago.

It was a little hectic since we had to rush to get the paperwork and the wire transfer arranged. I would've preferred a chance to take a look at the place myself, especially considering how much I invested into it, but it wasn't really an option since the agent said there were so many offers on the table and the owners wanted to close as soon as possible. She did hire an inspector to take a look at everything which gave me the confidence that, as long as Kate was happy, I was on board.

This isn't about some stupid house; this is about her and Roger's future.

I check the side mirror and see Jordan's Civic tailing the

truck. He and Scott are following behind to help us unload everything.

But there's something else I need to unload—right into Scott's ass.

This is where the real test of my restraint is going to come in. I flew in late last night, so I didn't have the chance to meet up with Scott and get him to take care of this need I now have for him, to give me that ass again and put me out of my fucking misery by letting me have what I've been craving since I returned home nearly two months ago. And ever since I started planning this trip, I've planned to make the best of it, which is why I booked a hotel room this time instead of just staying with Jordan again.

Even as I drive with my little sister in the passenger's seat, I'm hard as a stone, and I keep having to stop myself from adjusting the way it's caught in my boxers.

As we pull up to the house, I park alongside the curb of the street of two-story houses. While this one hasn't been taken care of as well as the others, it looks as good as it did in the pictures, which I feel like is all we can really ask for. Yeah, it needs a new paint job. The white siding and red shutters are fading. The grass in the front yard is dead, but that's to be expected. Nothing a good landscaper can't take care of.

Before we move everything in, I ask Kate for a quick walk-through. With my experience in construction, I can at least assess the damage and give her a realistic estimate of how much it's going to cost us to repair some of these issues. I'm fine with giving her the money for the renovation now and working out some sort of repayment plan later. I don't plan on her actually repaying me, though. I'll tell her it's a loan and not accept anything from her later on. She's the one who's in a bind, and I know if the shoe was on the other foot, she would give me whatever I needed without asking for anything in return.

Kate jingles her house keys before opening the door and welcoming us inside.

Jordan and Kate enter first, and I wave for Scott to follow after them. I grip his tight ass firmly, and he acts like he doesn't even notice because he knows we can't give anything away in front of Kate and Jordan.

God, it's been too long since I've been up inside him.

I still have a semi just thinking about how much I want to pull him aside and stick it in deep.

A minute is all it would take to spooge up in there, and he'd hardly have to wait for me to go again in a longer, much more satisfying encounter where I would let him remember what he's been missing.

What we've both been missing.

It's been a while, but he's the last person I've fucked around with. I've been so busy with work that I haven't even had time to play around with my regulars who've been blowing up my phone. In some ways, I think Scott fucking ruined me for women because I've been craving no one, not even other guys—except him.

I would've thought I'd had enough after all the sex we enjoyed while I was here before, but sex with Scott is better than all the fucking I've had in my lifetime—and that's a lot of fucking sex.

I keep wondering if it's the chemistry we have or his skills or a combination of both, but it makes no difference; all that matters is that he lets me have it again.

Kate starts her grand tour, guiding us through the spacious living and dining areas and into the kitchen.

"These cabinets definitely need to be redone," I say as I inspect them. "I was hoping from the pictures we might be able to reface them, but they're fucking wrecked on the inside from the water damage." I see the concerned expression on her face, so I try to set her at ease; I don't want her thinking that I fucking found mold or shit like that. "And we'll have to take care of the water damage on these floorboards. Redo the floors and patch up the ceiling in places, but that shouldn't be too bad."

"Like, how bad money-wise is that?"

"I can't be sure. Just let me figure it out, and I can give you an estimate. Okay, sis?"

"I guess," she says uneasily before leading us through the rest of the house.

"This is actually really nice. A lot of space, too."

Scott and Jordan are equally impressed. Maybe she lucked out, after all.

She finally takes us into the basement, and I check around when I notice some dust on the concrete floor beside a wall that's half concrete and half insulated wood boards. I inspect the tiny specks. They look concerning.

"Did the inspector notice anything wrong with this?" I ask Kate.

The guilty expression on her face doesn't set me at ease. "I tried to get an inspector to come, but he had to cancel last minute, so I asked the owners if they could extend the due diligence period. They said they were closing on another property, and they needed this one to close first or they'd overextend their credit. I either had to move forward or back out because they had multiple offers on the table, and one was a cash offer that came right after mine, so I knew they'd take it.

"So we talked about the issues. Anything I needed to be concerned about. And they were very upfront about the water damage. They never even stayed here. This was a house they were planning to flip, but they lost some money in some other investments, which is why they were trying to get it off their hands. Then they said, since they really wanted to close, if it concerned me that much, they would take five thousand off the asking price."

"So again, no inspection? And you didn't mention any of this to me?"

She shakes her head. "I just didn't want you to be concerned, and I thought it'd be fine. I figured we could use that money to fix the damages."

I sigh. "Holy fucking shit."

"What is it?"

"This is probably termites. There's no telling how much damage they've done to the structure, Kate."

I stop myself. I don't want to go off on her, but she has no idea what a wreck she made of her future.

"Can't we go back and ask them to fix it or something?" Kate asks.

"That's not how it works. The contract you signed said as-is. And if they didn't live here, I doubt anyone knew about the termites, so it's a shitty situation that you eagerly signed up for."

"What are we talking about in terms of cost?"

"That's the million dollar question... and I do mean the million dollar question because there's no telling until we get someone out here to figure out what needs to be repaired." It's a reminder that I had every reason to be skeptical about this deal. "Fuck, fuck, fuck."

Her excited expression dissolves, and though I'm sad that I have to be the one to disillusion her, it has to be done.

"It's not going to be millions, but this could be a serious mess."

Something a lot worse than if she had waited and found something a little more expensive and with fewer issues than this is likely to have.

I run my hands across my face. I wanted her out of Mom and Dad's, but I don't know that it's going to be worth it when she finds out just how expensive a mistake like this can be.

23
SCOTT

Mikey calls a friend of his who's an exterminator and asks him if he can swing by tomorrow.

I'm nervous that the change in plans will mean Mikey and I will have to wait until another time to mess around, but he coordinates everything seemingly with us in mind. After we transfer what we can from the moving truck into Kate's house, at least to store it while Mikey sorts out the mess, Jordan takes Kate back to their parents' with some of the stuff that she'll need now that she can't move in. If it was just Kate, Mikey said there wouldn't be an issue, but with Roger, the renovation will be extensive enough that it won't be a healthy environment for him—not with sawdust and chemicals in the air.

While Kate, Roger, and Jordan head back to Kirk and Dara's, Mikey and I return the truck to the rental service before heading back to his hotel room.

He doesn't talk much on the way back. And I keep quiet because he has a lot to digest, and more than anything, I can tell he's bothered by how he had to squash Kate's dreams.

He pulls himself from his daze and looks at me briefly. "Sorry. I know I'm not particularly exciting today."

"Considering what just happened, I totally understand."

"I don't think Kate realizes how serious this is. How much it'll cost. The more I poked around, the more extensive the damage looked. And it's to the foundation of the house. That friend who's an exterminator, the one I called, used to work with me when I volunteered for Habitat for Humanity during college."

Habitat for Humanity is a local housing project. They build homes for struggling families. Mikey hadn't mentioned that he used to do that. Yet another thing about him that surprises me.

"He'll come out and take a look at it tomorrow," he continues. "See what we can do."

"What's the worst case scenario?"

"I don't know. We're talking about potentially tens of thousands of dollars in damage. I could be overreacting, though. It just looks like it's affecting that one part of the house. I won't really know for sure until my friend takes a look."

"Kate can't afford the kind of thing you're talking about," I say. "You know that."

"Hell, neither can I. I'm gonna call into work and tell them I need to spend some more time out here. I can telework as long as I need to. I already finished up our big project of the year and now it's just supervising the damn thing, getting some of the changes made. That's the lucky part. Even if I need to stay out here to take care of some of this stuff. It'd be too expensive to get contractors, so I'll do it myself."

"Yourself? You can do shit like that?"

He smirks, and it's kind of a relief because it's the first time I've seen him look at ease since he saw that dust in the basement.

"What? You don't think I can handle some repairs? I told you I worked in construction. I could build that house from scratch if I needed to. Please. And I still build for some housing projects on the side. It'll be a hell of a challenge, but I'm the guy to do it."

"If you need any help, let me know. I can work on all my stuff from the house, so—"

"Are you saying that so I'll get balls-deep in you? Because I can tell you, that's going to happen either way."

I roll to my side to display my ass for him.

"Have at it," I tease.

Mikey laughs, and I like knowing I'm responsible for it. Then he looks at it again and growls. "You better not be too inviting."

"I think this is just inviting enough. Come on. You need a little destressing."

"We need to wait until we get back to the hotel, at least."

I glance around at the stretch of interstate.

"Do we?" I ask.

He glances at me, his jaw tense. Then he assesses the situation like I did.

He checks behind him before pulling over to the side of the road.

Holy shit, is he for real? I didn't think he'd actually take me up on my offer, but even the thought of this actually happening makes me hard.

As he puts the car in park, he unfastens his seatbelt before coming at me quickly, his lips pressing against mine. He slyly undoes my seatbelt, and as I move to him, the seatbelt pulls to the side and off of me.

Mikey's hand slides under my shirt. That familiar touch

and kiss send a rush of excitement racing through me that urges me toward him so that I shove him back into his seat. I climb over the console, gripping at his body, my hands seeming to need to feel all those parts of him I've been missing.

He presses against my chest, pushing me away and breaking our kiss. "What's wrong?" I ask.

"Come on. Get in the back." He tilts his head back, a stray lock of his bangs shifting down his forehead and revealing the sweat that's already collected from the mixture of humidity in the car and the heat we've stirred up through our make-out session.

I don't waste time. I climb over the console into the back seat and start unfastening my belt.

"Holy shit, you fucking needy bottom," he says. "I meant to get out the door, but this is just as much fun."

He crawls back as I kick my shoes off and remove my jeans, leaving them on the floorboard. He strips down while I toss off my shirt. I lay low so that passing cars won't see me. Mikey pulls a condom and packet of lube out of his pocket. He kicks his shorts off, then turns to me and smirks. He looks outside. "You think no one's ever seen anything like this before? It's not like anyone's going to recognize you. Unless this happens to be your dad's commute to go to his bougie buddy's parties."

"Shut up. And don't mention my fucking father before we're about to fuck."

He tosses the condom and lube down beside me. "Lie flat across the seat."

I obey, and he positions himself on his side at the edge of

the seat, his body pressed firmly against mine.

He looks at my lips and then into my eyes briefly before kissing me.

It's a soft kiss.

"God, you have no idea how much I missed this, you sexy motherfucker."

I like that, even though there's the possibility of someone seeing us, we don't have to worry that Jordan is going to come walking in at any moment.

It's just the two of us, pulling and tugging at each other as we lick and nip at each other's lips.

Fire erupts within me, and I can't tell if it's because I've had to wait all day for this or because my body's been craving him this much since all this began.

I want him to be back inside me, I want his fingers and hot breath moving across my body.

He kisses down to my chest, his nose and tongue sliding across my flesh before he leans back and says, "I missed this body so fucking much."

"I missed that cock filling me."

"I bet you did, you horny bastard."

I like the way he's smiling. The look he's giving me, filled with desire, and I can tell that he isn't worried about all that stuff that was stressing him out about figuring this house shit out with his family.

He growls a little as he buries his face into my neck.

And he takes me like he took me those days when we first met.

He claws at my flesh and takes to kissing me with such

recklessness that it makes me feel as though he just wants to be lost in all that I am, and it makes me feel incredible.

He suits up and readies me before he pushes into me. I call out, not feeling like I need to hold back all the things I kept quiet in our apartment.

"Fuck, Mikey," I groan, my hand against the back of the front seat, my left leg wedged between Mikey and the fabric upholstery as he tops me, his warm hands moving up and down my chest as he thrusts that cock against my prostate.

He cups his hand around my neck and pulls me up, holding my body in place as I continue shouting out my pleasure.

He glances around quickly before stilling.

"What's wrong?" I ask.

"Nothing. I want to fuck you on your side. Like me lying behind you."

He pulls out, and I slide toward the edge of the seat while he positions himself behind me. I raise my leg slightly as he pushes that cock back inside me.

He wraps his hand around my throat as I turn to him. We kiss, his hand moving up and down my side as my cock drips pre-cum across my stomach. His fingers move between the ridges between my abs, pressing against them as he massages his thumb through the grooves.

"You've been working out," he tells me.

And I blush because I have been—for him, in hopes that he was going to return and that I'd be able to be a little fitter.

Not much, but I can tell the muscles are firmer, more defined.

"It's a good thing," he says, not ceasing. "You were hot as

hell already, but these… ooh, it's like an early birthday present."

He licks my cheek.

It's so cramped in this space, but that's part of what makes it feel so good. Because it's wrong. Because we shouldn't be doing this. And because we're finally delighting in those sensations that we've been without for so long.

As he pushes against my prostate, I grab onto the seatbelt behind him and tug at it.

With each thrust, the pressure in my dick rises and rises.

"I can't fucking keep it in," I warn him.

"Then don't," he whispers into my ear. "I'm not going to."

And then I hear his familiar grunt, and just knowing he's spewing his load within me makes me shoot.

I twist my body so my warm cum gathers across my abdomen as Mikey's body jerks a few more times like his body's trying to make sure he got all the cum out.

We lie still for some time, recovering from the fuck before he stirs. "Get on top of me."

"I'm gonna get cum all over you."

"That's the point."

We shift positions and I lie on top of him, sweat rushing down my forehead and dripping onto him.

"I'm getting covered in all sorts of fluids now, aren't I?" he asks with a chuckle.

"You're going to get me hard all over again."

"Don't make that a challenge, because I'll fuck you as good as I did that first time."

We start making out again before he pulls away and says,

"Thank you."

"Thank you?"

"No. Sorry. That came out weird. I needed that so much after what went down this afternoon. It wasn't easy watching my sis be upset. Or having to break that news to her."

He moves his hand up and strokes his thumb across my cheek, staring at my lips like he doesn't want to talk anymore, like he just wants to kiss them again.

"No, I really get that."

"We should probably get back to my hotel so we can continue this in an environment where this is a little easier."

I laugh, making a snorting sound.

"Did you just—"

"Don't make fun of me."

"I'm pretty sure I'm allowed to make fun of you for snorting."

"You're awful."

"You don't even know the half of it yet," he says before licking my lips. "Mmm. Nice, hot, sweaty Scott." He spanks my ass, and my jaw drops. "Get your clothes on, you nasty exhibitionist."

"Yes, sir."

When we get back to the hotel, we shower off before heading into the bedroom and turning on the TV.

"Looking for Adventure Time?" I tease.

"Whatever. Shut the fuck up before I stick my cock in your mouth."

"Are you warning me or are you expecting me to keep talking so you'll do it?"

He smirks as he searches through the channels. "At least when I do have to come down here to fix this mess, I have something to look forward to."

His words give me goosebumps.

"God, you are such a fucking charmer," I say, annoyed.

"You say that like it's a bad thing."

"No, it feels good, but is this just how you operate? The doting? The compliments?"

He shrugs. "I'm just a nice guy, I guess."

But I really do wonder, if I was some girl—his trick of the week—would he say the same sorts of things? That shouldn't bother me, but it does.

He rolls toward me and rests his hand on my chest. "Scott, I don't ever say anything that isn't true. And you deserve to be complimented. I figure you must be used to guys spilling compliments on you as much as they spill their loads."

I laugh. "I guess that's accurate then, since I haven't had anyone since the last time I saw you."

"Really?"

"Yeah, I'm not like you. Can't walk out the door and find someone to sleep with."

"Most of my gay friends use Grindr. They don't even have to walk out the door."

"That's true. But you know what I mean."

"I've never had any issues, but I wasn't kidding you earlier when I said I've been so busy with work that I haven't really had time for any of the fun stuff."

I roll my eyes. "You don't have to tell me that. We're not fucking dating. It's fine if you've been hooking up with people."

"I seriously haven't. I'm not proud of it, so I'm not bragging."

"Then I guess we both have a lot of fucking we're going to have to get out of the way while you're here."

"We gotta do what we gotta do, I guess."

His gaze is fixed on me like he wants to take me again, and I sure as fuck don't understand why he doesn't just do it, because I'm already hard. But something shifts in his expression and he asks, "That guy... the one you were seeing. He complimented you, right?"

"What?"

"No. You said that thing about compliments like you don't get a lot of them, so I was just making sure that your man gave you the compliments you deserved."

I laugh. Not because it's funny that he never complimented me, but because the idea of him being that way is so far from the guy I knew. "Fuck no. He was more concerned about improving me than anything else."

"Improving you?"

"Like telling me I needed to get a better job. Make more money. Stop playing on my computer with stupid Photoshop shit. I think the nicest compliment I ever got from him was that I was kinda cute."

"*Kinda cute*? Oh, fuck him. You're hot. Like, dorky as fuck, but in a sexy way. Seriously. If that guy didn't see what he had, then fuck him. And you know none of that shit he or your dad think about what you do is true, right?"

"Sometimes it feels pretty true, especially when I'm not

making some amazing salary like one of my siblings. Oh, fuck. Sorry. I forgot who I was fucking around with for a second, Mr. Money Bags."

I'm just giving him a hard time, but he has a serious expression on his face.

"You know it doesn't mean shit how much you make. I hope he didn't bury that idea into that crazy brain of yours. You're happy doing what you love, and that means a hell of a lot more than money. Trust me. I've seen a lot of miserable people with a lot of cash. And that ex of yours is going to move on to someone like that and realize how fucking lucky he was."

"I don't know about that. He was never all that into me. We stopped having a lot of sex toward the end anyway. Just said he wasn't into it with me."

"I can tell you right now that's a bunch of bullshit. If he couldn't get hard, that's his problem, because you are hot as fuck, and the best…" He stops himself, then finishes, "The best fucking guy I've ever been with."

He makes a cheeky grin.

"Hardy har-har. Because I'm the *only* guy you've been with. Whatever."

"Damn straight. But obviously without any regrets. Now why don't you let me show you just how hot you are one more time?"

I must be grinning ear to ear as he kisses me again.

I pull away briefly enough to say, "I like the sound of that."

Then he pounces on me again.

24

MIKEY

Close call.

Stupid fucking, Mikey. Way to not keep your cool.

I almost told him that he was the best lay I've ever had.

I've never been weird about telling someone how good they are, but I've also never had the kind of sex I have with Scott. The mind-blowing sort that's left me knowing he's so much fucking better than any of the women I've been with. Which is a lot.

Although, he deserves to know. He deserves a lot better than he got from that fucking ex of his or his father.

I don't know why it grates on my nerves the way they've treated him, but I guess I'm starting to feel a little protective. He doesn't understand what an amazing guy he is and how lucky someone would be to have him in their life.

I'm kind of shocked that I'm standing at one corner of Kate's house with Otis, my buddy from Habitat for Humanity, and rather than being concerned about the mess Kate's in, all I can think about is Scott.

He didn't leave my hotel room last night, which gave us the opportunity to make up for lost time—something that was even better than I'd anticipated.

As Otis jots down notes on his clipboard, his mouth twists. His eyes are hidden beneath the bill of the cap he wears, which has his company logo sewed on the front. "Definitely got

173

termites. No ifs, ands, or buts about it. But it's not as bad as it could be. They've pretty much ravaged the foundation of this corner of the house. And from what I saw outside, I'm not sure how high they've gotten, but you'll know when you start ripping shit apart. I'll get back out here with my shit tomorrow and take care of them. Between this and the damage that you showed me earlier from that leaky roof, you've got some serious work you're gonna have to get done."

"That'll cost an arm and a leg, probably. Was thinking I might do it myself."

I keep going back and forth about it, but my job is flexible enough, and at least then I wouldn't feel like we were being screwed over by guys who could take anything from six months to a year to finish the repairs.

"How long do you think something like this would take me?" I ask him.

He clicks on the button at the end of his retractable pen before tucking it in the pocket of his navy blue button-up. "Eh... depending on the extent of the damage, maybe three months."

"Damn."

"What? You're not excited about sticking around in Atlanta for a bit? Come on. It'll be fun. We can meet up and have some drinks like the good old days."

"I might take you up on that."

"And if you need any help with this, you know how to reach me. I just wish I'd been in town last week when this was all going down. I could have saved you and your sister a lot of trouble."

"My sister was a little over-excited about this place. She has a lot going on in her life, and this was her first time buying, so she kind of made a few mistakes because she was blinded by some of the better aspects of the property. And I was so busy trying to finish up this big project at work that I didn't do what I needed to help out, so I guess this is what I get."

"Mikey, it's a nice place. Once you repair the damage, you'll both feel like she made a good investment. But you've got to throw about ten grand at it, I figure. At least."

I take a deep breath, reminding myself that it'll be worth it once Kate is moved in and in the house of her dreams.

"Cost four times that if you have contractors come out here."

"Don't I know it."

"I don't envy the workload you've got ahead of you, but if you need help, even just in the beginning with brainstorming how to figure this mess out, I can help you out. And if I don't know the answer, you know I've got friends in low places who I can ask."

"Thanks, Otis."

"No problem. Anything for you, Mikey."

I keep reminding myself this could be worse, but that doesn't make me feel much better.

Still, I know what I have to do. I can work out a deal with some people I know for supplies they get from wholesalers. And if Scott's willing to chip in with the help, we might actually be able to take this on ourselves with a modest amount of assistance from some of my old friends in town.

Despite how frustrating this all is, I keep reminding myself that the sooner I can get this done, the sooner Kate and Roger can get out of our parents' house and spend some time in their own place, a place where they can start their lives together.

I run some ideas past Otis about executing the project, and he offers me some suggestions. "It'll be just like the good old days," he says, slapping my arm. I can tell he's trying to ease my tension about the whole thing, but that won't be happening. Not today.

When we finish up, I drive my rental car back to my hotel and call Scott because I'm not going to promise Kate anything unless I can get some of these details in place.

I don't doubt Scott wants to help, but I want to make sure I can make it fair for him. I don't need to monopolize his time when he has his own work he has to take care of.

"Well?" Scott answers as if we haven't spent the past two hours apart.

"Were you serious when you said you'd help me out with this? You know, before we started swapping loads again yesterday?"

I'm trying to make light of it so that he doesn't feel pressured.

"I was totally serious. What do you need?"

"Just a few months of your time. A couple ten-hour days, really."

"Wow. It's that bad?"

"Not as bad as it could be, but we definitely have our work cut out for us. My buddy Otis walked me through the parts that we need to replace. He'll be back tomorrow, and when he's finished evicting our unwanted guests, we'll be able to get in there and work. I can't do it on my own, but I'm not going to ask you to come in and do it without any compensation. I can pay you as much as I'd pay anyone else to help. At least I'd feel comfortable knowing I can rely on you."

"Oh, fuck no. I don't want your money. It's on me. I know what Kate's been through, and I want to help her out."

"It's not your job to fix my family's issues."

"That's my point. It's not my job. I'm doing it because I want to."

I'm impressed, but not surprised. It seems like the kind of thing Scott would do.

It's not often you meet a guy like him. And I can't help but reflect on that first night I met him—so tense and rigid, so angry. It didn't seem like he would have helped me with a flat back then, let alone fixing my sister's mess of a house.

But generous as he is to offer, I don't want him to feel like I'm taking advantage. "There has to be something I can do for you, at least."

"I have an idea for that, but if we use it as payment for services rendered, I'm pretty sure that makes me a prostitute."

I laugh. "Well, if at any point it becomes too much for you, I want you to say so. I can hire someone, but it would be incredible if you could help me get started because I'm gonna be making up a lot of it as I go."

"Yeah, dude. I'll totally help out. It really isn't an issue. I mean, as long as you know what you're signing up for. I don't have a clue what I'm doing."

"Don't worry. I'm a good teacher."

"I bet you are."

I smirk. Good sex, good guy.

I haven't known him that long, but I like to think of him as a friend.

A friend with some great benefits.

25

SCOTT

Mikey moans as he offers his final thrust.

I could tell he came by the expression he made a few seconds ago, and as his body trembles in that familiar rhythm, I revel in the sensations that linger from my own climax.

I lie beneath him in his hotel room, cum covering my abdomen. It's like a lot of the sex we've had over the past few days since he's been back. We haven't done it at the apartment, and Jordan has been so busy between his TA work for summer semester and his thesis. Mikey and I have had time to mess around before I head home to act like everything is totally normal and I'm not fucking his brother on the side. But even though Jordan doesn't know what's up, I'm sure he's noticed how chipper I am these days, something he's noted a few times when we've seen each other around the apartment.

Mikey collapses on top of me, breathing intensely, the sweat on the ends of his bangs sliding onto my shoulder. "How can you still be this tight after how much I've fucked you?" he asks with a smile, turning his face toward me, our noses touching as I take in the scent of Listerine on his breath.

"Shut up," I reply, kissing his nose.

I enjoy the playfulness of what we share and how easy it is to chill with him and fuck since he's so at ease about it.

He kisses me back, and it's slower, more sensual than I'm used to. My flesh prickling, and as he pulls way, he glances me over before saying, "Oh, shit. Look who I gave goosebumps."

"Leave me alone."

"And now you're turning all red. I make you all sorts of flustered, don't I?"

"Easy to do when you're still inside me."

"You don't seem to be complaining." He leans into me and licks my lips. "I think this is gonna be a fun renovation, especially if we get to take these kinds of breaks throughout the work."

"Oh, will we have a lot of these?"

"As many as we can. I want to make sure it's worth your time, remember?"

"I think you've already made it more than worth my time."

He grins before sliding out of me. He disposes of the condom before returning from the bathroom with a towel. He slides back onto the bed, positioning himself beside me.

He wipes my abs with the towel. "Is it always like this?"

"What?"

"With another guy? This chill?"

"Doesn't seem like you had a problem being chill when you were with women."

"No. I didn't mean it like that. There's something different about doing it with you. It feels more like hanging out with one of my guy friends, but then we get to do the fun stuff, too. With a girl, I feel like there's only one thing we can really do, and we can chat and flirt or whatever, but then I'm kinda like… okay, can you go now? God, that makes me sound like a real prick."

"No, that's pretty interesting. But I'm sure that same thing holds true for some guys. Like, there are plenty of times when I've wanted to tell a guy he needed to get the fuck out."

"What? Are you trying to convince me that you're special or something?" Before I can answer, he says, "Because you don't have to convince me of that."

He crawls up the bed until his face is right in front of mine. He kisses me and drops onto his side, resting his hand on my side.

"So you don't like for girls to hang around?" I ask. "You sure seemed to like the way that redhead lingered at the door."

"We can make small talk, but it's not like I'd ever want to date them or anything."

"So how many girlfriends have you had?"

He cringes. "Girlfriends? Are you fucking kidding me?"

"No. I'm being totally serious."

"None. Why?"

"How is that even possible? Surely there's a girl somewhere in your life who at some point you spent enough time with that she might as well have been your girlfriend. Like in high school, even."

"Remember that story I told you about my parents? You think I was eager to get into a relationship?"

"There had to be someone, though."

His gaze drifts as though he's seriously thinking about it. "This one girl in high school… I guess she could count as my first girlfriend. We hooked up for months—"

"Hooked up? In high school?"

"Yeah. We made out at first, but she was a senior, and I was a junior, so she had some experience behind her and was eager to show me the ropes."

"And you were sixteen?"

"Yeah."

"Fuck. I was eighteen the first time I hooked up with a guy."

"And how many girls' cherries had you popped before then?"

"Oh, hell no. I didn't do any of that. I knew I was gay in elementary school. That was never an option for me. I had a girl who people thought I was secretly dating because we hung out together, but that was the closest thing I ever came to a relationship."

"You must have broken all the girls' hearts."

"Shut up. I just turned them down for dates. It probably is a lot harder to turn them down after you've had sex with them."

"Not really. When I was younger, I think it was trickier because I had to figure out how to approach it, but now I'm pretty clear, and the girls I typically hook up with know exactly what we're doing. And I don't typically do repeats."

"Like exactly what we're doing?"

"Yeah. This would be a big no-no. I wouldn't want to give anyone the wrong idea. I'm not giving you the wrong idea, am I?"

"Oh, fuck no. I'm just having fun, too."

His gaze shifts up and down my body. "Don't get me wrong. You're hot as sin and I think you're great, but I don't do the whole relationship thing."

"I do it, but I'm kind of enjoying that there's not that stress here. You know? Even the getting-to-know you period is exhausting. Does he like me? Do I like him? All that bullshit we kind of sidestepped, and we get to the best part. I always hated the game, anyway."

"Me too. But tell me when you start getting icky feelings for me, because I'm kind of amazing."

He rolls back onto the pillows and lounges so that his beefy body is on full display for me.

"I hate you so much," I say, incapable of concealing my amusement with his conceited attitude.

"Come on. It's okay. This is a safe place. You can tell me that I'm adorable and that you want to date the shit out of me. I don't mind."

"Right now, that's the last thing in the world I'd want to do, especially when you're fucking jerking your ego off like this."

"It is weird though. Having someone I can fuck around with on the reg like this. Definitely not a position I've ever been in before."

"Speaking of positions you've never been in before, wouldn't kill you to bottom, would it?"

"Really? You aren't going to be my perma-bottom?"

"Fuck you."

"How about I fuck you, and we'll call it even?"

"Deal."

He beams and moves quickly, pushing me back down against the mattress. And as he presses his lips against mine, there's that feeling again. He pulls away. "You can have this virgin ass whenever you want it, but you'd better go slow, because if you go fast, I'm liable to punch you."

As I let out a laugh, he kisses me. He slides his hand along my side, and now I really can't stop laughing.

"Ooh," he says. "How am I just now figuring out how ticklish you are? This is going to be fun."

"No, no, no!" I cry out, but it's too late for me as he assaults me with light strokes, sliding them down to my belly where I'm most ticklish. "Fuck!"

But as much as it's driving me crazy, it's so much fun too.

26

MIKEY

I hand Scott and Kate zip tools.

"This is how we'll remove the vinyl siding," I tell them. "Once we get the siding off, we'll need to remove the laths and insulation. We're going to go ahead and strip these all down so we can see the studs and figure out what we have to work on. We'll tear out all that's covering this side of the house on the first floor because we're gonna have to redo it anyway."

"Easy enough," Scott says.

I demonstrate using the zip tool on one of the panels beside me before retrieving a hammer from my tool belt and using the claw end to remove the nails from the top strip. Unhooking the panel, I slide it under my arm. I knock out a part from the top down and then demonstrate removing the laths and intermediate siding with a crowbar, which I also bought three of—one for each of us.

"Any questions?"

"I think that looks easy enough," Scott says.

"Yeah, I think we can handle this part." Kate sounds like she's fine, but I can tell she's already overwhelmed. I know it's because she feels guilty about all the repairs we need to do.

"For this part, at least," I add. "I'll get the ladder and get the higher pieces, and we'll stack them…" I glance around the yard. We're going to have a whole bunch of crap that needs to be chucked. Anywhere will really do right now. "Just at the other end of the house, since that's where we'll all end up anyway. Then—"

"Whoa, whoa, moving a little quick already, aren't we?" Scott asks with an amused expression. I can tell he's trying to get me to relax, but since we've been running around all morning getting ready for our first big day, I feel like all the pressure of this project falls on me. Scott at least reminds me that I'm not totally alone in this.

I fetch the ladder that I bought this morning from Home Depot along with plenty of other supplies to help us through the renovation.

As I work on my ladder, tearing apart the siding on the other side of the house, I see just how high the termite damage extends on the studs. At least it doesn't go up to the second floor on this part of the house, something that'll help make this slightly less of a pain in the ass.

While I'm moving the ladder over to get to the next area, I see Scott with a serious expression on his face as he carries some insulation and laths to the junk pile we've created.

He looks so serious about it, and I'm kind of relieved that he gets that this isn't going to be a cake walk. I definitely plan on making it worth his while, but I was a little nervous that he didn't get that this is just going to be work—and a lot of it.

I toss my shirt off pretty soon after we start because the humidity jacks up, and I notice that Scott keeps glancing my way, to the extent that Kate whispers something to him and he giggles.

Oh my God. They're like schoolgirls.

"Scott, did you have any questions about the siding?" I call to him.

"No, Mr. Bradshaw. I think we're doing just fine."

As soon as I get back to work, I hear my sister try to whisper, "You are shameless, flirting with my straight brother."

If only she knew.

When we finish up, we head inside. I fucking have a film of sweat covering my body, and as I review some of my initial plans with them at the table we moved into the kitchen the first day we got here, I notice Scott keeps ogling me.

I want to make a comment so bad, but I restrain myself. Goddamn my sister feeling responsible for this. If she'd left the two of us to this project, I'd already have him bent over with his elbows on the kitchen counter as I take him from behind.

And now that I'm thinking about that, I'm getting hard. Fuck.

The doorbell rings.

"Chinese is here!" Kate announces before she heads for the door the way she used to when our parents would order take-out when we were younger.

As I hear the door open, I lunge at Scott and wrap my arms around him, pushing him back against the pantry door. He seems stunned for a moment, but it's not long before he's sliding his hands up and down my slick body. I kiss him in such a frenzy that I forget to breathe. The sweat on his lips tastes so good, like it did when we fucked in the car the other day.

He opens his mouth, releasing a soft groan. I can tell he's stifling it to keep Kate from hearing.

I reach down and feel the hard erection in his pants. "Stop

flirting with my sister's straight brother," I tease him.

He chuckles until he snorts again. "Oh my God. I don't normally make that sound," he whispers, but I don't give him a chance to offer any more of a defense. I just crush my lips against his.

When I hear the door close, I back away quickly and return to the table. Scott stands at the pantry door, frozen, looking like I just sucker punched him.

When Kate enters with two big brown paper bags, she glances at Scott like she's trying to figure out how he got over there.

"Are you looking for the plates?" she asks. "I have some in a box in the living room."

"Oh, yeah. That was it."

He heads into the adjacent living room to fetch them while Kate and I pull out the containers of Chinese.

After we finish eating, we clean up our mess before Kate asks, "Is there anything else I need to do?"

"Little sis, you just need to stand there and look pretty."

She glares at me. "That's the last thing I'm going to do considering this is my house, and if you think I'm not going to be here to help out, you're mistaken."

"You have a regular day job. You don't have the luxury Scott and I have, and you have your little fella who you need to spend time with, so whatever you can offer is fine."

Plus, the less time you spend around here, the more opportunities Scott and I have to take breaks and fuck, so please let us handle this.

"Thank you again, Scott," she says.

"It really isn't an issue."

"It might not be an issue for you, but it's a big help for me. I feel like this is all my fault."

"It isn't your fault," I tell her. "It's a frustrating situation, and I understand why you did what you did, but we're going to figure this out, and we're going to make this your dream home. You got that?"

She forces a smile, but I can tell my words don't bring her much peace of mind.

"Well, I don't know what I'm going to do to make this up to you guys, but I will, okay?"

"You don't have anything to make up for." I move close and offer a hug.

"Oh, Mikey, you're all sweaty! Stop!" Scott laughs as I pull away from her. "So gross."

I look over her shoulder at Scott, who shrugs like he doesn't understand what her issue could be.

We chat a bit more before she leaves, and as soon as I close the door behind her, Scott says, "She feels so guilty about this whole thing."

"It's my fault. I was so frustrated at the situation and didn't know how much money was going to be involved. I had told her all we needed was to get an inspector out here, but I totally understand why she did it. No matter what I say, she just keeps beating herself up about it."

"You have to admit, it's kind of fun that we get to play slumber party in this place until we get it fixed."

"Judging by the look on your pretty face, I know what you're expecting to get out of this 'slumber party'."

I hook my arm around him and pull him close to me, offering a kiss, tasting that sweat on him again. "Yum. I've been waiting to do that ever since you started working out there."

"You already kissed me before the Chinese food came, remember?"

"I wasn't talking about kissing you."

His eyes widen with excitement. "Well, well."

"You did good today, by the way. Looks like you'll pick up this stuff real quick."

"You're not the only fast learner. But are there any big tips that you need to offer me before we really get into this project?"

"You know how to hit a hammer?"

"Obviously."

"You think you can drill?"

"Does anyone not know how to drill?"

"Then I think we'll be as good with this as we are in the bedroom. I'm not asking you to do major electric or plumbing."

"Well, even if we're not doing any plumbing, I don't see why we can't have a little plumbing roleplay?"

"Oh, God, is that one of your fantasies?"

"Yes." He looks surprised by my response. "Is that weird?"

"A little, but it's cute. You're too adorable." I offer a peck on his lips. "But before we get to any of that, we have some real work to get done…"

His gaze drifts to the floor, like he's disappointed by my response.

"Fuck it," I say before pushing him back against the door.

I tug at the hem of his shirt, practically peeling it off his sweat-soaked body.

"We just need to get some of this out of the way so you can't distract me with that perky ass of yours."

I undo his belt and unfasten his fly before yanking his pants down with his briefs, revealing his full erection.

"God, how the fuck am I going to be able to work when I know I could be sucking on this beautiful dick?" I ask him. "Gonna have to go hours without violating you."

"Hours? I don't know if I can handle that."

I shake my head. "I was going to suck you off, but now that you're talking stupid, I think you need a dick in your mouth."

I step back, undo my pants, then pull them down, and without question or hesitation, Scott gets on his knees and starts servicing me.

"That's fucking right," I tell him as I thread my fingers through his hair.

He deep-throats my dick with that skill he's always eager to demonstrate, one I kind of which I could give him in return. I need to step up my game with him. There are so many things he's so much better at. And I pay attention as he takes my dick so that I can show him the same pleasure when the roles are reversed.

27

SCOTT

It's seven in the morning, but I feel pretty damn chipper. Between last night and this morning's fuck sessions with Mikey, I think that I'll be able to hold off needing sex for at least a few hours, maybe until we break for lunch. We can't start work until nine because of the homeowner's association regulations, so we review plans together in the kitchen, Mikey's hand on my leg stroking gently as he reviews what needs to be removed and fixed. When we can start working, he walks me through how to repair the studs. He demonstrates as he removes one, replaces it, then nails it in. I start to show him my work on another when he eyes me uneasily as I hammer.

"What is it?" I ask.

"It's nothing. Just watch me."

He slides between me and the stud I'm working on—so now it's the stud working on a stud.

"This is a little trick that's gonna help you," he says. "When you're hammering…" He slides a couple of nails from a pouch in his tool belt before placing one between his lips and the other up against the board. "*You* hammer a nail like this." He taps lightly until the nail goes in. He takes the other out of his mouth and positions it. "This is how you hammer a nail." He lifts the hammer and drives it forward. Hard. It goes right into the board.

"Gotta be careful not to top like that," I say. "You gotta

ease a guy into that."

"You haven't complained yet."

He lifts my chin with his finger and kisses me.

"God-fucking-dammit," he says as he pulls away. I'm confused until he looks down at the bulge in his pants. "Guess lunch is going to come sooner than I was thinking."

"Something's gonna be coming soon, that's for sure."

He smiles. "You keep distracting me, and we're never going to get this done."

Not a problem for me, considering I'd be happy if we could keep this up for a lot longer.

We work until lunchtime, making steady progress, but I can tell I'm moving a lot slower than him. I don't want to rush anything and do a bad job, but I don't want to be the guy holding us up either. The only guy who should be holding something up is Mikey, and that thing should be me while he's driving that cock into me. "I feel like I'm sweating a lot more than you," I tell him as we enter the kitchen.

Mikey opens the refrigerator and grabs two beers. "That's 'cause you are." Mikey twists the cap off of one and hands it to me. "And not even just now. You're always like this in the bedroom. I don't get how a person can sweat that much."

"I don't hear you complaining."

"No, no. No complaints. I'm just amazed." He removes the cap on his bottle and takes a sip, his lifted arm granting me full view of that jacked body.

I lean back against the counter and take in the beautiful display before saying, "Like, honestly, please tell me you do steroids."

"What?"

"That body. I just need to know for my own sanity that you're, like, shooting up in the ass to get these big-ass muscles."

"Protein shakes all the way, but I guess you can get those in the ass, too, can't you?"

"Oh, aren't we suddenly hip with butt sex?"

"I'm not doing too bad. I keep getting requests."

"The guy who needs it from you must need it all the time. I can only imagine what sort of saggy hole he must have by now."

"Actually," he says, approaching me, his brow cocked in a way that's so fucking sexy that I want to throw myself back on this counter and let him have his way with me, "he has the tightest hole ever."

He sets his beer beside me, kneels down, wraps his arms around me, and hoists me into the air. Setting my ass on the kitchen counter, he kisses me. It's that slow kiss again. I notice it because most of the kisses have been frenzied, like we're making up for lost time.

As he pulls away, he scans my face. "You look worn out as fuck."

"Wow. You just lost all nice points for the day."

"Not what I meant. I was just thinking that you still look fucking hot even when you're drenched in sweat and still wishing you were in bed."

"You have no idea how much I wish I was in bed right now."

He grips my ass cheeks with either hand, and a deep, low

growl slips past his lips. "I'm not caving to you, temptress."

"Oh, am I a temptress now?"

"You've always been that. Luring innocent straight boys like me from the ladies. They would be so unappreciative."

"Don't I know it."

"Speaking of temptresses, what does your dad think about some dude stealing you away from your job to work on his sister's house?"

"Are you asking if he thinks we're an item?"

He laughs. "Not what I meant. Like, this must seem random to him."

"Not at all… since I haven't mentioned it yet."

"Oh, really?"

"I know my dad. He's not going to be cool with me spending what he sees as all these work hours working essentially for free."

"You're helping a friend out. You gotta give your dad some credit."

"I think you might be giving him a little more than he deserves. I'm pretty confident Dad would see this as unpaid labor. I know I make him sound like such a dick every time I talk about him, but he's a really good guy."

"I wish I could say the same thing about my father."

It's sad how quickly his expression can shift from playful to intense.

"This is none of my business," I say. "And you don't have to answer if you don't want to, but have you actually talked to him about what happened when you were younger?"

"What the fuck is there to say? He knows what he did, and

he's certainly never brought it up. Neither of them have."

"I know, but I don't mean for them. Just maybe to get it off your chest. You don't think it might help you to tell them how you felt about it back then?"

His jaw tenses.

"I'm sorry. I wasn't meaning to bring up a sore subject. Well, obviously I was, but only to make it better. I just meant that maybe it would be therapeutic to talk to them about it."

"Like you talk to your dad about shit?"

"Fair point. Maybe I'm projecting a little bit here."

"But you make a valid point. Maybe a point that makes me uncomfortable. I've thought about bringing it up again. But every time I do, I imagine what he'll say. How he'll make up excuses. Or blame me for bringing up something that doesn't matter. Or that time when I tried to destroy our family."

I see a tear forming in his eye. He turns away from me, and I don't comment on it because I don't think he wants to know that I can tell how affected he is by this.

"At least," Mikey says, "when you talk about your dad, even if he's being totally unreasonable or a jerk about something, you know he cares about you. That he doesn't agree with everything you do, but he's not blaming you for the demise of your entire family. When you tell me that he's worried about your job, it's something that he doesn't get. He doesn't have a clue what you do every day. Mine was just such a heartless, selfish bastard to me. I wish I could get in a time machine and go back and tell myself that I needed to tell Mom right when I saw the messages on his phone. But he scared me, Scott. He scared me to death. And even now when I think about it…" I can feel his arms trembling against me. "It's like I'm eleven years old all over again, and he's got this hold over me. And that's why I blow up the way I do. Because I'm constantly keeping this thing bottled up, and there's all this pressure inside… building and building until I explode. But even after I've let it out, I haven't actually gotten rid of what causes all the pressure. And Mom, what she did… The betrayal. The hurt. It's all just too fucking much. They were the two people in the world who I was supposed to be able to trust… who I felt like would be there for me when the shit hit the fan, and they destroyed any chance of that ever fucking happening."

I don't know how to make him feel better after what he's shared or how to take away his pain, so I kiss him. He kisses me back, cupping his hand behind my neck and pulling me closer.

The tension in his body relaxes as he slides his other hand up and down my back, his tongue flicking against mine.

"We might… need a little… break after all," he says, his words barely audible between our kisses.

And I'm so fucking hard and want to set him at ease so much that I sure as fuck am not going to be the one to discourage this.

His hands are tight against my flesh, like he doesn't want to let go, so I start undressing without his help, maneuvering and shifting to get my jeans out from under my ass and forcing his hand back as I pull my shirt off over my head.

He pulls away long enough for me to kick my shoes off. Then he drops his jeans while I kick out of mine.

As he comes back at me, he lifts my legs and places them

on either shoulder. With his hands around my legs, he slides me toward him across the counter so that my ass just barely hangs off.

He sticks his cock between my ass cheeks, rubbing up against me and making make me need him inside me so bad.

And I still see that, as into this moment as he is, there's hurt in his expression, too. I want to do whatever I can to soothe that.

"Please tell me you have a condom," I tell him. "I don't think I'm going to be able to stand you just rubbing on me like this. I need you hitting my fucking prostate."

He kneads his hands against my thighs as he growls. "I left them upstairs."

He continues stroking that dick along my ass crack.

"We just won't do that, it's fine," I say.

"Fuck that." He starts off, and then I see him dive to the floor. "Shit!"

As I prop myself up, I see he's fallen, his hands before him as he's crouched on the hardwood floor, his jeans still around his ankles.

"Thank God you caught your fall," I tell him. "Wouldn't have wanted you bruising that dick of yours."

He rolls onto his back, his full erection resting against his abdomen. He plants his hand against his face. "Well, that was smooth of me, wasn't it?"

His face is red, and now it's my turn. "Are you blushing, Mikey?"

"Don't. Shut up!"

"No. I get to savor this moment because I don't think I've

ever seen it happen before. Mikey Bradshaw is blushing because he just fell on his ass in front me of."

"Technically, I nearly fell on my cock, but whatever."

He's trying to cover his face with both hands, so I hop off the counter and crawl on top of him, seizing his wrists and pulling his hands away from his face.

"What the fuck are you doing?" he asks. "Isn't this embarrassing enough as it is?"

"No, it's not. It's my job to make it as embarrassing as possible."

I pin his wrists on either side of him, and he's still struggling, but not as much as I know he can, because he's too busy laughing at my attempt. "You fucking asshole," he says through the laughter.

And it's so adorable that soon I join in.

"Oh, I almost forgot how ticklish you are," he says before pulling one of his hands sharply out of my grip. He goes right for my side, tickling where he knows I'll respond quickest. I twist and spasm as my laughter escapes uncontrollably.

He takes charge, rolling on top of me, seizing my hands, and pulling them over my head, pinning me down. "Now look who's on top."

"It's where I prefer you anyway," I manage to get out as my fit of laughter transforms into a series of chuckles.

He kisses me again. I'm still trying to fight these fucking giggles. But between how good his lips feel against mine and how scattered my thoughts are from our little wrestling match on the kitchen floor, it's easy to get lost in the heat between us. So I let myself do just that, enjoying how hard his cock is against my pelvis.

He growls before pulling back and saying, "Still need to get condoms."

"Be careful this time," I tell him.

"Shut up."

He goes ahead and kicks off his shoes and removes his jeans before running to grab them from the rooms we've made for ourselves upstairs. He's back in no time, though, and he's got me on the counter, pushing into me.

I rest on my elbows, leaning back as he fucks me, his hand drifting down from my chest to my cock.

He strokes it, and I enjoy all the stimulation, the energy that radiates through me, each time exciting my nerves more and more. He firms his grip on my cock.

"Ooh, I can tell you really like that," he says. "I think I deserve a big load for the way you tried to make me your little bottom earlier."

Between the pressure and the way I find I'm twisting with how he fucks me, I know it's going to be soon.

"God!" I call out, but he relaxes his hold. "Fuck, what the fuck are you doing?"

He winks. "Torturing you." He leans over me and adds in a whisper, "You didn't think I was going to let it be that easy, did you?"

He rises up and grabs one of my ankles, pulling it up and twisting my body as he sets it on his shoulder so that I'm sideways as he continues claiming my ass.

I reach for my dick, but he snatches my hand.

"Not happening, buddy," he tells me. "You're gonna come

like this whether you like it or not."

I can tell he's just being playful, that if I really wanted to come, he'd let me, but I love that I'm his to serve right now. He wraps his arm around my upright leg and pulls it close to him as he gets in deep. And soon, it's too much, and I shoot across the counter, calling out as my body spams from the sensations the orgasm moves through me.

"Fuck, fuck, fuck!" I shout as he rams me and shakes with his own climax.

As our bodies relax, he moves my ankle from his shoulder down to his side, shifting me onto my back. He leans back down, and I meet him halfway for a kiss, his hand stroking the back of my head before we pull away and gaze into each other's eyes.

I could seriously look at those blue eyes all day. It's like they pull me out of this world and into the bright blue water of an ocean. But as much fun as we've shared, I know there's still sadness behind those eyes as Mikey is haunted by that experience with his parents, tormented by it because of what fucking assholes they were to him. Inside his body of muscles, there is strength. It makes me think of his tattoo: *Strength is Within.* But there's weakness, too. Maybe that's why he works so hard on his tough exterior; it's a shell to protect him from the rest.

Whatever the reason, all I know is that the more I get to know him, the more I realize that what he has going on inside is at least just as beautiful as his incredible body, and I'm starting to suspect that the more I get to know him, the more beauty I'll discover within him.

28

MIKEY

Stressed as I've been, we've fallen into this project fairly easily.

I thought the beginning would be the most difficult part, but with Scott, Kate, Jordan, and Otis's help, we've been able to get things done fairly quickly.

It's been five weeks since we began the project. I haven't had to give Scott too much instruction. He picks up everything fairly quickly, and it looks like we just have another two or three weeks before we'll be able to wrap up.

But it's sooner than I would like, because I'm not eager to stop doing… well, whatever the hell we're doing.

Since we started this project, Scott and I have spent about as much time fucking as we have working.

It's been days and nights of sweating and panting. Feeling his hot breath against me, his hands clinging to my body as he needs me to fill him with my dick. Most of the time when we finish up, we're so exhausted from the day of repairs that we just wind up on one of our blow-up mattresses, which I'm fine with. Hell, I don't even see why we keep up the pretense of staying in two separate rooms. Although, the ruse is helpful for when Kate and Jordan come over to help out.

Dinners are quick and easy meals. Soups and microwavable dinners, which we're getting tired of, but we squeeze in the occasional pizza or Chinese.

But as busy as we've been, I'm pleased that Scott's been able to keep on top of his work. I don't want to feel like this project is monopolizing his time. I know how seriously he takes what he does, and I wouldn't want him feeling like I'm disrespecting that or thinking it's any less important than my job, because it's not.

I clean up the scraps in the basement—all the shit that's collected since we threw up some beams for support and replaced some of the rotted wood on the foundation.

I hear footsteps coming down the stairs before Scott walks in and grabs some of the shit I've piled by the studs beneath the stairwell. We have to patch up the ceilings and floors a bit still and repair the cabinets, but this cleanup marks the conclusion of the more extensive work on the house, which is a fucking relief.

Scott's not wearing a shirt. His body glistens from the sweat he's accumulated throughout the day. His skin's also tanned nicely over these past few weeks, and his muscles have bulked up—all of these things making him even hotter than when we first met. Not that he wasn't hot as hell then, but it seems like working on this house has just made him that much more attractive.

He doesn't even look at me as he continues collecting scraps.

This level of focus is why I think he's so good at graphic design. Even when I see him just sitting at his computer, he is totally absorbed in what he's doing.

He glances at me for a moment, offering a smile, his eyes lighting up in a way that makes me feel like he's just excited about the prospect of this making it easier for us to fuck.

I size him up again, appreciating how delicious he looks. If we didn't have so much to do right now, I'd distract him from his work and take him right here. I want to fuck his brains out. I want to give him my fat dick and make him squirm and sweat a little more, until his sweat and cum are dripping onto the basement floor.

Stay focused, I tell myself. But I don't want to focus right now.

I just want him.

He's about to leave when I call after him, "What do you say we do something tonight?"

His smile broadens. "Weren't we already going to?"

I approach him. "I mean, I'm certainly not going to let a day go by without paying you, if that's what you mean."

"Ooh. I'm getting paid now, boss?"

This little boss/employee roleplay is something that we've joked around about for the past month and a half.

"Yeah. In buckets of cum."

"This sounds like it might be sexual harassment, Mr. Bradshaw."

"It is."

I kiss him, and he gives right into it.

I like that about him. He submits to me. He doesn't play games. or act coy like he doesn't want it. He just opens himself up for me to pleasure in whatever way I choose.

My dick gets hard fast as I push him back against one of the studs under the stairway. A wicked thought rises within me, and he must have the same thought because he grabs my crotch.

He unzips my fly. "Well, well. Look what just sprung up."

I kiss him as he pulls my cock out and strokes it back and forth. The lingering tension I've been feeling from all the work we've put into this house dissolves.

"You want me to suck you off, Mr. Bradshaw?" he asks, his expression deadly serious.

"I think I'd like that."

I move in to kiss him, but he leans back and kneels down.

Sliding my pants to my knees, he takes my cock into his mouth.

I curse as I enjoy the sort of break I've needed all day long, even after our morning fuck.

He works it some before pulling it out of his mouth and gasping for air, as if he's been so into it that he fucking forgot to get a breath in.

He grips onto my hips and guides me back against a board behind me—the frame for an unfinished wall.

I lean on it for support as he blows me, relaxing the back of my head on the wood as I enjoy his skilled tongue—one that he's gotten good at using.

"Fuck, Scott. Fuckin' A."

He cups my balls in his hand and applies just the right amount of pressure. I twist my fingers in his curls, gripping on and forcing him to take me deeper. He gags softly, but it's clear by the way he forces it back that it's not discouraging him, and it's sure as fuck making me leak.

I tug his hair back so that my cock springs free from his lips. Then I lean down, hook my hands under his arms, and pull him to his feet. He looks annoyed that I interrupted his work.

"Don't look so upset now," I say as I squat and retrieve a condom and packet of lube from my back pocket. He glances down and then back at me. There's lust in his eyes. "See? I wouldn't let you down."

"I notice you always have one handy these days."

"Because I'm not letting us get into a bind like we did the first day we tried this."

He grins. "You mean because you don't want to trip over your pants?"

"Same difference," I say before wrapping an arm around him and pulling him to me, claiming his mouth with mine.

I press my free hand against the small of his back, enjoying the feel of his sweaty body against my shirt. I tuck our supplies in his front pocket because I'm not in any rush. I want to enjoy the feel of his smooth body and the grooves and dips between his muscles.

I explore with rough gropes before unbuttoning his shorts and unzipping them to reveal the massive bulge in his briefs.

He shrugs, his expression filled with guilt. How does he always manage to look so fucking adorable?

I take the condom from his pocket, curl my thumbs in either side of his shorts and briefs, then force them down. His cock springs forward, and I don't waste my time.

I grab his hips, spin him around, and push him toward the wooden beam. When I'm prepped, I slide into him, letting his body adjust to my girth and listening to his movements as I feel my way inside him.

I like the way his ass grips onto my shaft as I push deep

within.

He looks over his shoulder, his mouth hanging open.

"God, you feel too fucking good," he says as his body trembles beneath me.

"You should feel this ass."

I slide my hand up his side, trailing up his chest to his neck, which I grip onto and pull back on. He turns his head a little more, and I lean forward and kiss him. I pull away briefly and lick across his cheek, enjoying that familiar taste of him while I thrust. I reach down with my right hand and grip onto his fully erect dick, running my thumb across the head.

"You're leaking for me," I whisper into his ear, since I've learned through our fucking that he likes when I do that. Since I've listened and explored the things he likes, I know just how much it gets to him.

And the quaking of his body reminds me of how good I am at turning him on these days.

I continue whispering, "You like me taking your hot piece of ass. Makes you real hard, doesn't it? Just makes you spill all over the place like the greedy little bottom you are."

"Yes. Fuck yes."

I entangle my fingers in his hair, grip on, and tug back so that he has to tilt his head up, because another thing I've learned is how much he enjoys being dominated. Sometimes I think he just needs to be tied down and forced to obey my every command.

"Tell me you like it when I own you like the dirty bastard you really are."

"Yes! Fuck me, Mikey. Fuck me harder."

I obey.

He writhes in pleasure as he takes my dick.

Then a burst of inspiration takes control.

I slide out of him and spin him back toward me. I like the confused, thrown expression he's making. It's like he feels rejected by the fact that I didn't go ahead and spill my load inside him.

But I know he'll like this, considering how much he enjoyed that day when I fucked him on the desk.

Leaning down, I lift him by his thighs and use the tips of my fingers to guide my cock back inside. His arms around me, holding on tight, I watch his face as he calls out, "Fuck, Mikey!"

"I love it when you scream my name."

"Make me come, Mikey, please."

And I take him. I take him the way he needs to be taken, watching his head roll back and forth as he calls out without inhibition—just like I've heard him ever since we started this recurring fuck buddy arrangement.

There's a wicked part of me that wants to fill him up without this condom between us.

I'd never do that to either of us. I'd never be so irresponsible, but it's a wicked thought I enjoy while I claim this ass.

He tightens his hold around me, and I can feel that I'm getting close.

"Fuck," I say. "I'm not coming before you."

"Just do it," he says.

"No."

"I'm about to go, so you might as well."

I stop moving. If I so much as push one more time, it's over for me.

He has his hand gripped tight around his cock, jerking it furiously. "Please, it'll take me over the edge," he says. "Just come. I need it."

I offer him a little push, thinking that at least I can stimulate his prostate a little, but I realize it's too much as the pressure in me builds too fast, and my body forcing another series of thrusts, my muscles seemingly forcing me to go through the motions until I'm coming.

"Fuck..."

Scott shoots his own load onto himself.

I push up against his body, keeping my face next to his, the sweat sticky between us as we settle from the intensity of yet another amazing fuck.

29

SCOTT

I feel filthy, disgusting, and so fucking sexy from the way Mikey took me.

My legs tremble. My body shakes from the excitement that soars through me.

Mikey pulls his jeans and tool belt up, securing them around his waist as I do the same with mine. As soon as mine are on again, he grabs my ass and presses me up against the board again.

"I have a funny feeling I'm going to have a big black mark where you had me against that board," I tell him.

His expression shifts to concern.

"Relax. It's a sex injury. Not like you fucking kicked the crap out of me."

He grabs my shoulders and spins me around. "Oh, nah. It's a little pink. You'll be fine. But did it hurt?"

As I turn back to him, I can tell he's genuinely concerned.

"I'm sorry. That was a joke. I didn't mean to actually get you concerned about it."

"I don't want to hurt you."

"Mikey, trust me, any pain I've experienced has been trumped by the pleasure, so it's nothing." But his face is locked in a frown. "Dude, come on. Chill." I move to him and kiss him. "I would tell you if I didn't like something we were doing."

"Just want to make sure. I don't want to scare you off. You know I was serious about what I was saying. That we do something tonight. More than sex, I mean."

"Like a date?"

His sad expression shifts to confusion. "What? No. Not like a date. Like friends hanging out. I think we deserve to have a little fun since we've been go-go-go on this house."

"Go-go-go on a lot of things besides the house."

He smiles and wraps his arm around me, pulling me close so that our torsos are flush.

"Come on. We've been doing this long enough that we can fucking go out and have fun together. I don't think of you as just a fuck buddy, Scott. I think of you as a friend." His words make me kind of sad, and he must notice since he goes on with, "What? Why is that a bad thing?"

"It's really nice, actually. It reminds me that I don't have many friends. I mean, I have Jordan, but I'm not like you where I can go out and meet people like that. If I go to a bar by myself, I typically leave by myself, too."

"Well, I can tell you're a little guarded, especially with people you don't know."

"I'm sure that wasn't totally clear when I confronted you that first night after you were fucking that girl," I say, teasing.

He chuckles, but his expression turns serious again. "Sometimes I wonder what you're so guarded about. Why you try to keep people out all the time? You're too amazing to keep all this goodness all to yourself?"

"Oh, now I'm amazing?"

"Yeah, you are." He says that so seriously that I can't

really make a joke of it, but I don't want to hear it either. I start to turn away from him, but he grabs my chin and forces me to look at him. "You're amazing."

I blush for the thousandth time since we've known each other.

"And no matter what your dad or your siblings think of you, you don't have to feel like you're less important than anyone else."

Those blue eyes of his seem to peer into mine and see all my faults. How insecure I am. How I've never felt good enough, not just for my family or Sam… but for anyone.

"Okay, can we avoid turning this into a Dr. Phil episode?" I ask. "Please?"

"You'd prefer if we turned it into a hot porn?"

"Didn't we just do that?"

"Fair enough."

"So what were you thinking for tonight?"

"Dave & Buster's, maybe."

"Oh, really? What if someone sees us out and tells Jordan?"

"Then we'll tell him we were out having some fun. Come on. We could use a few games to relax."

"You really are just a big kid, aren't you? Well, except with sex, that is. With that, you're just a big man. A really big, girthy man."

He wears that conceited smile—the one that makes me never want to compliment him again, but how can I not when there are so many things about him that are worthy of praise?

"Well, your boss needs you to get back to work first," he

says. "And if you're real good… and I do mean real good, he'll treat you to some fun tonight… and then some fun after, too."

"Yes, sir," I say. I turn to head off, and he slaps my ass once again. "I think I'm going to file a complaint with HR for that one."

"I'll warn my lawyers." He flashes that smile of his once again, and I find myself excited about tonight.

It's totally a date, I think. Of course, I know it can't be, considering our lives. But after all we've been doing, it just feels like saying it isn't a date is just us being in denial about how good this all feels and how much we like each other.

* * *

I keep trying to remind myself that this isn't a date, but considering how much time I spent picking out this snug black polo and these jeans that shape around my ass just right, that's hard, and Mikey's looking about as adorable as ever in a navy shirt that his biceps stretch to the point where I think if he flexes too much, he might tear the fabric.

"You look hot tonight," he tells me, clearly thinking about the same things I am.

"Whatever. You just like that you know you're getting steady action."

"No. You're hot as fuck in that shirt, and you know it. I think you just wore it to tempt me."

"Doesn't seem like I have to do much to tempt you."

"You really don't."

I roll my eyes. "So what the fuck made you choose this of

all places?"

"Are you kidding? I love Dave & Buster's. This is where I'd bring Kate and Jordan when I was in high school. Hell, we'll still come here occasionally when we can all get together. I think we need to bring Kate here so we can cheer her up. Like, do it to celebrate finishing the renovations. She and Roger deserve something special, some sort of treat once we get her moved in."

For some reason, the mention of Roger and doing something special for Kate sparks an idea: "What if we got the baby room together for her?"

"What?"

"Like, what if we went shopping and pimped out a baby room for Roger?"

"Oh, man. I think that'd be an awesome idea. She'd flip out. We could get it all set up for her…"

"Yeah. Paint the walls blue. You know, do the whole nine yards with it."

"Why's the wall gotta be painted blue?" Mikey asks.

"'Cause it's a boy?"

"You don't know. Maybe he won't always identify as a boy. Why would you want to push that on him? Reinforce these gender stereotypes?"

"Are you being serious right now?"

"Yeah. No. If I had a kid, I wouldn't want to just have the pink or blue. And yellow is a fucking awful color, so I always figured I'd go with something a little less confining. There's this shade of orange that I really liked when I was at Home Depot one day, picking out colors for my place in California. I always thought if I had a kid, that's the color I'd pick."

"I want to critique your choice of the color orange, but first, I want to seriously know, how much thought have you given to having a kid?"

"*A*, as in one kid? Oh, I plan on having several. Like three or seven. I'm not sure."

I can tell he's making light of it, but there's something serious to what he's saying, too. "Be real with me for a second. Like, you want kids?"

"Don't you?"

"I haven't given it any serious thought, I guess. I'm more surprised that you have."

"I guess that's what five years' age difference does. I mean, I'm getting near thirty, and I would seriously like to have a kid at some point."

"Don't you need to get a little more serious with someone for that to happen?"

"Look at you and all your traditional values. I figured, considering you were raised by a single dad, you'd understand more than anyone. I can always get a surrogate on my own. And I'm happy to do that."

My jaw drops.

He's smiling as he asks, "What?"

"This isn't something I would have expected from you. Like, at all."

"It's not something I typically bring up while I'm driving nails into boards or my cock into asses."

I laugh, and as I do, I realize how loud I am and glance around, nervous someone may have overheard more than my laugh.

"No, but seriously," he says. "That's a really cool idea for Kate. I'll do it, though. I've asked way too much of you already."

"Are you kidding? You don't get to take all the credit for my awesome idea. I'm totally helping out. You've seen that I'm not having an issue keeping on top of my stuff."

"Only because you wake up at three instead of seven in the morning now. But I've notice you don't dress as nicely as you used to."

"Yeah, not easy when we don't have a working washer and dryer, and it's kind of made me feel a little wild working in a tank and shorts."

"You're cuter in those anyway. But you look good dressed up, too. You're a sexy motherfucker all the way around."

I don't resist the compliment. I've had to give in a little with that, otherwise I'd be constantly contradicting him.

"But back to your brilliant idea. I'm not going to turn down any help on the baby room from you," Mikey says. "Look how fast we're moving. First date and already talking about fixing up baby rooms together."

"Wait. What? Is this a date?" I seriously want to know, because that's what's been lingering in the back of my mind ever since he suggested this.

"I was just fucking with you. Why? Do you want it to be a date?"

"I mean, it's kind of datey. We can at least admit that, right?"

"Fair point."

"But obviously we can't really do anything serious, considering our lives, so that would be ridiculous."

"Yeah," he adds, shaking his head quickly.

But that doesn't keep it from feeling like a date, or me from liking him.

"So… how are your projects coming along?" he asks, changing the subject. "You know, I think it's kind of weird that I still haven't actually seen any of these projects you're always working on."

"I just get weird about people seeing my stuff. I don't know. It's personal. Too personal."

"I'd like to see it, if you would let me… at some point. I'm curious, but if you don't want me to, I understand that."

"I'll totally show you sometime. Something that's finished, though. I can't stand for people to see my unfinished projects. I don't want them seeing all my errors and mistakes and how crappy everything looks when I'm not done yet."

"You know, it's okay not to be perfect," he tells me.

"That's easy for someone who has the body of a god to say, isn't it?"

He has a bright gleam in his eyes, the sort that stirs that same desire I get when I think about him taking me like he did earlier today.

"It must be a rare talent to be so full of yourself and so charming at the same time."

"I can do a lot of things at the same time," he says with a wink.

"I've learned."

"What can I say? I know what I can offer in bed."

"You know what you have to offer in everything. Trust me, between that and this body, I honestly can't understand why the fuck you mess around with me."

His expression goes from playful to serious. "Why do you always say crap like that?" he asks, his words harsh.

"What?"

"Like there's something wrong with you or you're not good enough. I mean, I tell you how awesome you are all the time. Do you just not listen to me?"

"In one ear and out the other."

"Well, one of these days I'm gonna make it stick."

He glances around like someone might be watching us, but there's no one in view of our corner booth. Just the two of us in our own little world.

Leaning across the table, he plants a kiss. I enjoy the taste of his lips and how the sensation that it fills me with stirs life in my jeans.

Mikey has this power, just like the confidence he exudes—some inexplicable way of igniting passion within me so effortlessly.

It's the sort of fireworks that everyone talks about in movies and songs. The explosion that makes coming when we're together even hotter, even more powerful than it's ever been by myself or with another man.

But at the end of the day, I know this is what he can do for whoever he's with, any girl or guy.

He really isn't human. Just a sex god who walks among mortals and gives us a glimpse of what it feels like to touch the sky when we submit to his power.

When he pulls away, I acknowledge that my thoughts might have gone off the deep end.

He sets his hand on my cheek and runs his thumb across my face, awakening another sensation within me. Why does he have to touch me like that? Why does he have to leave me wanting more?

"You're special, Scott," he says, even though I feel like I'm the one who should be telling him that.

I force a smile because I know this is the kind of thing he must tell everyone. Or he's just trying to make me feel better.

He shakes his head, clearly knowing that his simple advice isn't going to help me any.

"You lovebirds want me to give you a minute?" our waitress asks, who stands beside us smiling as she holds our plates.

I tuck my head low as I lean back against the cushioned booth.

"Thank you," Mikey says politely as she sets the plates down in front of us.

"You don't have to stop on my account," she tells him. "How long have you two been together?"

Oh my God. This night could not get any more embarrassing.

What the fuck is he going to say? I sure as fuck am not answering that question.

"Not long enough," is his reply, and I don't look at him as he says it.

I can't.

"Well, time fixes that." She chuckles before whispering to

him. "Sorry. Didn't mean to make your man blush."

"He'll live."

She heads off.

"And there's the blush again," he says.

"Can I die now?"

He laughs, and despite how tense I am, it offers some relief.

30

MIKEY

I don't think he understands how mad he makes me when he talks about himself like that. Like he isn't good enough. Like there's something wrong with him.

He underestimates how much it annoys me. I try to downplay the severe reaction I have to it now, but sometimes I want to slap some sense into him. I wouldn't be fucking around with him if I didn't think he was incredible. And I sure as fuck wouldn't have done it as much as I have if it wasn't the kind of sex that leaves me breathless, exhausted, and wishing I could go again one more time to recapture that magic. Maybe it's because he hasn't fucked enough people to know the difference between fun fucking and what we have, or maybe Sam fucked him up enough that he has this distorted view of himself.

But what I feel for him is beyond the sex. He's a good guy. Hell, he helped me out with my sister's house for free, and then demanded to help create a baby room to give her a fun surprise. Who the fuck does that?

Scott does.

It's so hard to find people who aren't like Mom and Dad, who are just in it for themselves.

If we were in different positions in our lives, this would be a date, not just us hanging out. And in a way, I know I'm thinking of it as one because I like Scott, and I enjoy getting to know him more. Even tonight, with the simple conversations we've had, I want to keep asking questions. I want him to tell me everything about himself. I want to know about the first guy to break his heart. I want to know about what video games he liked to play when he was younger. I want to know the kind of music he's into. Although, from being around him, I already know that Shakira and Shania Twain are on his list. I don't think he realizes that it's hard to mistake either of them even when he has the earbuds of his iPod in.

There's so many questions I have, so many things I want to know, but then there's that rational part of me that wonders why we should do this to either of us when, in a few short weeks, it's all going to be over. We just have to take what we can, enjoy this now, and then be ready to move on when this project comes to an end.

We finish eating our meal before heading to the games with the Power Cards we got from the front desk after we arrived. I guide Scott to the Skee-Ball lanes first since it's always been one of my favorites.

"You good?" I ask him.

"Eh. I'm okay."

I gesture toward the lane. "Bottoms first."

He steps up and swipes his card in the slot on the side panel. The balls release. He grabs one and takes his first aim. He misses all of the holes for points, and the ball rolls into the return slot. He tries again and again, each time missing horribly.

He glances at me, flustered.

"Don't worry. It's okay that you're shit at Skee-Ball. I can teach you when your turn's up."

"I promise. I'm not this bad. I just have to get my technique down."

"Oh, you have a technique? Really?"

"Whatever."

He's about to go again, but he stares at the holes, biting his lip like he's thinking real hard about it.

God, I hope for his sake he at least gets it in the ten point slot because I don't know how he can miss after this without me making fun of him at least a little bit.

He takes aim before throwing the ball underhanded, it jumps as it hits the ramp and lands right in one of the two one-hundred point holes.

"Shit, wow," I say, but despite how impressed I am, I have to believe there was a little bit of luck involved there.

Still, he cocks a brow, and as he turns to me, I can tell he's gained some confidence.

"Look who's the conceited one now."

He takes another turn and lands it in the same slot. Then again. And again, maxing his points for the rest of the game.

When he finishes and I check his score on the digital screen, I gasp.

"Tops up," he says with a bow and a gesture to indicate it's my turn.

And fuck if I'm not intimidated.

I take my turn and don't do nearly as impressively as he did.

"I think I just got sharked," I say as I finish what I like to think is a good game for me. "Personal best."

"Don't worry. I'll get you a big, fluffy stuffed animal."

"Like hell you will. How did you do that?"

"My brothers and sister were smart, so I had to be good at other things. When we'd go out as a family to places with arcade games, they'd kick my ass, so I started going to the mall and practicing at the mini-arcade there so I could at least have something I could be awesome at."

"Just so you could beat them?"

A devilish smile overtakes his face. "Yeah. They didn't have a fucking clue how I did it, either."

"You never cease to amaze me, Scott."

We play a few other games with Scott doing about as well as I do on them. When we finish up, we stop by the shop to claim prizes with our points. Scott picks out a big panda, which he offers me as a gift. I resist at first, but he's being too cute for me not to accept it. As we head back to the car, he's grinning, obviously pleased with himself.

"A lot better than that little rubber ducky you got with yours," he tells me.

"Don't talk about Ducky like that!"

He laughs and wraps his arm around me as we walk together to the car.

If only every night could be as much fun as this one was.

After we head back to the house, we have a little fun time in Scott's room. The blow-up mattress isn't the most comfortable thing in the world, but we've made do with them, and once we finish up, I cuddle with him, as we've unashamedly done on many of the nights we've spent together. Neither of us question it, and it doesn't seem like either of us want to.

"Kind of weird having someone watching us fuck," I say, eyeing the stuffed panda that I threw down on the floor beside the bed.

"Do we need to turn him the other way next time?"

"Nah. I figure he can't really do much, so he might as well get a show."

Scott laughs, and I kiss his forehead.

"You mind if I pull up my email on your laptop real quick?" I ask. "I need to check to make sure my assistant has some things ready for a meeting tomorrow."

He eyes me skeptically.

"What? I'm not going to, like, look at your password or anything."

"No. That's not it. It's cool. There's not a password on it anyway. I don't exactly keep anything that important on it."

"I'll just check it and then we can pull up a little Netflix, maybe?"

"Yeah. I saw *Howl's Moving Castle* on there earlier, and I was thinking I'd really like to watch that. It's by the same producer who made *Spirited Away*."

Since we started spending nights together, we've started watching movies together, and Scott's introduced me to a few cool anime films that I'm surprised I actually really enjoyed.

I roll off the mattress and push to my feet. "Oh, yeah, that'd be awesome."

As I walk across the room to his basic desk, he whistles. "That's one pretty ass you've got there."

"It's yours whenever you want to take it."

"I know. I should be taking advantage of the invitation. I

guess I'm just so greedy to have your cock in me that I just haven't gotten around to it. That isn't bothering you, is it?"

I sit at his desk and turn to him. He's sitting up, his expression far too serious. "If I was bothered by it, I'd say something. If you just ever gave me that ass, I'd be totally fine for the rest of my life."

I don't even realize how that sounds until the words are out of my mouth, but it's true, so whatever.

I turn back to his laptop and open the screen before moving his wireless mouse across the pad. The main desktop screen pops up, and there's a beautiful image of a shirtless angel, his wings spread out, as he emerges from a raging fire beneath him.

"Shit, shit, shit," shouts Scott. I turn to find him hopping to his feet, his dick swaying about as he hurries over.

"What's wrong?" I ask him.

"Sorry. I meant to close that when I was done."

I look back and notice that the image of the angel is opened up in Photoshop. "Holy shit," I say. "This is the thing that you think is full of issues?"

"It's not finished yet." He leans over me and closes out of the screen.

"Are you fucking shitting me right now? That was beautiful."

"It's not like I made that hot man. I got him from a photographer I met online, and then I just put together the other images from stock photos. But it needs a lot of work."

"I can't believe you haven't shown me this shit already. It's really good."

"Thanks."

But he doesn't sound like it means anything to him, and I want him to understand how incredible I think this is.

"I'm not saying that to be generous or to just say it. Like, I don't even know how you did that."

"A little Photoshop and a lot of hours."

"This is such a big part of your life, Scott. I would love if you would show me some of it. At least, stuff that you would be okay with me seeing."

"Really?"

I can tell I'm one of the few—if not only—people who have asked to see his work. That frustrates me. His family should be more supportive. His dad, especially. I don't doubt that he loves him, but this is his son's life.

"You mind if we take it over to the bed?" I ask him. "And then maybe you can pull up some of the ones you're proud of? I can at least see those."

"I'd actually really like that."

We take the laptop onto the blow-up mattress. He opens several image files before setting the laptop on my legs and pulling up the first. It's the image of two men holding each other in a garden with a snake descending from a tree.

"Obviously I couldn't Photoshop the men kissing. I'm not a miracle worker, but they were on a bed initially, so I had to move them into this scene, which was a field initially that I had to turn into a jungle for the Garden of Eden."

"And who was this for?"

'Oh, this was just something I did for me. Like for fun. Did you just want to see stuff I work on for clients?"

"Fuck no. This is exactly what I wanted you to show me. How did you get into this? Like, how did you first know this was something you were into?"

"A lot of fucking around on the computer when I was a kid. When I first knew how to use Paint, I would cut out different images that I saw online and sort of put together these scenes that I thought looked cool. One of the first ones I did was an ocean, and I grabbed a bunch of different images of fish from online. I mean, you'd think it looked crappy as fuck, but I was eight when I did it, so I thought it was the shit. I even had this cool shark image—"

"You've been doing this since you were eight?"

"Oh yeah. And I just got deeper and deeper into it as I got older. Never really could shake it. It was like my own sort of art.'

"It's not sort of art. It *is* art."

"Thank you."

He smiles, but I'm so fucking pissed right now. "I don't know how your family can see this shit and not admire what you do."

"In fairness to my dad, he didn't really ever get to see most of this stuff. When I was little, I tried to show him a few of these, and he wasn't interested. And by the time I was in high school, they became very dirty. Like my discovery of porn collided with this, and it was just filthy picture after filthy picture. Thank God I had my own laptop because Dad would have been horrified if he'd seen half the things I'd created."

"Oh, God. Now *those* I want to see."

He beams as he takes the laptop from me again. "I can't

believe I'm showing you this."

He pulls up an image, and it's three men fucking, but they're in a beautiful bedroom, something I sincerely doubt was the case when he pulled this photo from whatever porn he was watching.

"You filthy bastard."

He laughs. "I know, right?"

"I wish you wouldn't give a shit what your dad thought about this."

"Me, too."

"So your dad has no idea how long you've been doing this and how much it means to you?"

"Not really."

"If you told him that, I don't think he would be so dismissive of it."

"What? Show him these pictures? I'm sure that would go over well."

"No, but seriously. I can't imagine that he could know how deep you are into this and still give you shit about getting a real job. Like the way you talk, he thinks this is some flighty thing you just one day woke up and decided to start doing. This is kind of like how I was with engineering. I've been doing it forever. It's second nature to me. I'm an expert, and I know it. You are, too."

"Well, yours led you to a much more socially acceptable career."

"You have a career with this. If you can pay bills, then you're good, you know what I mean?"

"Yeah, but it goes a little deeper than that with Dad. When

he was younger, he was a photographer. I don't mean that it was just a hobby for him. He was featured in some big magazines. He still has this scrapbook with all of these awards he won and publications he was in. He doesn't talk much about those days, but he says it wasn't enough to pay the bills, and when my mom wound up pregnant with my first brother, he realized he had to settle down and get a serious job—one that could support a kid and a family. So he gave up his dreams. Didn't even touch photography when I was growing up. Not just artistically. He wouldn't even take a picture of us going on trips or anything. So, considering he had to give up his dream…"

"You think he wouldn't consider it responsible of you to go off and do something creative rather than get some job that's considered normal… or like him and your other siblings?"

"Pretty much."

"Sounds like a tough life."

"Doing something creative?"

"Trying to live up to your father's expectations."

He frowns.

"Sorry." I wrap my arm around him. "I don't mean to make tonight so serious. The whole point was that you could relax and chill. And I'm enjoying getting to see these sides of you that you haven't shown me before."

"It's nice showing them to someone else. Now pull up some more of these bad boys. We can go through the whole Scott Wintry catalogue if you want."

"I don't know if we have time for that, considering we

have to be up bright and early."

"Your boss won't mind if you come in a little late."

"Well, Mr. Bradshaw, I think we can work something out. Maybe if I show you some pictures, you can do something for me."

"Fuck that. I'm getting in you again tonight, even if you refuse to show me anymore pictures."

My dick hardens just at the thought of another go, and I kiss him, excited about sharing this part of his life with him.

31

SCOTT

We sit at the kitchen table eating the lasagna Dad made for tonight's family get-together. Miranda chats with Dad about an issue she's struggling to figure out with an account at her job. They're so engrossed in the discussion, I think I might escape Dad's usual rambling since he hasn't focused any attention on me since I arrived.

For the first time in many family dinners, I don't feel worried or stressed because I'm still riding on the high of what a great time I'm having with Mikey. It meant a lot to me last week when we looked over my projects together. It was nice sharing that part of my life with someone outside of my clients. Even more importantly, it felt good not just to be appreciated by anyone, but to be appreciated by Mikey. I know we still have a few weeks of work left, but I'm already thinking about how I'm going to miss him when he returns to California.

As Dad and Miranda's conversation settles, Conner scrapes his fork across the bottom of his plate to collect some scalloped potatoes. The sound hits my ear just the wrong way.

"Oh," Conner says, as though he remembered something important, "what was that shit doing in the back of your car?"

Fuck, shit, fuck.

Before I left Kate's house, I loaded up boards, boxes of screws, nails, and some other shit we either don't need or that we bought the wrong sizes of at some point for the renovation.

I'm planning on returning them to Home Depot on my way back to Kate's place. Mikey said he'd do it, but I figured since I was already coming here, taking care of the errand would give him more time to spend at the house working on the ceiling repairs.

I certainly wasn't thinking that Conner would have taken a peek and asked me about it in front of Dad.

"What kind of stuff?" Dad asks me, his fork and knife in his hands before him as he stops eating to wait for an answer.

"It's just for this project I'm working on."

"Another one of your projects?"

"No. Not related to that at all."

"Then what is it?"

It's almost like he knows what I'm up to, even though he can't know anything. But it's that sort of father's intuition that seems to act outside of the boundaries of logic and reason.

"Scott?" he presses.

How can him just saying my name make me feel like he's got me handcuffed to a chair and a light in my face as he demands answers for some crime I've committed? No wonder Mikey totally lost it when his dad was talking to him like that at dinner that night when he blew up and ran off. Moments like this make me want to fucking explode.

"I'm helping my friend with some repairs on her house," I blurt out. "That's it."

He sets his silverware down and wipes his hands on the napkin in his lap, his face scrunched up in confusion. "Repairs on a house? What do you know about fixing a house?"

"A lot now."

"Scott, please at least tell me you're getting paid for this."

"Why would I be getting paid? I'm helping a friend." I won't feel ashamed or let him intimidate me, not about this. Just like with my graphic design work, I'm proud of the work I've done. "We're getting it done pretty quickly," I add. "My friend Mikey and I work together really well, and I've learned a lot about houses… stuff I never really knew before. It's kind of fun."

"So, like, on an average day, how many hours do you dedicate to this *project*?" Dad asks.

"Um… maybe six or seven." I'm intentionally misleading with that estimate, especially because I know if he heard eight or higher that he'd freak.

He purses his lips and tilts his head back. "How are you paying your bills? *Are* you paying your bills?"

"I have a job that I keep on top of. That's how I pay the bills." My words are laced with anger and resentment. I'm liable to pull a Mikey at any moment. "I wouldn't be doing it unless I could keep up with that."

He sighs, and I hear the disappointment behind it, that same disappointment that's so familiar to me. "Sometimes I think you're just trying to make me worry about you. Is something wrong? Do you need help? Scott, I try to talk to you and help you when I can, but you have to talk to me."

"I do talk to you, Dad. I don't need any help, but for some reason, you always think I do."

"You can't tell me that there's not some reason why you've taken on some construction job—for free—if there isn't something going on. Are you rebelling against me? Are you trying to slap me in the face after everything I've done—?"

"This doesn't have anything to do with you."

"Why are you raising your voice?"

"You just barked down my throat about helping my friend out in my free time, which you have no control over, and that doesn't affect my income at all, so excuse me for getting a little defensive. I'm sorry if it annoys me when you don't let me live my life the way I choose."

"I have never stood in the way of anything you chose."

Even in his words, I can hear his disapproval of me being gay—that conversation that rarely comes up but is always there, lurking in the back of our minds, reminding me of the day I told him and he was so upset, as if it was the end of his world rather than the beginning of mine.

"No, you never stood in my way," I tell him, "But you never supported me either."

"I supported you every day. I fed you. I clothed you. I gave you a home."

"That's not the kind of support I'm talking about. Yes, those things matter. I get that. Trust me, you have buried that into my head. But I'm talking about a sort of support that means just as much."

He's quiet. He doesn't say anything, just grabs his fork and knife and continues eating.

But I can't. I throw my napkin on the table.

"Sorry," Conner mutters, clearly feeling guilty that his simple observation started this fight between me and Dad.

I push to my feet. "It's not your fault."

"Where are you going?" Dad asks.

"Thank you for dinner, and thank you for raising me, but I don't feel welcome tonight."

I head for the door. I know he's not going to be happy, but tonight, I don't care. I won't let him sit there and judge me and my life. Maybe it's because I finally get that Mikey is right and that I've deserved some encouragement all this time.

I return the shit in the car to Home Depot and then head back to Kate's house.

When I walk into the kitchen, Mikey sits at the table in just his sweats eating from a Healthy Choice plastic tray. I can't help but smile and enjoy seeing him smile back as he chews on some of the lasagna—one of his favorite microwavable meals, I've learned. He swallows, which reminds me of other times he's swallowed.

"Are we out of Froot Loops?" I tease, since we've both been bad about eating that for breakfast, lunch, and dinner.

"Had some as an appetizer. How's the fam?"

"Could have gone better."

"What happened, if you don't mind me asking?"

"No, that's fine." I sit across from him, and as I'm about to share my evening, this strange sensation comes over me. Here he is, sitting before me, and I can't help but feel like this is an exchange boyfriends would have. I mean, it's better than the way Sam and I interacted, for sure. It reminds me of how nice it is to have him in my life and how I'm going to miss him when he leaves.

I tell him about the evening, and why it bothered me so much.

"That's a good thing," he says when I finish.

"Yeah, well, I don't feel that great."

"He deserved it with the way he always hounded you."

"I know, but I just… I don't know. I think I need to give Dad some time to think about what I said. To realize that I'm not ashamed of who I am or what I do. Whether that's with guys or work."

"What did he do when you came out? Did he freak out?"

"I was in high school, and I had this guy who I was attracted to. I wasn't going to say anything, but I felt like I needed to tell Dad because it was something that had been itching at me since I was a kid. Everyone else was either off at college or working at that time, so one night, I told him over dinner, and he got quiet. He told me that it was going to make my life harder than everyone else's and that I needed to be careful about who I told. Didn't remind me that he loved me. Or tell me that everything was going to be okay. If anything, it was all a warning. And after that, I never felt like I could talk to him about it. It was like it was this burdensome thing that he didn't want to hear any more about. I felt so guilty about it that I spent those four years working on my bachelor's in accounting to please him… but when I finished, it still wasn't good enough. Then I had to get a job. And with Conner and Miranda, it was more money, and I realized that if I spent my life constantly doing the things I thought he wanted, it was never going to end. I'd always be trying to do the next thing and then the next thing to please him. That's when I started picking up more graphic design gigs. Quit interviewing for accounting positions."

"He's still in your life, though, even after all this. He does love you."

"I know that. And we'll be fine. It's just... maybe we needed to have this discussion, you know?"

He nods, gets up, and walks around the table. Kneeling, he hugs me.

"What are you doing?" I ask with a chuckle.

"I think you just need a hug to feel better."

I don't resist because it works.

"You want to share my Healthy Choice with me and then watch some TV? What was that *Howl's Moving Castle* you were telling me about the other day? That sounded good."

"That would be really nice."

We wind up on his mattress, his laptop in front of me as he cuddles me from behind.

One of the scenes makes me laugh, and Mikey says, "Look at them trying to get up the stairs. Good God. There's so much fucking sweat in these anime movies."

I laugh some more, and the moment offers the first real escape I've felt from what happened at dinner.

"There we go. That's the Scott I wanted to get back."

I turn to him, and in the blue light from his laptop, his face is lit up, his dark eyes shimmering in the reflection. "I really like this one."

"Yeah. I'm glad you started showing me these. I didn't know much about anime except from watching Dragon Ball Z and Sailor Moon when I was a kid."

"Oh my God."

"You little dick. Don't you make fun of Sailor Moon." He tickles my abs, and I immediately curl into a ball.

"No, no!"

"More? Is that what you want?"

He persists, and adrenaline races through me as he tackles me, and I'm begging him to stop.

I set the laptop on the floor to protect it from the wrestling match that's about to ensue.

I grab his wrists to stop his attacks, but he rolls on top of me and runs his fingers down my body, making those tickling sensations race through me.

I laugh so hard that my face starts to hurt and tears stream from my eyes.

"Let me hear the snort," he says. "Let me hear the snort!"

"Stop! No, please!"

"Not until I hear it."

Just the thought of him waiting to hear that ridiculous noise forces it out.

"Fuck!" I say before I release another. "Goddammit."

I try to curse again, but I'm laughing so hard I can't even speak. I push on his chest before he grips my wrists and pulls them over my head, pinning me so my wrists dip into the air-filled mattress. I chuckle as my body continues working to recover from the attack.

"You fucking asshole," I say as I'm able to speak again.

He gazes down at me with a serious look on his face. I can't read it, but then he leans down and kisses me. Not the lust-filled sort that we usually share before fucking, but still so powerful.

When he pulls away, he has his eyes closed, like he's really taking in just how good the kiss was. Savoring it. It's one of the things I've come to appreciate about him: how much he delights in every moment, how good it feels to him.

"I'm real proud of you for standing up to your dad," he says as he opens his eyes.

His support means the world to me right now. I allow myself to imagine something more here with Mikey, and it's lovely. He's become a good friend.

He offers another kiss.

"Shouldn't we get back to the movie?" I ask.

"Yeah. But I need to send one quick email to Jim about that project we're working on."

"Everything okay?"

"Yeah, yeah. Just some stuff that we got back from the client was kind of all over the place. They didn't like some of the changes we had to make, so we're trying to smooth things over. Work is work, you know? It'll take me a second, but then I'll be right back in your loving arms."

He rolls off of me and grabs the computer, his ass cheeks shifting as he walks, stressing their impressive definition with the dents in the sides that are shaped just right.

I need to appreciate every moment I have with that ass while I still have it, I remind myself.

32

MIKEY

"Just a week left," I tell Scott as he runs his roller down the side of the wall. "Can you believe it?"

We apply the orange coat I showed him at Home Depot—the one I told him about during our date at Dave & Buster's.

I only meant to say that it's amazing how time flew, but as he turns to me with a sort of sadness in his expression, the hard reality hits me like a brick: in just a week, I'm going to be back in Los Angeles without my Scott.

Back to real life and probably unable to get these incredible times we've shared out of my brain.

When he came home last week from dinner with his dad, it was so much fun messing around in bed together, and I got so swept up in our kiss that it made me hope—wish—that we could have something more. It's why I made up the excuse of emailing work. I needed to get away from him for a minute, to clear my head. I've never been that way with someone before. But Scott, he's changed me.

"It's kind of amazing," Scott says, glancing around the room Kate selected for Roger. "I mean, we took on a fucking extra project after all we did. As if we didn't have enough to work on."

I laugh. "Right?"

But this one's been fun. We've spent some of our free time hitting up Toys "R" Us as well as a few thrift stores, finding furniture and toys to fill the room. Most of the stuff is packed in the hallway until we finish the paintjob. We're not finished shopping for it, but we've enjoyed our little project together, picking out baby furniture and toys. Feels like everything we do together is fun.

"I can't wait to see the fucking look on her face when Kate sees this," I say.

We haven't had to worry about her interrupting since I told her that we don't need her for any of these final repairs. And the truth is, we don't. Scott and I have made such an amazing team that we haven't needed much outside assistance throughout the whole project. And we really haven't asked for it since we've both been trying to make this last as long as we can—to spend just another moment in each other's arms.

"I don't think I can tell you enough times how appreciative I am that you sacrificed so much time to help us with this," I say to him.

"And I don't know how many times I have to tell you I was happy to do it. And Kate deserves this. I mean, the night after Sam left me, Jordan took me out to dinner on him, which you know is a rare fucking thing. And it meant a lot because I was feeling really lonely and vulnerable. He reminded me that I wasn't on my own in any of it. And that helped. I'm hoping this will remind Kate of that, too."

"It will. I know it. Speaking of Jordan, I figured he could take a little time to help out today."

"He already had hiking plans with his friends today. I'm just glad he was able to have some fun. Between TAing and his thesis, he hasn't had a lot of time off. Give him a break."

"Maybe in his leg."

Scott chuckles. "Whatever. You'd give him a kidney if he needed it."

He leans down and collects some more paint on his roller before adding it to the wall.

Just a week left of this.

I don't know how to feel about that. I'm relieved we're finishing up, for Kate, at least. But I also don't want to walk away from this part of my life with Scott. In the beginning when it was just fucking around, I wasn't thinking about leaving being an issue. He was just a nice guy who I enjoyed having sex with. It was incredible sex, but that was all there was to it. That was all there was supposed to be to it. Now, I feel like time is being snatched from us. We've had just enough to leave me wanting more—to leave me feeling like there could be something special here. When I try to sort it all out in my head, the crazy thought keeps pushing forward that it wouldn't be so bad to find a way to tele-work for a while longer. Maybe even relocate.

I have a convenient job for it, and considering Scott can work from pretty much anywhere, it wouldn't be impossible for us to make some sort of arrangement. I don't expect him to pick up his life and move for me, but we're in the position to actually give what we have here a shot.

As much as that thought's been crossing my mind, another one always chases it away: It's too soon. We just started doing this. Scott didn't sign up for a relationship, but even as he glances at me as he's painting, I find myself appreciating the way those light brown bangs curl across his forehead and the way his biceps stretch the tee he wears.

But it's more than his looks. More than the fucking.

We've shared something so meaningful, something I have to believe we both want to continue exploring.

"Put down that fucking roller," I tell him.

Scott eyes me suspiciously, but obeys. I put mine in the roller tray with his. As I lean down, he looks up at me, and I give him a quick kiss. As he reciprocates, I enjoy the feel of those soft lips. I close my eyes and appreciate his taste as much as I can since this could be one of the last moments we have alone together.

We rise to our feet, tilting our heads either way and matching each other's movements, igniting that familiar spark.

We're so in harmony now that it's effortless how we strip each other of our clothes. I grab the condom and lube from my pocket, musing on how planning ahead in case a moment like this arose while we were working was one of the best decisions I ever made. Also a sound investment in Trojan Magnums and Swiss Navy lube.

"Not exactly a lot of places to fuck in here, are there?" Scott asks, pulling away from our kiss as he glances around the room—empty aside from the plastic floor film lining the walls and the painting supplies.

We don't have much to work with as far as places to fuck. Just the carpeted floor.

"This'll have to do," I tell him as I sit down and lie on my back beside a pile of our clothes.

Scott laughs. I think we're both amused that we've gotten to the point where we can have sex anywhere. Although, I'm impressed with that more than anything else. Scott gets on his knees and lies alongside my body, taking the condom and lube from my hands. As he suits me up, he offers the occasional kiss.

"I keep offering to bottom for you," I tell him. "You never take me up on it."

"I keep being greedy." He straddles me and descends onto my cock.

There's no apprehension in his expression. No worry about if I'll move too quickly, which I would notice occasionally in the beginning.

There's just an expression of delight that I enjoy seeing as he fills himself with me before sliding his feet back along the carpet and getting on his knees. I wrap my hand around his neck, gripping as I push within him. He kicks his head back and groans as he turns to stick my thumb in his mouth and suck on it. His tongue flicks about.

With my free hand, I grip onto his side and knead my fingers into his muscles.

I thrust.

"God, you're right there, Mikey."

He didn't have to tell me, though. I can see it in the way he opens his eyes—the way they're rolled back as he's just lost in this experience. This is one of my favorite views when we fuck.

I sit up and wrap my arms around him.

I'm greedy for his body. Hungry for it.

My lust consumes me as I continue to take him. He groans and calls out between kisses. I stifle him, shouting my name a few times with my lips.

Grabbing his dick, I stroke it softly, not wanting to bruise the flesh.

Pre-cum leaks from his dick, and I collect some in my hand, using it to lubricate his cock some more. Soon he's got his head pulled back as I kiss his neck, his body twisting, his ass pushing against me. I rock my body as I try to get deeper inside him.

We're on a mission—a desperate, passionate mission—and it feels like I'm nearing the finishing line.

"My balls are so fucking full, Scott."

"Holy fuck." But it's not Scott's voice.

The blood in my face drains, and I turn in the direction it came from.

Jordan stands in the doorway, his cap tilted to the side, his eyes wide and his mouth hanging open.

"Fuck," Scott says, sliding off my dick quickly. He rolls to the side and covers his dick with a nearby shirt. He grabs his jeans and tosses them over my stiff erection before springing to his feet.

I'm in so much fucking trouble.

Throughout the whole time Scott and I have been playing around, we never said anything to Jordan. We just did this in secret.

Is he going to feel hurt? Betrayed? Like I've just been taking advantage of his friend this whole time?

"Jordan, I'm so sorry," I say.

I'm expecting an outburst. Rage. Fury. Confusion. Hate, even.

But a smile spreads across his face. "Holy motherfucking shit!"

Why did he say it like that? And why the fuck is he grinning?

"Oh, dude, this makes me feel so much better. Here I figured I was the only one who was gay."

Now I'm the one who's confused. "Wait. What? You're gay?"

"Yeah, but doesn't it make sense? We're both brothers. I mean, genetically, there was some possibility this could happen."

He's right. Even though I'm technically bi, now doesn't seem like the appropriate time to explain the details of my sexuality. In fact, he's already too involved in my sex life in this moment, as I sit on the floor with Scott, naked, and with a condom still on my dick.

"This is so cool," he goes on. "Oh my God. Oh my God. I'm just so happy to know I wasn't the only one. I wanted to tell you. Kate told me I *should* tell you."

"Kate knows?"

"Of course Kate knows. She's my sister."

"I'm your brother."

His expression twists. "Really? The brother who has been fucking my friend and roommate is now telling me that *I'm* the one who was keeping secrets?"

I like to think this means we're on an even playing field, and I should be appreciative that that's the case and just let go of this.

"Do you know what this means?" he asks.

FU:FIXER UPPERS

"What?"

"We can totally go to gay clubs together now."

"Hey," Scott says. "I'm really appreciating this whole brotherly communication thing, and the fact that you guys are talking about stuff you've never shared before is totally awesome, but if I'm gonna be honest now, I think this would be better if we put clothes on and had an actual discussion… dressed."

"Agreed," Jordan says. "Let's go to Blake's!"

His eyes are wide, and if I'd caught him making that face without any context, I'd think he won the lottery.

This is not how I thought my brother finding out about me fucking his friend would go down.

33

SCOTT

Well, that was weird as fuck.

I was so embarrassed when Jordan walked in on us in the middle of having sex, seeing me with a big fat hard-on and his fucking brother's cock buried in my ass. He shouldn't have found out like that, but I don't think I get to complain, considering that's the best case scenario in terms of Jordan not totally wigging out about what we were doing.

But it got out of control.

We went from fucking around to so much more. We got caught up in each other, in enjoying the fun and the playfulness of it all. In the process, it's gotten far more serious than either of us planned.

I like Mikey a lot, and it's not going to be easy for me when he goes back home—something I keep being reminded of as we share what I know are the last days we'll have with each other. I'm going to have to say goodbye and be okay with that.

We Uber to Blake's, Jordan telling us about how his hiking plans fell through before rambling about how excited he is about his discovery. He tells us the story of when he first starting feeling attracted to guys in elementary school and about one of his first crushes. Even the driver is excited to be in on the news.

Jordan asks Mikey questions about the same sort of stuff he's sharing, but hardly gives him time to answer before he continues telling us about his own experience. I don't think he's trying to monopolize the conversation; he's just held this in for so long that it's like a dam was finally lifted, releasing a wave of emotions that have been trapped behind it all this time.

When we reach Blake's, we order some drinks before taking a nearby table.

"This is so exciting that I can actually do this with you guys," Jordan says, glancing around Blake's with excitement.

I notice a few glances from some guys, but I think everyone's checking out Mikey, which doesn't surprise me.

"Why couldn't you do this with Scott before?" Mikey asks Jordan.

"I mean, I love you Scott, but I've still been coming to terms with all of this. Really it wasn't until Belize that I figured out a lot of shit. That so-called 'girl' I met when I was there, that was actually a dude. That's the person I'm going to see up in Asheville this weekend, after we do the big reveal with Kate. His name's Brian. We've been talking and texting since I got back."

"That's really cool," Mikey says.

It's nice seeing how supportive he is of his brother. That despite how we were both totally thrown, he can shake all of that off and still manage to say the right things to him.

"And Scott's been so busy," Jordan continues, "that we haven't really spent a lot of time together. I mean, I guess now I know why he's really been spending so much time working on this house. So are we going to tell Kate right away, or do you want to wait?"

"What?" Mikey asks.

"I think it would be kind of cool if we could keep the secret a little bit longer so that I can be in on it."

"That's ridiculous," I say.

"Yeah. Yeah. You're right. That's weird to say, isn't it? But this must have been going on for a while. At least before I came back, because you guys were totally acting weird. I really wouldn't have guessed *that*. Mikey, I thought you were, like, the straightest guy ever, which is one of the reasons I didn't want to come out. I figured I was going to disappoint you."

"You thought you were going to disappoint me?" Mikey sounds horrified by his brother's assumption.

"Well, yeah. I sure as fuck didn't care if Dad or Mom thought it wasn't okay. I just thought you wouldn't think I was cool."

"Who you fuck doesn't have anything to do with whether or not you're cool."

"You don't have to sound angry."

"I'm sorry. I'm not angry. I'm a little bothered by the fact that I did something or said something that made you think you couldn't talk to me about this."

"Growing up, you were always talking about girls. Like, always. Was that all bullshit?"

"I'm bi."

"Bi? Are you sure?"

"He's definitely attracted to girls," I say, throwing in my two cents. "I heard him having sex, like, the first night he got here, and it bothered the crap out of me."

Jordan eyes Mikey suspiciously. "Where were you having sex?"

"In your bedroom," Mikey replies, as if he wasn't eager to divulge that information.

Jordan chuckles. Then laughs. "Please tell me you changed the sheets."

"Yes. Of course." Mikey sounds annoyed more than anything else right now.

"Relax, big bro. That's all that matters. So, guys *and* girls, you greedy thing," Jordan jokes.

Mikey tenses his jaw. This is obviously not the way he was expecting for today to go down.

"Well, Scott," Jordan continues, "who knew that you would end up being a part of our big, gay family?"

I can't stifle my laugh. And it's the most relaxed I've felt since we got caught in the act. "I've been really happy to be a part of your big, gay family for sure."

"Clearly." He takes a sip of his drink and scans me up and down. "You know, Scott, I had a crush on you for a long time."

"What?"

"Of course I did. Why do you think I kept hanging out with you all the time? And joined that study group for Bio 101?"

"I assumed you just wanted to do well in the class."

"I did, but I was totally into you. We'd be in bio, and I'd feel some biology working up on me, especially when you'd come in wearing one of your tight button-up shirts."

"I don't think I want to hear this," Mikey says.

I can tell he's getting a little jealous, which I kind of enjoy.

"Come on," I say. "I want to hear how your brother had a crush on me."

Jordan blushes. "Oh my God. I shouldn't even be saying anything. I'm just so relieved. You really have no idea how long I've wanted to tell you about this."

Mike stirs his cocktail in his hand as he says, "I just wish you didn't have to find out the way you did. Wasn't the best of circumstances."

"Not the best of circumstances? I'm pretty sure those were the *perfect* circumstances. I definitely did not have any questions about you judging me when I saw you sitting on the floor of our sister's house penetrating one of my best buddies in the world. Making him scream out. Roll his eyes back. And don't think I wasn't thinking about joining in."

"Oh my God!" Mikey exclaims.

"Kidding! Kidding! Relax, Mikey."

But it does make me consider something I hadn't before. "How long were you standing there?"

"Just long enough to figure out what was happening." Although, judging by the guilty expression on his face, I suspect he was there perhaps a few moments longer than he needed to be. "But, sorry," he goes on. "I've been monopolizing the conversation and making it all about me. What about you guys? This has been going on now for, I guess, three months since you've known each other. Talking to each other. Doing other things with each other. So what's the deal?"

"What do you mean?" Mikey asks.

"Like, what's seriously going on? Is this just friends with benefits? Or is there something more?"

We're silent. It feels like we're both waiting for the other person to say something. I look at Mikey, but he doesn't look back.

"That wasn't a trick question."

"I really like Scott," Mikey finally says, and it feels like there's a *but* to that.

"I really, really like Mikey, too."

"Can we define 'like'?" Jordan presses. "As in, you… would-date-each-other 'like'?"

"We've kind of already gone on dates," Mikey replies.

At this point, we'd be lying if we didn't call them dates.

Finally, our gazes meet. Mikey smiles. It feels so good and nice knowing that as much as we haven't talked about it, we really have been on the same page about where we stand.

"So it's kind of serious at this point?" Jordan asks.

Mikey nods. "I think we can both agree that it did get serious."

"So what's in the books for you guys after this is all finished? Will you try to make this work long distance?"

It's something I've thought about, that's lingered in the back of my mind, this idea that maybe we could find a way. But at the end of the day, from everything Mikey's told me about his past—about his long list of sexual escapades—he's not like me. Yeah, I could sit around and be fine and happy texting or Skyping him, but I've seen what happens with other couples who've tried that approach. When one of them is as hypersexual as Mikey, it's a hard reality.

I'm not stupid or delusional about that.

"I think it just ends once he leaves," I blurt out.

Mikey shouldn't have to say it. I don't want him to feel bad or like he's hurting my feelings.

And I've needed him to know for a while now that I'm not a kid. I didn't have these big dreams of the kind of couple we could be. Admittedly, there were the usual sort of fantasies I have when I'm messing around with someone, especially for as long as we were, but I'm a realist, and I know no guy as amazing as Mikey could ever really wait around for someone like me. I would never expect him to.

"Yeah," Mikey adds. "We both went into this knowing it was a temporary thing and that we were fine with it staying that way. There's not really room in our lives for each other as it is right now."

I almost wish he hadn't said that, but it's the truth, and I have to accept that now.

Maybe this conversation with Jordan was for the best.

Jordan's expression turns serious. "So," he drags out. His gaze shifting between us. "I don't have to buy a bridesmaid's dress?"

Mikey laughs, but it seems forced. "No, not today."

"Well, at least you boys had fun."

"We had a lot of fun," I reply, and as I look at Mikey, his expression says it all, that what we shared meant something, but he also looks kind of sad. I'm sure it's because we've just been forced to face the reality that this is all about to come to a screeching halt.

"Well, fuck him," Jordan tells me. "As soon as he leaves, we're going out to all the gay bars. We're going to get you some dick. I used to restrain myself because I didn't want to seem gay or anything. Now, I don't give a shit. Let's party to die!"

Mikey's jaw tenses up, like the thought of me running around hunting for tricks bothers him, but he doesn't have a right to judge when he's going to be doing the same thing in Los Angeles.

Jordan takes another sip of his drink. As lighthearted as the atmosphere feels, after all that happened today, there's a tension between me and Mikey that hasn't been there before, now that we've answered the question we've both had but neither of us wanted to ask for a few days, at least.

34

MIKEY

We hang with Jordan a little while longer at Blake's before Ubering back to Kate's.

I'm glad I had that conversation with Jordan, but now I'm on edge and want to confront Scott about what he said. Not exactly the sort of conversation I can have with an Uber driver in earshot, though. It isn't until we get out at the house and make our way up the driveway that Scott, who's obviously been sensing my tension, turns to me.

"Everything cool?" he asks.

No. Everything's not cool.

"It bothers me that Jordan didn't feel like he could talk to me about being gay," I tell him. "That something I did made him think I would have judged him or thought less of him because of that."

"Don't beat yourself up about that. It's hard enough coming to terms with it yourself, let alone tell other people about it. He didn't tell me, and I'm gay. You didn't tell anyone about you being bi."

"Fair point."

"And your family isn't exactly one for talking things through, you know?"

Unfortunately.

As we reach the door, I pull out my key. "Well, I guess tomorrow we should go baby shopping after we finish up the

257

paint job."

The way Scott looks at me, I can tell he notices I'm not as chipper as I usually am around him.

Truth is, bothered as I was about Jordan having felt like he couldn't share that with me, I'm just as bothered by Scott's reply when Jordan asked us about what our plan was after we finished working on Kate's house. I thought things were going really well, that maybe we could find a way of working out what was starting to blossom between us.

Clearly, I was misguided. Scott doesn't seem to be interested in that. He was so quick to answer Jordan about it, too. He didn't even need to talk to me or get my feelings about what I wanted out of this.

Although, if that's how he feels, that's his right.

We head inside, and I close the door behind us. I find, maybe because I'm slightly inebriated, I can't let it go. I just have to make sure what he said to Jordan is how he really feels and it wasn't just a quick thoughtless answer he was giving to him, because we hadn't really had a discussion yet.

"Scott. Did you mean what you said to Jordan about not wanting to try anything beyond this?"

If he says no, he says no, but I'm not the kind of guy who's going to lie about how I feel. I may have not even really understood how I felt for a while, but this is probably the most special connection I've allowed myself to have with another human being, and I'm not giving it up that easily.

"Because I would really like to give it a try," I confess. "We can do something long-distance. We can Skype or talk on the phone or text. I really like you Scott."

"I really like you, too, Mikey. I've had so much fun every day and night we've spent together. You are unbelievably amazing, and you deserve to be with someone unbelievably amazing."

"You are amazing," I tell Scott, because right now, I'm fighting for us.

And why am I the one fighting when what he said just sounds like a compliment, not an obstacle?

He looks hurt. Sad, even.

"I do care about you, Mikey, but I don't think it'll work. I've seen people try to make long distance relationships work. People get hurt. People cheat. People lie."

"Doesn't mean you can't give it a chance. Come on. We've both been experiencing the same things. Tell me you don't think there's something special."

"There is something special. I will tell you that a million times, but the reality is that we live in two different worlds. You have a life in Los Angeles. My life is here."

"We could work it out. We could figure something—"

"There's no reason to," Scott says, aggression in his tone, like he just wants me to stop, like he's tired of me fighting for this.

A silence stretches between us. I don't think he realizes how hurt I feel right now.

How rejected.

It makes me feel like the past few months have just been in my head. Like I've been taking it further in my mind than he has, but as I reflect on the nights of cuddling and sweet kisses, I can't believe that's true.

But there's another part of me that feels this is for the best. I remember my parents—their bitterness, their anger. They loved each other once. I remember that. I remember being young enough when they were still in love, and there were sweet kisses and affectionate gazes, and it changed.

It turned on them.

Scott gave me a reason to believe that maybe I could find something special and meaningful, and it was worth taking a chance on. Now, I just feel like I've been kidding myself.

"Mikey," he says, his tone seeming to be an attempt to soothe me.

"No," I say because it's too late to fix what he's done. Obviously he's made up his mind, and I've made up mine now. "If you are so sure that you don't want this, then I would never try to make it happen. It is complicated with long distance relationships, and I can't ask you to do that if that's not something you want. Let's just do what we've always done and agree that this is going to end when it ends, and that's fine."

"Are you mad at me?"

"I'm not thrilled," I admit, "but you have every right to want what you want."

That's a fucking lie, because I'm pissed as fuck.

He approaches me and puts his arm around me. What normally feels like this loving safe hold has twisted into something cruel—this desire, this want that I can never really fulfill because he hasn't given me the chance, because he doesn't want to give *us* a chance.

"Come on," he says. "Let's go watch a movie or something. Curl up in bed like we normally do."

"I care about you, Scott, but I think tonight I need to be by myself."

His eyes widen. It's clear that he's surprised by my words, considering we haven't spent any nights apart since we began the repairs on the house. We've ended up in either one of our beds without exception.

"I understand," Scott says.

Why won't he fight? Why doesn't he care?

My chest tightens. I don't think I realized how much I cared about Scott until he convinced me of a future where I couldn't have him.

"So I guess we'll just see each other tomorrow to get supplies for Roger's room," Scott tells me.

"Yeah. That works." He starts to walk away and then turns back around. I want him to say anything that will make me think that what I've been feeling isn't totally irrational. "I'll wake up early and get started on the painting so that it can dry by the time we get back."

It feels like someone just sucked my soul right into the floor.

I'm devastated. *You've wrecked me, Scott. You've destroyed me.*

"That sounds good," I tell him. "I'll see you tomorrow."

He heads off, and I get ready for bed, feeling so alone in this house that brought me so much companionship and joy. I keep cursing Scott as my rage twists in knots within me. This is what happens when you let yourself care about someone—something I've rarely let myself do outside of Jordan, Kate, and Roger. This is why I don't let myself get attached. Why my life has just been a series of one-night stands, because I know what it's like to be betrayed. I know what it's like when the love that I thought I was being showered with is suddenly withheld from me. It takes me back to when I was eleven years old confronting my mother, telling her what I thought she needed to know, expecting love—and instead getting anger and bitterness and blame.

It feels lonely, so fucking lonely.

35

SCOTT

It's the big day.

Kate finally gets to move into her home. She's all smiles as we walk her around the house, showing her the finished work. It reminds me of when I sent the final proof of an image I've been working on to a client.

The sleeves of her light-blue blouse are rolled up to her elbows as she rests Roger against her shoulder. "Oh, my God, it's perfect!" she exclaims as we walk her through the kitchen to show her the fixed ceiling and cabinets. Roger squirms as he tries to spin around to look. "You want to see, honey?" she asks.

"Here, I've got him." Mikey takes him from her.

"Thank you."

"I want you to enjoy the house while you can. You have plenty of time to carry him around this place in the near future."

"Don't I know it."

"Hey, fella," he says, and all I can think of is that night he told me he wants kids.

I'm gonna miss this project we shared. I'll miss him.

Since we talked about not trying to make this work long distance, we haven't hooked up. We finished up the house and the baby room just as friends. I can tell I hurt Mikey because he wanted us to take things further, and it isn't that I didn't want to, but I would never ask him to do that. He's a hot item, and he can get any guy or girl he wants; I'm not going to hold up his sexual needs because he's got some crush on me.

I'm not holding him back from finding someone better and more interesting than me once he's back in LA.

And even though it hurts getting the cold shoulder from him, I know it's for the best. It doesn't keep me from missing the fuck sessions and hating that the last time we fucked might really have been the last. If he knew how much it hurt depriving me of that, I don't know how he could keep doing it to me, but it's his right to be upset.

"I hope you don't mind that I invited Mom and Dad," Kate says. "They've been here for me for the past few months, and it's all finished and perfect, and when Mom asked, I wasn't going to say no."

"I understand," Mikey tells her, but the thought makes me tense up now that I know the truth behind his anger, about what those fuckers did to him. "I can take them being here for a little while. But I at least want to show you this before they arrive."

After we've shown her the rest of the changes downstairs, we lead her up the stairs to the second floor. Despite the tension that's lingered between Mikey and I, even as we've set up the baby room, there were still fun moments. We've still been playful, teasing each other about fucking picking out kid's clothes and toys together. And even though the changes to the house are great, this is what I'm really excited about. I can just imagine the look in Kate's eyes when she sees the room for the first time.

With Roger still in his arms, Mikey opens the door for

Kate.

She puts her hands to her face and releases a shrill cry before she rushes into the room, glancing around at the crib with the star-themed mobile. Stuffed animals are piled around the panda I won for Mikey, and beside them, there's a bookshelf Mikey made with some of the scraps from the renovation. We've stuffed the shelves with picture books we purchased at the local Goodwill.

And of course, the walls are that orange that Mikey picked out.

"You guys," she says. "You shouldn't have done this. This is too much."

"Nothing is too much for you, little sis."

Tears stir in her eyes. "I don't know how I'm ever going to repay you guys for this."

"That's not what this was about. This room was a gift for you. We did it because you deserve this after everything you've been through. To start your new life over in the house of your dreams."

"Thank you, thank you, thank you, thank you." She bursts into tears.

"Oh, come here." Mikey hugs her as she cries into his shoulder. "Get over here right now, Scott."

As I move close, she hooks an arm around me and pulls me in for a group hug. "You guys are just too incredible. This whole thing was too much, and I'm just—"

"You can repay us all when you take us out to dinner. And drinks are on you. Fair?"

Mikey's clearly trying to help her relax.

She pulls away from us and smiles. "Fair."

I hear a car pull up the drive.

"That must be them," she says.

She pulls away and looks into Mikey's eyes. How can she not detect the tension and see how uneasy he is right now?

Every muscle in my body has tensed. I shouldn't be this on edge, but I am. I don't want Mikey to have to face that bastard or his asshole mother, not when they're just going to be cold and inconsiderate of his feelings, not caring about what they did to him.

Kate leads us down the stairs, and Mikey soothes Roger as he starts to cry, surely sensing Mikey's discomfort. As we reach the bottom of the stairs, Kate heads out the front door. Mikey turns to me, and as we look into each other's eyes, it's clear that in this moment, we're allies.

He needs me right now, and I'm happy to be here for him.

"You guys are going to die when you see how great it all looks," Kate says as she follows the concrete path to the driveway to meet them halfway.

Jordan's Civic and his parents' Audi Q5 are parked outside. Guess they followed him here.

"I did help out quite a bit," Jordan says, adjusting the bill of his cap to the side as he makes his way to the house, "so you gotta give me some credit." He winks at us. "Let me see my little, most adorable nephew in the world!" He skips up the steps of the front porch, ignoring us for Roger. "Hey there, little guy." Roger's still fussing a little. "What did the evil Uncle Mikey do to you this time?"

"Whatever. Here. Why don't you be the grown-up for five

seconds?" Mikey suggests, handing him over.

I know why he's really doing it, though. Roger's sensing his uneasiness, and it's only going to get worse the longer they're here.

Jordan takes Roger and cradles him. "Buddy, how's it going? You miss me?"

He rocks Roger in his arms while Kate leads Dara and Kirk inside. I offer the greetings I know they expect before she gives them a tour. Jordan takes Roger up into his room to play with him, and Mikey slips out the front door.

I figure he wants to get away to keep from blowing Kate's big day. I don't know if I should, but I follow him outside around to the backyard.

He turns and sees me coming toward him. "I was kind of hoping you were following," he says.

"Are you okay?" He shrugs. "You can shrug with Jordan and Kate all day, but you don't have to do that with me. I'm here for you, you know that."

"I really do, Scott. Thank you." He glances over at the back of the house where we replaced all the siding. "We did good. We did really good, didn't we? I know I haven't been the easiest to deal with these past few days, but I don't want you to think for one moment that I haven't appreciated everything you've done."

"You've been fine. You didn't do anything wrong."

"Neither did you. And I'm sorry if I've made you feel like you did just for feeling the way you feel."

"Thank you for saying that."

This conversation reminds me of how hard it's going to be

when he finally leaves.

He's too good of a guy to be hurt by me. He'll find somebody, though—some hot guy in Los Angeles who is as hypersexual as he is and can keep up with him the way I have. They'll have fun, probably even more fun than we've had. I have to stop thinking about that because it's driving me crazy and filling me with jealousy, which I don't have a right to feel.

36

MIKEY

Scott and I head in through the back door into the kitchen. Kate, Mom, and Dad are chatting by the cabinets. Kate's eyes are still lit up with excitement, but Dara and Kirk's gazes shift our way.

I can tell, as I always can, how uncomfortable they are about me being here.

I usually feel like I'm on my own when I see them, like it's me and the rest of the family, but not today. Today I have Scott, and he can't know, but having someone here who knows about what really happened, who's on my side, that means so much to me.

I don't feel so alone.

I've been bitter after what he told me the other night, but I know he's a good person, and I meant what I said when I told him it's not his fault for not wanting to be with me like that. I've been a little bit like a kindergartener being told he couldn't play with his favorite toy. Not that he's just a toy to me, but it feels cruel for him to deprive me of something that's been so life-giving. It's as if he told me he wasn't going to let me breathe oxygen anymore.

And the past few days of not fucking with him? Those have been the worst. I figure Mom and Dad will just leave me alone, especially after my outburst last time, but Dad slips away from them and makes his way over.

"Scott, how's it going?" he asks.

"Very good, Mr. Bradshaw."

He reaches his hand out, and Scott reluctantly takes it for a shake. "I just want to tell you how appreciative I am of everything you've done for my daughter and my family."

Scott smiles, but I can tell he's irritated, that he's having a hard time appreciating my dad's words knowing what he knows.

There's this impulse rising within me. It's always been there when he's around. This desire to tell him, but now that Scott's here, for some reason, it's more powerful than usual. I feel like I should tell him exactly what I've always thought and felt about everything he did wrong. I bite my tongue, though— like I always do.

Dad turns to me. "You did good for your sister. How are things going, Mikey?"

He's nice enough, but that's what pisses me off. Once again, he's just pretending everything's okay. But it's not okay. *I'm* not okay.

"They're fine." I force the words out.

Dad scans me over. "When do you head back to Los Angeles?"

"Monday morning."

"Well, good. I hope you have a safe trip. I wish we could have gotten to spend more time with you while you were here, but I understand you were busy."

This is so like Dad. Fucking in denial about the fact that I'm so pissed about what happened. Acting like there are other reasons why I can't make time to be with them or blow up whenever we wind up together. I just can't hold back my rage: "I wasn't busy. I didn't want to see you."

His gaze shifts to the floor. "Then I guess you can be on your way and continue pretending we don't exist." He sighs, stressing his disappointment before he turns and walks toward Mom and Kate.

My face fills with heat.

The bastard. The fucking bastard. Turning this back on me like I'm the douchebag who caused this rift in our family.

In a moment, the rage, the hurt, the pain, and that impulse to say what I've been holding in all these years pushes through me.

"Fuck you," I say through gritted teeth.

Dad turns around. I figure my face is about as red as his is turning. "What did you say to me?"

"Fuck you!" My shout is uninhibited, filled with the rage and hostility that's been pent up in me for years.

It's venomous. It's the rage not of a man who's nearly thirty, but an eleven-year-old boy who never stood up to this bastard.

Kate and Mom turn to see what all the commotion is about.

"What has gotten into you, Mikey? Are you trying to start another fight? Another spectacle? What is it with you and all these goddamned scenes you want to make?"

"I'm tired. Sick and fucking tired of you acting like I'm making a scene when you know exactly what I'm mad about."

"You're just trying to start drama again."

"I'm not trying to start drama. I just know that you owe me

a little more than you've ever given me."

"What do I owe you?"

"An apology, to say the least. I was a kid. I was young. I was confused. I didn't even know at first what I was looking at on that phone. You didn't just not take credit for what you did. You made me feel like I would destroy this family. Like I was the one who was doing something wrong by just knowing the truth. You made me feel guilty because you wanted to shut me up."

"I don't know what you're talking about." His denial is obviously for Mom and Kate's benefit. And maybe Kate won't believe me. Maybe she'll side with them, but for the first time ever, there's at least one person in the room who knows the truth, and that feels incredible, freeing, empowering.

"Mom, do you not know what I'm talking about either?" I ask, giving her the chance to atone. "Because, as far as I'm concerned, you're just as guilty."

"What is going on?" Kate asks, glancing between everyone.

I feel like shit. This was supposed to be her special day. But right now, I can't hold this in anymore, not the way I have in the past.

Mom remains silent. It's apparent she doesn't want to get involved.

"Kate, we have no idea what your brother is talking about right now," Dad says. "He's lost his mind, as far as I'm concerned. He's just trying to poison this family against each other, I guess, because he has some ridiculous vengeance against me for a reason I can't imagine."

"You can't imagine it, Kirk?" I ask. "You can't imagine why I'm so fucking pissed at you after all these years?"

"I don't have a clue."

I don't see a reason to hold back. Not anymore. "Then I don't mind reminding you. Because you had an affair with a women named Sheryl, and you made a kid who stumbled across evidence feel like if he told anyone, our family would be on the streets, and that it would all be my fault. And Mom, when I came to you, you told me that you didn't believe me, only to later assure me that you knew all along what was happening. You both fucked me over, that's what you did."

"Is this true?" Kate asks. "Is it?"

I look between Mom and Dad, waiting for them to reveal their part in all this, to fess up to this crime that they committed against me so many years ago.

"I don't even understand why this is coming up now," Dad says.

Kate approaches him, her hands balled into fists. "But is it true?"

"Affairs happen all the time," Mom says quickly, coming to his defense.

Kate doesn't look nearly as confused as she did when this conversation began. "I knew about the affair, though, and I was willing to forgive that. Or at least try to push through it with you, Mom. The affair was one thing, but this? Making your child feel responsible for ruining their family? That's another. Am I wrong thinking it's the person having the affair who should be accused of that? Did you two really do this to Mikey?"

"I don't know what anyone's talking about." Apparently, Dad's sticking to his story.

Kate stands upright, her jawline sharpening. "Get out of my house."

"What? We let you stay in our home for weeks without paying any rent, and—"

"Do I owe you for that? Is that how family works? Because up until now, I actually thought that family works by not dragging their children into their affairs. Lyle may have been a lot of things, but at least all he did was cheat. At least nothing happened to Roger, because I can tell you right now, Dad, if he had ever done anything like what you did to Mikey, I would have been dragged to jail because the cops would have needed to pry me off of him." She turns her attention to Mom. "And Mom, you should be ashamed for not being there for your son. This all makes sense now. It was always hard to understand why Mikey was so upset, why he kept lashing out at you guys all through high school. Jordan and I never got it, but now that I do, you need to leave."

"How can you believe him?" Dad asks.

"And now you're doing it all over again?" I ask, horrified that nothing's changed after all these years, that he's not even willing to give me this moment.

"Get out," Kate tells him. "Now."

Dad grunts. "Come on, Dara."

"Baby, we're so sorry," Mom tells Kate.

"I'm not the one you should be apologizing to. And that's why you need to leave."

Mom tucks her head low and follows Dad out, still not

offering any words to me, maybe because she's just so ashamed of what she did.

As soon as they're out the door, Kate turns to me. "How could you have kept that in all these years? How could you have not told us?"

"I didn't want to take your family away from you the way mine was taken away from me."

"Do you think it was better for us to live that lie, like when I lived the lie that my husband still loved me?"

"I'm sorry, Kate."

"I don't need you to be sorry, Mikey. This family's been strained for so long, and Jordan and I especially haven't really understood the reason why. It's kind of a relief to know that it wasn't just in our heads, and to know what really happened. You shouldn't have had to deal with that on your own."

"Yeah, well, Jordan shouldn't have had to face being gay alone, either."

"He told you?" Kate asks.

"Yeah, and I'm bi, by the way." I figure now's the time for total honesty—a first for our family.

Her expression, which has been serious up to this point, twists into a smirk. "Really?" She sounds shocked.

"Yeah, really."

"I guess today is just the big reveal of all secrets, isn't it?"

"Apparently."

"Scott," she says. "Anything you would like to share?"

"I think if there is anything else Mikey wants to tell you," he says, "it's probably better that it'd be him."

Her gaze shifts between us as she takes note of the clue he

just dropped for her.

"You dirty boys. Haven't you all been busy?"

"I recommend you play catch-up with Jordan," I say. "I'm not interested in describing the details of my sex life to my sister."

"I don't need the details of the sex part, but everything else, I'm down with."

We laugh together, and it's such a huge relief. All those things I've carried on my own are finally out in the open, finally off my chest.

And I'm just so goddamned happy that Scott was here for me. For this. I couldn't have found the strength without him.

I chat with Kate some more about the truth before we talk with Jordan, too. It's time for me to be free. I deserve that.

As I talk to them, Scott stays close, and I can feel his support right here with me. I need it, too.

When we finish up, I drive Scott back to his and Jordan's apartment. He has his things in the trunk—all his belongings that he brought with him while we worked on the house. Jordan offered to drive him, but I insisted. It's not just that I want to see him some more for as long as I can before I have to go; it's also that I want to talk to him about what just happened.

I want to thank him, really.

"You know I couldn't have done all that work without you," I tell him. "And I wouldn't have had nearly as much fun."

"You could have done most of it, I'm pretty sure. I just did what you told me."

"You'll never really know how much help you were.

Thank you."

"It was an honor to serve." Scott waves his hand before him as he leans forward in a symbolic bow. "So now, do you mind if I ask you about what happened back there with your parents? I don't want to push."

"You're not pushing. I just couldn't stand it that time, watching them pretend that everything was okay and then Dad grating my nerves like he always does, trying to make it like my distance from them, like never seeing them, was about something that *I've* done. And really, that was the first time that's ever happened where I felt like I had someone who was on my side. I've always been afraid that they might find a way to turn Kate and Jordan against me if I said anything and that I'd feel so fucking alone. But with you there... at least I knew you had my back... and that was nice."

I've been giving him the cold shoulder the past few days, but I acknowledge all that he's brought into my life, how amazing he is, and how he's changed my life in ways I'll never fully understand.

"So thank you for being there. Kate was right. We've had too many secrets for too long, and it was time we faced them. Maybe now that the house is fixed, we can start repairs on what we've neglected for far too long. Our family."

"I'm really proud of you."

Is it terrible how good it feels knowing that he's proud of me? I shouldn't care as much as I do, not when he doesn't even want to be with me. But at the same time, I've realized over the past few days—even as I've abstained from giving him what we've shared so many times, hurting both of us in the process—I can't force him to want to make this work. And regardless of how he feels about me, I care about him.

I keep hoping he'll change his mind and want to find a way to have me in his life, but this is so new. It's just been a few months, so there's no reason for him to feel any way that he doesn't.

As I pull alongside their apartment building, all I want to do is invite myself up. I want another moment with him—against him, touching him, being inside him.

He looks around uneasily. "So it's just this weekend and then you're gone?"

"Yep. Kind of surreal how everything's gone down, isn't it?"

"Yes, it is. I did have a lot of fun, Mikey. I hope you know that, and I hope you know just how incredible I think you are. I know it bothered you when I said I didn't want to do this long distance, but I didn't meant to hurt you."

"I get that."

"I guess this is the last time we're going to see each other before you head back."

I can't help myself. "It doesn't have to be. Do you want it to be the last time?"

Scott shakes his head, and it gives me some hope—maybe more than it should. Maybe I should just walk away now so that I don't get hurt, but after the moments we've shared, I can't shake them. I don't want to shake them.

I cherish what he gave me and the way I've opened up to him, the way he's opened me up, and the transformation that I felt like I've gone through by being with him.

"We could get together before I leave, if you wanted to," I say. "Jordan'll be leaving tomorrow afternoon to see that Brian guy in Asheville. Why don't I come over and make you some dinner, and we see where things take us from there?"

"I think I have an idea where things will take us. Or at least I'm hoping."

"Don't get cocky."

"Well, I would really like to do it."

There's this lightness about Scott, but I can feel his guilt, too.

He opens the passenger door and gets out, and as he closes it behind him, there's this ache in my gut—the pain of knowing I'm going to go another night without him.

How could we share so much—get so close—and now feel so distant? Does he not understand how I feel, how much I care, how much I want him?

* * *

I knock on Jordan and Scott's door. Scott answers, smiling.

In a hunter-green polo that fits snug, the hem tucked behind the clip of his belt, he looks hot as ever.

I pull out the flowers I have behind my back. Red roses. It's corny as fuck, but this is the kind of treatment Scott deserves. I don't mind being corny for him. Tonight's my night to dote on him and savor what I can. I won't let anything, not even my ego, stand in my way.

"Roses? Are you kidding?"

"Do I look like I'm kidding?"

"I didn't take you for a roses kind of guy, Mikey."

"Maybe you haven't noticed some of the best parts of me yet."

He glances at my crotch. "I think I've noticed the best part."

"Fair enough."

In my other hand, I have a brown paper bag filled with groceries, which he eyes. "So what is this mystery dinner you're making us?"

"It's a surprise," I tell him. "I mean, for another five seconds until I get this stuff out and you help me make it."

He laughs. "That's the Mikey I'm familiar with, and I wouldn't have it any other way." As I start unloading the bag onto the counter, he glances at the ingredients. "Meat, tomato paste, spaghetti noodles," he notes. "You're making spaghetti? Like, one of the easiest dishes in the world?"

"Spaghetti and meatballs, and I make amazing meatballs."

"Is everything you say going to sound sexual?"

"It just works out that way, it seems."

As I unload a few more items from the bag, Scott goes on, "Oh, and some Brussels sprouts and rolls. I know what I'm handling."

"We do make a good team."

"Yeah, we do." I can hear the sincerity in his tone.

We work together on the dinner—laughing, joking, falling back into that rhythm we found when we were staying at Kate's. I let go of the anger I've been holding towards him. And when we finish, I set the table while Scott plates our meal. I head into the kitchen, and Scott carries the plates past me to the table. I grab our wine glasses and a bottle of Chardonnay I opened before we began. When I return, I set the bottle in the middle of the table and our glasses next to our plates, then head back to the kitchen.

"We have everything, I think," he says.

"Not yet." I grab a candle I picked up from the store and dig through the drawer for a lighter. "Just a final touch," I say as I place the candle in the middle of the table and light it. Scott's expression is so serious. "You can feel free to give me shit about this, for sure."

He shakes his head. "No. It's actually nice. Thank you."

I set the lighter down beside the candle and take my seat. "I think we deserve a toast."

He grabs his glass and lifts it in the air.

"To a job well done, and to something special that we discovered along the way."

We clink our glasses together, and I'm kind of wishing Scott would change his mind—that he would say something, anything to let me know that he wants this to go on. I know it's a fantasy, but I can accept that. I'm fine with doing whatever I have to do to spend the night with him and just have this moment.

37

SCOTT

God-fucking-dammit, Mikey. Why do you have to be so charming?

As he sits across from me, the glow of the candle he placed in the middle of the table creates a sparkle in his eyes—as if they weren't beautiful enough already.

He's always looked like a god, like the universe conspires to make him even more beautiful to me with every passing day. It doesn't seem fair. I imagine I still look like the same geek to him that I've been since we've known each other. It's not just the gorgeous shell that makes him beautiful, though. It's knowing everything that's underneath, seeing how much more he is than just another hot guy.

"Are you excited about finally getting home?" I ask him.

"Yeah, it'll be nice. Get back to my own place. Actually sleep in a comfortable bed. Not a hotel bed—"

"Or a blow-up mattress."

He laughs. "Yeah. Not that we had particularly bad nights on blow-up mattresses."

"No, not all. No complaints from me. Maybe some stiff muscles because of it, though."

"Not sure you can blame the mattress for that."

Tonight's different than it's been since we had that conversation about if we would keep going or not. I see the appreciation in his eyes again for what we've done, what we've shared. That makes me really fucking happy because I don't want him to leave mad at me or feeling like I was a jerk for saying we shouldn't try.

I look over at the entryway where I stood, arms folded, judging him, being so fucking mad for how he kept me up that first night. "It all comes back to this place, doesn't it?"

"You hated me that night."

"That's what happens when you wake up hearing some girl screaming at the top of her lungs. I'll be honest, if I knew what she'd been screaming about, I probably wouldn't have judged as much."

"And if you'd known how easy it was going to be for you to get this guy in bed, you probably would have found a way to be friendlier sooner."

"I think it all worked out just the way it was supposed to."

I meant that to be friendly and playful, but I catch sadness in Mikey's expression.

"We did have a lot of fun," he admits. "And I'm going to say really honestly, Scott, I never met anybody like you, and I don't know that I'll ever meet anybody like you again. But I do feel fortunate to have you in my life."

"I feel the same way about you."

If only he knew. Maybe he can't ever really know. I wish I could express it in words, but no one's ever been as kind or generous or friendly or given me that fucking amazing sex before.

"Wouldn't be a tragedy if we had another night." I say it, slightly joking, but as the words escape my lips, I know that there's something serious there.

"There's no reason we can't."

"You're not mad at me?"

"I'm frustrated that we're in this shitty situation. I wish we had lives that would make all this easier, that we weren't just together for this amount of time, but I know how the world works. We both knew what we were getting into, but I don't want to give that hot sex up cold turkey. Already done that for a week, and it's driven me pretty fucking crazy."

I chuckle.

"I'm being serious." His words are so intense, they silence me. We just stare into each other's eyes.

He gets up from the table, walks around, and reaches his hand out.

I'm not really sure what to think.

"Come on," he says. "One more night."

I take his hand. I'm not sure either of us are really thinking about if this is a good idea, but only about how much we want it and the fact that it'll bring back all those good feelings and memories—the memories we created together.

We brush our teeth in the bathroom together, the way we did at Kate's place for the past month and a half. When we're done, I start to head from the bathroom into my bedroom when Mikey grabs my shoulder and spins me around. He crushes his lips against mine, his hands moving in a frenzy across my body, his light scruff rubbing against my face. Tonight feels more desperate. There's a sting to it. It's not like it got when we were doing this at Kate's house, when we knew that night after night, we'd be together. Now we know this is the last chance, and I'm determined to make the best of it.

I pull his shirt off over his head and throw it aside, kissing down his body to those broad shoulders, down his biceps, back to his pecs, then right back to his lips. I don't know which part I want to kiss most because I'm going to miss it all.

We make our way to the bedroom, losing more and more clothes. Soon I'm rolling on top of him, and he gazes at me with an expression I haven't seen before.

"I want to bottom tonight," he says.

I'd almost forgotten that he was a virgin when we got together the first time he fucked me. "You've never—"

"I want you to be my first, Scott."

I feel honored and privileged, because this is something special. It's something I want to share with him because I care so deeply for him, and I don't know that the same will be true about the next guy who has this opportunity.

Even thinking about another man being with him drives me crazy, but all I can do is enjoy this experience; it's the only thing promised tonight.

I reach over to the nightstand and retrieve the condoms and lube from my drawer. A part of me feels like he's going to object or take them, but he just lies there in anticipation. I kiss him as I finish rolling the condom on, my dick so hard because this is something I want us to explore together. I used to fuck Sam all the time before we stopped having sex, but we didn't have this chemistry—this sensation that burned through every nerve in my body, setting fire to a passion that possesses me when we fuck.

I grab Mikey's thighs and push them back. Pressing my face against his ass, I lick and slide my tongue inside him before slipping a finger in, pushing slowly. I work my way deeper, easing him into the experience. I wait until I think he's ready before I add another finger.

He rolls his head on the pillow behind him, moaning as I stimulate his prostate, rubbing in circles the way others have done for me.

"God, Scott, just like that. Right there."

He grabs his dick and strokes it. "Get inside me. I'm ready."

I'm nervous and excited all at once. I rise onto my knees, pressing the head of my dick to the rim of his hole. He gazes at me, smirking in that way that always looks so fucking adorable.

"I want it to feel good," I tell him. "You tell me if it's too fast or if you're not comfortable... or you change your mind, and—"

"Do it, Scott. I trust you."

With his invitation, I slide in.

His body tenses up at first, and I rub my hand on his abs, hoping to soothe him, remind him that I'm here and I care.

He arches his back and raises his arms over his head, pressing his hands against the headboard, completely surrendering to me in this moment.

I keep going, and we find our rhythm together, moving in sync, his moan being the only encouragement I need.

He laughs suddenly, loudly. I stop. "Holy shit," he moans.

"What?"

"You didn't tell me it felt this good." There's something wicked in his expression—the excitement of what he's discovered.

"Oh, just wait and see."

"Go for it."

I wrap my arms under his legs, lifting him slightly, and then I take him. I give it to him hard and fast, the way he's given it to me plenty of times. He curses, his body twisting with each thrust as he arches his back. I rest his body back on the mattress before I lean down, wrap my arm around his neck, and press my lips against his. He keeps moaning even as we swap licks and nips. I can feel the pre-cum oozing out of the head of his dick.

"I'm pretty… sure you're going… to make me… shoot," he warns me between kisses.

"Oh, we can't have that yet. You haven't tried my favorite position yet." I pull out, grab his ankle and guide him onto his stomach. I pull on his legs so that he gets to his knees. Then I push back into him from behind. He sets one hand on the pillow beside him, and the other at the top of the headboard, his beautiful back on full display.

I stroke a hand down it to that hot ass before I impulsively slap it, the sound of my hand against his flesh filling the bedroom. He looks over his shoulder, smiling. "Do it again."

I obey as I drive into him.

He kicks back his head. "Oh, fuck yes, Scott. Fuck me just like that."

With each thrust, he pushes his ass back, inviting me in farther. I get lost in the experience the same way I've gotten lost in it when I bottomed for him. I'm lost in the sensations— the heat of our bodies, the taste of his tongue, the feel of his flesh. My thoughts, worries, and insecurities dissolve as I only become aware of us and what we give each other.

He chuckles softly. "Oh my God, Scott. Jesus, that feels great."

Instinctively, I reach around, grab his dick, and press my body against his back.

I kiss the side of his face, and he turns to me, his mouth meeting mine. He leans back so we're both upright, and I wrap an arm around him, resting it on his firm torso, keeping him close as I become immersed in our kiss.

I'm hypnotized by this moment.

My body forces me through movements I can hardly control because it's just like everything in me wants to get to that final explosion.

"Fucking come in me, Scott. Please." His words followed by his hot breath against my face is too much, and I feel the power of my release. Just as I do, he calls out, and his cum spills from his dick, wetting my hand. He twists, turns, and grunts. His muscles are stiff, and I'm still clinging to him in the same position as we breathe heavily together. I didn't realize how in sync our breathing was until now.

He reaches back and runs his hand across my face.

He doesn't stop kissing, and I won't either because I don't want to let him go. I don't want to escape this perfect, blissful moment. I want to keep it for as long as we can.

And judging by the way he's keeping me close, he does too.

He pulls away long enough to whisper, "Let's make the most of this, Scott. Let's just give each other that."

My kiss is my agreement.

38

MIKEY

I sit at my desk in this office where I'd spent most of my time before I went to help my sis out.

Being back here almost makes that time I spent with Scott feel like a dream—a beautiful, amazing dream. I don't like the distance, and even though we talk on the phone and text every day, two weeks of not seeing him has been hard. I didn't think I could ever come to appreciate another human being the way I came to appreciate Scott, and I'm only sad that circumstances aren't different.

I work on a project that just came in this week—a new client with a design one of our competitors fucked up last year.

It's been pretty easy falling back into my routine. One of the perks of working in the office is that I don't have to motivate myself to get work done, as if it's the hobby and fixing a house is my job. As hard as that was, at least I know Kate's happy with what we did. I've talked to her several times since I returned to Los Angeles, and I can hear the playfulness in her voice again, reminding me that there is hope.

That she's in a place where she can move on.

My phone vibrates beside my laptop, and I snatch it. I used to cringe when my phone would go off and just avoid looking at it, but now there's always the possibility that it's Scott, and I want to talk to him again, especially today because I know he's talking to his father for the first time since they got into it about what Scott's dad thinks isn't a real job.

"Hey, Stud," I answer.

"Hey, Tight Ass." It's his new nickname for me ever since we shared that magical night—the night that changed my fucking life.

"You excited about chatting with your Dad?" I ask him.

"Just thrilled. It's not for a few hours, but of course, that's all I can think about, you know?"

"It'll be fine. Just remember he loves you. He's not like my asshole parents. Everything he's done has been to improve your life."

"I know that, and I would never cut him out of my life for good, but I just want to be clear that it's my life. I'm happy with the choices I've made, and I want him to be supportive of those choices. I don't feel like that's a lot to ask."

"I don't, either."

"Sorry. I don't want to make this all about me. How's your day been?"

"Ah, it's pretty good. Some of the guys are going out tonight. There's this bar in Beverly Hills where they do a trivia night. Feel like I need to catch up with everybody. When I got back, it was just straight back to work, playing catch up. Now I feel like I can actually chill a little bit."

"Don't work too hard. There's only one thing I'd like you to do when you're hard."

"Bring it out here any time you want."

"Don't tempt me."

"All I want to do is tempt you, Scott."

I'm not kidding. I still want to be with him. I thought being back out here would make it easier to move on—and maybe I will after a while—but this is tough. All I know is that even if we can't be together, I want Scott in my life so much, and I won't let him go.

"Well, I better get back to this," he says. "I have three book covers I gotta get done by tonight before I meet with Dad."

"Oh, that silly hobby that you do?" I tease, and he laughs.

"Yeah, you know. That stupid thing that pays the bills."

"I gotta get back to my hobby, too. Call me when you're finished. I might not be able to answer since I'll be out, but definitely let me know how it goes."

"I appreciate that," Scott says.

When we say our goodbyes, I'm sad again. I'm missing him, even just knowing that I'm going to go a few more hours without talking to him. I shouldn't miss him this much, but two weeks has felt so much longer. Time without Scott stretches on and on, reminding me he's not next to me in bed and that I can't wrap my arms around him. I can't do all of the naughty, dirty things that enter my head every time I think about him—things that I know he would love, things I've learned he would love.

Once I've finished up at work, I head home to relax, watch some porn, and turn on an anime flick on Netflix because it reminds me of him.

When it's time to go out, I get dressed, throw on my leather jacket, and meet the guys at the bar where we laugh and talk about some drama at work. They tell me about their families, their kids' soccer games, the PTA meetings, and people they're dating. I never envied their lives before or wanted to settle down, but Scott changed all that.

When the gang gets caught up in trivia—passionate, eager, and maybe a little too dedicated—I head to the bar for my next drink. Hanging with people is more my thing, not really trivia.

Three girls chat at one corner of the bar. They're an attractive crew. One at the end, with straight blonde hair, wears a dress that reveals a decent amount of cleavage. She's hot, and as her gaze catches mine, I make that instinctive smile that I would make to a girl back before any of this stuff with Scott ever happened.

As she grins, I look away.

I'm not out to get laid tonight.

Although, it wouldn't kill me to have a wild, steamy encounter with a beautiful woman—giving her everything she wants, everything she needs, listening to her body, asking her what she needs me to give her.

I chase the thoughts away, turning my attention to a screen behind the bar playing the news. The weatherman talks about what a beautiful week it's supposed to be. It just makes me think that I need to find a way to con Scott into coming out here. The beautiful weather will definitely be more appealing when he's struggling through intense humidity of a Georgia summer.

"Hey, there," I hear beside me. I turn to the beautiful blonde, who now stands right next to me. "This seat saved?"

"No, it's not."

She makes herself comfortable on the stool, leaning forward and resting an elbow on the bar. "My name's Jenny."

"Mikey. You look awfully lonely without a drink." It's the

sort of line I would have used back in the day.

"Lonely? Well, I am kind of lonely, now that you mention it. I wouldn't mind a vodka cranberry."

I order her one from the bartender, and she keeps shifting her gaze about, but letting it always settle on me, her eyes filled with desire. I know that look. I've seen it on plenty of girls before, and this isn't the kind of girl who I'm going to have to work hard to get. Hell, she's doing most of the work for me.

"So, what brought you out tonight?" I ask her.

"My girlfriends. It's my friend Carol's birthday party."

"Happy Birthday to your friend."

"I'll pass it along." She leans close to me like she's trying to emphasize her impressive breasts. "You have the most beautiful blue eyes. Has anyone ever told you that?"

I want to tell her plenty of women before her have said the same thing, but I go with, "It's come up."

"A man who knows what he's got. What other sort of compliments do you receive from women?" Her gaze drifts lower. "I have a funny feeling you get a lot of compliments there as well."

"No complaints."

Her lips, bright red with lipstick, curl into a smile. "Look, Mikey, I'm gonna make this real easy for you. I'm honestly not the best of friends with Carol. She's my coworker's friend, and they're both starting to get on my nerves tonight. I'm only in town until the end of the week. You're cute, and you seem like no drama. So to save us both the stupid lines, I just want to tell you, if you're game, I'm game."

I should take her up on this offer. We could Uber or Lyft

back to my place or go to wherever she's staying and just have a little fun.

Maybe that would help me shake Scott.

The truth is, though, I don't want to shake him.

"I think I'm going to bow out tonight," I tell her.

"It could be real fun."

"I believe you, and I would, but the truth is, I'm kind of getting over someone."

"Oh, really? What's her name?"

"His name? It's Scott."

"You could have just told me that you're batting for the other team."

"I bat for a lot of teams."

She snickers. "I like you, Mikey. So who's this guy? Tell me about him."

"He lives in Georgia, and we've had a thing going on for a few months. I've never had anything like that. Never any sort of connection with another person, but this guy, I mean, he changed my whole world. I didn't even think I would ever want something like that."

"Why not?"

I don't have to think about that. I know it's my parents, not only with how they made me guarded by betraying me, but by being the shittiest example of what a relationship was. In some way, I think I've always been afraid that's how relationships are: filled with lies and misery and resentment. And I think I've just been avoiding them because I don't ever want to end up in that nightmarish place with another person.

"It's a lot of things," I tell her, because I don't plan on

sharing that kind of information with a stranger.

"But this guy's different?"

"Very different. Amazing and wonderful and special."

"Then what are you doing not being with him right now?"

"The project we were working on together, it ended, and I had to come back here to continue my life, and like I said, he's in Georgia."

"There's not any way you both could have worked that out?"

"We could have. We still could, I figure, but I don't know. He didn't really push for it or say anything that made me believe he'd be interested in finding a way that we could make this work."

"That doesn't sound fair, does it? If distance is the only thing keeping you apart though, do you think that, if you went and lived in Georgia, he would want to keep seeing you? That he would be interested in that?"

"I know it."

And I do.

As confused as I was when I left Georgia about how he felt, I'm not anymore. I know he keeps talking to me because he genuinely likes me. And I felt how much he cared in that night we shared before I left—the night I don't think I'll ever be able to get out of my head.

"You'll have to forgive me for pushing, but if he really is this special, what's stopping you from finding a way to be out there to make this happen?"

It's a good question. "Doesn't that seem crazy? Three months and then uprooting my life?"

"It's a gamble, but if it's something you could do, why wouldn't you?"

"Well, he certainly hasn't offered to do that."

"Maybe he thinks it seems crazy, too."

And the way she throws my words back at me like that makes me really question how I've been approaching this.

"But you must not really think something is there," she insists.

"That's not true."

"If you did, and if he really cared about you, you'd be with him right now. Not in this bar."

It really is that simple.

If I want to keep seeing him, all I have to do is go back out there and be with him.

My life is such that I could find a way to work outside of LA—even tele-work a little longer. I certainly have the credentials and the contacts to get work in Georgia. But Jenny made a good point. As much as I put this on Scott, as much as I've said that it's about what he wants, I never offered up that I would be willing to move my life for him either. I would be willing to do that for us, and I know it's because it's a big step—a risk—and for what? Something I've never really let myself believe in?

At least, until I met Scott.

Until I *fell* for Scott.

"Is he worth the gamble?" she asks.

"He is."

I answer too quickly. So quickly, I don't doubt the words as they escape my lips.

I want to be with Scott.

Yeah, it has been fast and crazy and beautiful, but I've had enough sex and I've lived long enough to know what I want, and what I want is him. And maybe this is a huge mistake, but goddammit, I think it's worth fighting for this because, even in these two weeks, I've discovered that a life without Scott isn't a life I'm interested in.

"I think you're making a lot of sense, Jenny."

"I do that from time to time. What do you say we get another drink? If I'm not getting laid tonight, I want to at least get wasted."

"It's on me."

She's right. She's so fucking right. For the first time in my life, I'm really sure about something.

And in my heart, I desperately hope it's something Scott would be willing to do.

He might not be ready. He might think it's too fast, but I'll try anything at this point. I don't need him to care about me the way I care about him, because this is confusing as fuck, but I do believe that one day he'll feel for me the way I feel for him.

I have to believe this connection we share is real.

39

SCOTT

I approach the door to Dad's house.

The house I grew up in.

The house where Dad always made me feel like I needed to work harder, to do a better job, to do the things he wanted me to do with my life.

I knew I would talk to him again. I don't have Mikey's horrible parents, and I know my father cares about me, but I don't know how we're ever going to get through this when he refuses to take my life and my choices seriously. Since our fight, he's left a few curt voicemails and texted a few times, but other than that, I haven't wanted to approach the problem. I've been sad enough without Mikey being here.

I miss him so much, and the idea of him going out tonight and winding up in the bed of some hot trick makes me uneasy. But he has every right to. I don't have a say in what he does. I let him go.

I knock and wait before Dad opens the door, his expression stoic. I can't really tell what he's thinking, but then again, I was never all that good at that. I'm glad it's just the two of us right now, unlike other family nights when he and my other siblings gang up on me.

"How've you been?" he asks.

"Been good, Dad. You?"

"I would've been better if you would have talked to me.

Come on in." He guides me into the kitchen. "I'm making fettuccine, your favorite. You okay with that?"

I see the concern in his eyes. It's kind of nice seeing him worry about our relationship. It reminds me of what Mikey told me, that he loves me despite the hell he gives me sometimes.

"That will be really nice, Dad."

He heads over to a pan and pulls off the lid before stirring the contents. I sit at the kitchen table, waiting for him to finish.

"It wasn't easy raising you guys by myself," he tells me, "and I made a lot of mistakes. I know that. I know you don't necessarily believe this all the time, but everything that I've done, I've done so that you could all have happy, meaningful lives." He sets the lid back on the pan and the spoon down on a small plate on the counter next to the stove.

"I do know that."

He turns, his lips curling into a frown. "I knew from the time you were a kid that you were going to have a more difficult time. You didn't take to reading as fast. And you struggled with math in elementary school. It was different with your brothers and sister who were all ahead of their classes all through school. They excelled on standardized tests, and you were just… average."

He makes me feel average when he says it like that.

"I don't mean it that way," he adds, as though he's sensed my offense. "I meant that I understood you'd have to work harder than your brothers and sister to survive. Because with them, their skills and talents set them on paths to success. You weren't as easy, and you didn't want the things they wanted. And I know I handled you coming out in the worst way a father can, but it was never about you liking guys. It was about me worrying that it was just one more setback for you. I don't care who you love. I just want you to have the same opportunities as everyone else in the world."

"But I still needed your support."

"I get that. I should have been there then. I know that one was wrong. And it hasn't hindered you—"

"Would it have mattered if it had?" He stares at me like he's confused about what I'm saying. "If it had been some sort of obstacle," I clarify, "would that have made you love me any less? Or care any less?"

"Of course not."

"Then why do you always make everything about that?"

"Because I know how hard this world can be. That's all that was ever about. I want you to have a great life—"

"How can it be great if I'm not happy?"

"It frightens me how much you sound like I did when I was younger. You reminded me of myself, and I think that's why I wanted to push you... if only to prevent you from making the mistakes I made."

"Do you really feel like photography was a mistake?"

He's quiet, standing still for a moment before approaching and sitting in the chair next to me. "I was a stupid kid, and I thought that was all I wanted... to look at the world through my lens and capture its beauty. I was taking pictures when I was eight years old, using my dad's Polaroid. And I had success with it, but I couldn't make much money. Definitely not enough to make ends meet. And it wasn't until I was out in the world, with a kid to take care of, that I realized exactly how wonderful it would have been to have a career that I could have fallen back on. Instead, I wasted so much of my life… spent years and years doing something that I loved, but I was struggling… always. And it was hard and painful. And such a fucking handicap when I entered the business world. It's taken me a long time to make up for that. But I got to tell you, when I started earning money—serious money—I appreciated it. It gave me security. And it made me realize how stupid that kid was to think that following creative passions could have ever amounted to the comfort of being able to have all the things I need."

"I'm making money at this, though. I'm successful whether you want to acknowledge that or not."

"God, I just want to shake you and remind you of how hard this world can be, and that even though it might be going well today, it can all be gone tomorrow."

I can tell he's talking about Mom. "I know that, Dad. But I don't know how many times I have to tell you that I am making money at this, and it's no different than Miranda or Conner or Darren's jobs."

"It *is* different, though, because it's a creative field. What separates you from any of the other competition you have? Why should they get it from you when they can get it somewhere else cheaper or from the next guy who comes along with more talent?"

"Because I've proven that I can do this. Because I'm worth the money they pay me."

"How can you possibly know that?" He looks into my eyes, but something in his expression has changed. It's like he's not fighting me right now, but he's genuinely curious.

"Because I worked hard to get here. I didn't wake up one day and think this would be fun. I've been busting my butt since I decided that this was what I wanted to do. Starting off working for free for buddies who believed in me and encouraged me... until people started offering to pay me because they saw value in what I was doing. Because every referral, every opportunity that has come my way, has come because other people have seen value in what I do. Far more than you've ever seen."

"That's... impressive."

"What?"

"I was never able to feel very confident that my pictures had any value. I mean, I loved it, but I didn't think I deserved to get paid for it. And people sure as hell weren't lining up to pay me for them." For the first time in a long time, he appears to be giving what I'm saying some serious thought. "I thought I would be happy because then at least I wasn't chasing this elusive dream that would never pan out, and I guess in a way, that's what I've always felt like you were doing."

His words leave me with a question I've had for a long time. "Don't you miss it, though?"

"There's not a day that goes by where I don't regret leaving it behind, but now all I see when I look at a camera is failure. I see this thing that I loved that I can't have because I gave up, and it hurts so much."

We're talking about our passions, but it feels like we're talking about Mikey, too. About how I don't feel worthy, or like I wasn't good enough—how I gave him up.

It's funny that I can feel worthy and confident about some things and not others.

It hasn't been easy being without him, and it's been harder and harder every day. And just like Dad, all I feel is this deep regret over what I let go. I did what he did with photography, and that scares the shit out of me.

I don't want to end up like Dad. I love him, but I can tell what his decision has done to him, how it's tortured him throughout the years, how something he once loved has turned him into this jaded man who can't even let himself fucking use the camera on an iPhone app because it just reminds him of his own failure.

It's one thing if it didn't work out with Mikey, and my fears were realized and he ended up moving on with someone else. It's another to not even try.

And I do want to try. So bad.

I'm glad we had this discussion, because it's offered me some clarity—clarity I needed right now.

"Well, I've done that too, Dad. Given up on something because I didn't think I was worthy. But I think I need to change that. Do you mind if I make a call real quick?"

"Sure. I'll finish dinner. This was kind of getting depressing for me anyway." He smiles, but I can tell there's still sadness in his eyes over reflecting on the past—on his own loss.

I get up and start to head out, but I stop myself in the entry to the hallway and turn back to him. "Dad, you could take pictures again. It's not too late to turn back and pick up the camera."

I see the knowing look in his eyes, but I can tell what's really there right now is fear, like maybe he's still too afraid to pick it up again, like he's still not good enough.

I step outside and call Mikey, but my call goes straight to his voicemail. "Hey, this is Scott. I was just giving you a call. Wanted to talk about something that came up with my dad tonight. Everything's fine. But something he said made me think about us. And I guess I'm calling to say, you make me happy, Mikey. And I think I made a mistake. I don't think. I *know* you make me happy. When we talked about a long distance relationship before, I was worried that maybe I wasn't someone you could be with. That you would get back to your life and move on, and maybe if we ever did something together, we would end up that way, but I don't know. I guess I'm saying I'd like to see what happens, if that's still an option. Which I hope it is."

I hang up. God, that's gonna be fucking embarrassing if he gets my message and isn't interested anymore. But I can't believe that's how he'll respond. Not after all the conversations we've had since he left.

Although, considering how dismissive I was of the idea of working on this, I can't be sure he'll still be interested.

I finish dinner with Dad and play catch-up while waiting for Mikey to call, but he doesn't.

I'm disappointed and a little sad.

I know he said he had to hang with some of the guys from work, but what if he heard my message and he needs to think it over? What if he's not as sure about us as he was when he was here and he's already reconsidering the idea?

I return home that night, still not having heard from him, and I can hardly get to sleep because of it. I keep thinking he has to reach out at some point.

Nothing.

* * *

I work my way through the covers I need to get done for my client, side-eyeing my phone sitting on the desk right beside me just in case he calls, but it's five in the afternoon now.

That's it. I weirded him out. Or he realized, now that he's home, this isn't what he really wants. I get that. I understand. I just wish he would call me back and say it.

I like to think he hasn't heard my message yet, but I doubt it, especially since he wanted me to follow up with him.

There's a knock on my door. When I answer, Jordan stands there. "Hey man, how's it going?" he asks me.

"It's going okay. Any chance you've heard from Mikey today?"

"No. But I talked to him last night. Why?"

And my suspicion is confirmed that he just doesn't want to talk to me right now. "No reason."

"I was gonna order a pizza if you wanted any."

"Yeah, that'd be great, thank you."

I return to my desk.

I've officially given up.

He's definitely not calling. And I don't want to, but I'm so sad thinking maybe I fucked it all up by telling him that I wanted something more. Maybe we would've been better friends if I'd kept my mouth closed, but that wouldn't have been enough. At least now I can say I tried. I didn't give up on something I really wanted like my dad did.

Half an hour passes, and there's another knock at the door. I wait for Jordan to get it, but I don't hear him stir, so I call his name. "Jordan! I think the pizza's here!"

The knock again.

Figuring he might be showering, I answer the door for him.

Standing outside in his leather jacket, Mikey lifts his head, those bright blue eyes glistening.

"Hey," I say, and all my senses are totally thrown because I can't figure out what the fuck he's doing here.

He scans me up and down before he comes at me, pushing me back against the wall in the entryway, his lips crushing against mine. His hands move around my body slowly as he pulls me to him.

I don't even care why he's here right now. Just that he is.

I enjoy the feel of his body and delight in it the way I have so many times before. How can I miss him this much when it's only been two weeks? Two of the longest weeks of my life.

When I can finally think straight again, I ask between kisses, "What are you doing here?"

"You called."

"You could've called back."

He pulls away, looks into my eyes with a sneaky smirk on his face. "Felt like what I had to say needed to be said in person."

"And what is that?"

"I'm falling in love with you, really hard. I mean, there was no turning back before, but Scott, I don't want to be all the way across the country from you if we're gonna try to make things work. I don't care what we have to do. If I have to come here or if you want to move out there, but I want you in my life. You're such a stupid shit for having thought you didn't want me in yours."

"Shut up," I say. "I always knew I wanted you in mine. I just didn't think—and don't laugh at me—I didn't think I deserved you."

"Scott. Stupid, stupid Scott. If anyone doesn't deserve someone, it's me who doesn't deserve you. And it pisses me off that you still don't see that. So I guess I'll have to make it my mission to prove you wrong."

I grin before he kisses me again.

"Ooh!" comes from beside us.

I turn to see Jordan standing there. He has that same smirk on his face that I'm used to seeing on Mikey's.

"Is there even pizza coming?" I ask.

"I mean, there *can* be if we order some. I just thought this would be a funny way for you to find out Mikey was here. He texted me when he was at the airport that he was on the way."

"You guys are both assholes."

"Well," Mikey says, "I think you're falling in love with at least one of these assholes."

"Yes, I am." I kiss him again. We wrap our arms around each other, holding each other close.

"Okay, I'll go order the pizza," Jordan says as he leaves us alone in the entryway—the place where we first met when I was pissed as hell at him.

And now I've gone and fallen for him.

EPILOGUE

MIKEY

Five Years Later

I'm on my knees, hammering a nail into the board of a shelf I'm making for the baby room. It's a bookshelf like the one we made for little Roger. Scott liked it so much, he wanted one for our kid.

Work's been so busy, I haven't had time for this project, but we've had nearly two years to prepare the room, so most everything else is in place. We picked out the crib together at Toys "R" Us the day we signed the papers with the surrogacy program, and the periwinkle paint on the walls was the subject of several heated debates until Scott finally caved and admitted it was fine for us to paint a girl's room blue. Many, but not all, of the toys around the room used to be Roger's—ones he's too old for now, including a familiar panda that still reminds me of those early days with Scott when we were just getting to know each other. That was back when our relationship was so new and I never could have realized exactly how much I would come to love Scott Wintry.

As I finish hammering, I inspect the bookshelf, making sure it's sturdy.

As a rock.

"Need a hand?"

I turn to see Scott standing in the doorway, hands in the front pockets of his jeans, a gray tee tight against his chest and revealing the groove between the muscles in his torso.

"Just finishing up." I set the hammer on top of the shelf and approach him, offering what I intend to be a soft kiss, but as soon as I taste him, I can't help myself. I slide my arm around to the small of his back and pull him close to me.

My dick goes hard, and I push him back against the wall across from the doorway.

He sets his hand on the back of my head.

"I thought you had to work," I say when I manage to pull away for a moment.

"I finished up early. Thought we could make time for something special since we both have a little spare time on our hands. Past few days have been so busy."

This isn't like the days when we first met when Scott was taking on freelance projects to make money. Three years ago, he was approached by a major ad company, and now he works exclusively for them at an incredibly salary that blows mine out of the water.

I'm proud as fuck of him, too. Not just because his skill and talent landed him the job, but because he busts his butt and still makes time for his own work—art that I can tell satisfies him beyond a paycheck.

"Something special?" I ask him. "What did you have in mind?"

"I think you know exactly what I had in mind."

I growl before kissing him again and moving my hands under his shirt, kneading his flesh.

He grips onto my ass.

"Gonna… have… to get this out of… our system," he says between my kisses, "while we don't have a little one running around taking up all our time."

It reminds me of this journey we're on together. It's a journey we agreed we were ready for just months after we married each other. That was three years ago when we picked out the matching black titanium bands we now wear and took vows that I haven't regretted for a moment. When the conversation about a kid came up, we both agreed. I think Scott may have wanted this even more than I did. And now we're days away from the due date when the woman who we were introduced to through the surrogacy program will have our little baby girl.

"I'm happy to see you're so excited about little Esmerelda-Sue," I tease.

One night when we were first deciding on names, we each joked that we would pick strange names for her.

"Esmerelda-Sue, that's ridiculous," he says. "I think you meant our little Donatella-Marie."

"Over my dead body."

I kiss him again.

He claws at my shirt, as annoyed with my clothes as I am with his. We can't even make it all the way to the bedroom before we're pulling them all off, scurrying to get free, our dicks hard as ever.

"Get that fucking dick in my mouth," I say, dropping to my knees at the doorway to our bedroom. I take his cock in my mouth, licking, sucking, and enjoying that taste that I can never get enough of.

Fucking in this house always feels so good—this beautiful house we purchased together after we got married. It was another fixer-upper, but this time, we eagerly signed on to the challenge, knowing how well we work together and how much fun we had working on Kate's house.

Through all these projects, everything we've shared—every conversation, every kiss, every fight—has only brought us closer.

When we finally make it into the bed naked, him beneath me as I rub my cock against his thigh, he grips onto my neck as he slides his tongue past my lips. I eagerly accept it.

I would have thought that after five years it wouldn't have felt this powerful, this intense, but each day I spend with Scott only makes me crave him more. I can't ever get enough of him.

I never could have imagined being with one man could have felt this good or would've meant so much.

Everything I've shared with Scott means more in the world to me than any of the meaningless hook-ups I had before him—what I realize now was an empty life that I lived until he changed my world.

He grips my right bicep and pushes, guiding me onto my back. He straddles me.

"Ooh, aggressive Scott has come out to play."

There's a wicked gleam in his eyes. "You have no idea."

He leans over to the nightstand, opens the drawer, and retrieves a set of handcuffs. It's a toy we picked up several years ago when we were at an adult toy store at a leather bar in Atlanta.

"Oh, really?" I tease. "You think I'm just gonna let you dominate me?"

"Yeah, you will, you fucking bottom."

Scott slides off me and pushes me onto my stomach.

I don't resist him because I want this as much as he does.

He hooks one of the cuffs to my right wrist and wraps it around one of the vertical slats in the headboard before cuffing the other to my left wrist.

"Be gentle," I say. "It's my first time."

"Oh, it's been a long time since then. I was there, remember?"

"Do I ever."

He reaches back for the nightstand, and I know what he's going for: lube.

"I don't think I'm gonna need any," I tell him.

He turns to me, those hazel eyes lit up with excitement.

"Just a little spit and a lot of love," I add.

That's what he gives me until I'm feeling his hard cock deep within me. He pulls up, guiding me onto my knees and grabbing my hair, pulling it back—another thing he's shown me I enjoy.

As he pushes in again and again, I revel in having him filling me.

I love barebacking with my husband, because when we

lost the need for condoms, it felt like there wasn't a barrier between us anymore, like we could be totally and utterly one another's.

He fucks me good—the way only Scott could know how to fuck me, in all the positions I enjoy so much. He slaps my ass sharply and then rubs over where it's tender.

"Again," I demand.

And he obeys before drilling into me some more.

This is what marriage is for us, being able to explore and experiment without inhibition, not hiding anything we enjoy from one another, being totally open to share whatever fantasy fills our thoughts—whether we discover it in an adult store or in a porn.

When the pressure swells within me to the point where it's almost too much, Scott has me on my side, my leg upright against his torso, my hands still bound to the headboard, and he pushes deep.

"God, I wish I could touch it. I need to rub it out," I say.

"Are you asking me to get you off?"

"I'm begging, fucking begging."

He grins, still hitting my prostate just right. Then he grabs my cock and strokes it while continuing to stimulate my ass.

"Fuckin' A. Spew in me, Scott. Get it up in there."

Scott's movements quicken, build, and climb before I hear the grunt I know all too well.

He's filling me.

It's so gratifying to know, and as he pushes in once more with his hand still around my dick, I shoot, my cum spreading across the sheets.

Sweat runs down my body as I catch my breath.

Not pulling out, Scott lowers my leg and lets me rest on my chest as he collapses onto my back. His lips press against my cheek as he wraps his arms under mine, clinging to me in a way that makes me feel so needed and appreciated.

"Someone was in a toppy mood today," I say.

"Shut up, you needy bottom."

He leans back and slaps my ass again—for good measure, I'm sure.

"Mmm," I say, pushing my ass back and still enjoying the sensation of his hard-on lingering within me. "Can we just do this for the rest of the weekend?"

He laughs. "I think that sounds like a really good idea."

He lies back on top of me and we lie there for a few moments until we hear a buzz.

One of our phones.

"That's probably your brother," Scott says.

We're going out to dinner with them later tonight—me, Jordan, my sister, and Scott—so we can catch up.

Ever since I came back to live in Atlanta all those years ago, I spend a lot more time with my family—at least the only family that matters to me. It was the best decision I ever made, because I feel like Kate, Jordan, and I share a deeper connection with each other than we ever did when there were all those secrets in our home.

But over time, we've bridged the gap, and now I talk to them more than ever. I go grocery shopping with Kate, and I'll hit the bars with Jordan and his partner of three years now. Kate hasn't settled down with anyone yet. She's enjoying her life as a single mother, dating and taking her time finding someone who, as she says, needs to be just right.

I'm still cuffed to the bed with Scott's cum in me when he slides out and steps off the bed. He retrieves his phone out of the pocket of his jeans.

"Holy shit," he says. "It's Stephanie. She's going into labor now. Holy fuck."

I sit up so quickly, I'm not even thinking, and the cuffs pull before there's a snap.

The vertical slat in the headboard snaps in two. "Shit."

"We'll fix it later," Scott says. "Let's just get ready."

After he uncuffs me, he frantically starts getting into his clothes. I run to the bathroom. "I still fucking have to get you out of me."

We get ready as fast as we can before hopping into our car. Scott drives, me calling Kate and Jordan while Scott calls his Dad so we can get everyone to meet us at the hospital.

Scott has a much better relationship with his father these days.

It's taken them time, and it hasn't always been easy, but they're working on things, and I'm proud Scott hasn't walked away from his father, that he understands how much his dad loves him and is trying to be supportive.

When we get off the phone, we're both upright in our seats, tense and alert. There's a swirl of excitement racing around inside my belly. I turn to him, and he looks at me with those beautiful hazel eyes, that expression so distant from the one he made the first time I saw him when he was so pissed off. Now he's looks scared as hell, and it's so fucking adorable.

"I'm really nervous," he says, tearing up.

"I am, too."

I rest my hand on his thigh, checking the road before throwing him a quick glance and assuring him, "But we're gonna do this like we do everything. Together."

I feel like the luckiest man in the world, and I'm so excited about this next chapter of our lives.

THE END

ABOUT THE AUTHOR

A good ole Southern boy, Devon McCormack grew up in the Georgia suburbs with his two younger brothers and an older sister. At a very young age, he spun tales the old fashioned way, lying to anyone and everyone he encountered. He claimed he was an orphan. He claimed to be a king from another planet. He claimed to have supernatural powers. He has since harnessed this penchant for tall tales by crafting worlds and characters that allow him to live out whatever fantasy he chooses. Devon is an out and proud gay man living with his partner in Atlanta, Georgia.

Find Devon:

www.facebook.com/groups/devonsreadingroom

www.twitter.com/devon_mccormack

www.goodreads.com/author/show/7327303.Devon_McCormack

Made in the USA
Las Vegas, NV
23 November 2024